EVER
CONSTANT

The Treasures of Nome

EVER CONSTANT

TRACIE PETERSON AND
KIMBERLEY WOODHOUSE

BETHANYHOUSE
a division of Baker Publishing Group
Minneapolis, Minnesota

© 2022 by Peterson Ink, Inc. and Kimberley Woodhouse

Published by Bethany House Publishers
11400 Hampshire Avenue South
Minneapolis, Minnesota 55438
www.bethanyhouse.com

Bethany House Publishers is a division of
Baker Publishing Group, Grand Rapids, Michigan

Printed in the United States of America

Library of Congress Cataloging-in- Publication Data
Names: Peterson, Tracie, author. | Woodhouse, Kimberley, author.
Title: Ever constant / Tracie Peterson and Kimberley Woodhouse.
Description: Minneapolis, Minnesota : Bethany House Publishers, a division of
    Baker Publishing Group, [2022] | Series: The treasures of Nome
Identifiers: LCCN 2021037712 | ISBN 9780764232527 (paperback) | ISBN
    9780764232534 (cloth) | ISBN 9781493436019 (ebook)
Subjects: LCGFT: Novels.
Classification: LCC PS3566.E7717 E84 2022 | DDC 813/.54—dc23
LC record available at https://lccn.loc.gov/2021037712

Scripture quotations are from the King James Version of the Bible.

This is a work of fiction. Names, characters, incidents, and dialogues are products of the authors' imagination and are not to be construed as real. Any resemblance to any person, living or dead, is purely coincidental.

Cover design by Jennifer Parker
Cover photography by Joanna Czogala | Arcangel

Kimberley Woodhouse is represented by The Steve Laube Agency.

Baker Publishing Group publications use paper produced from sustainable forestry practices and post-consumer waste whenever possible.

22 23 24 25 26 27 28   7 6 5 4 3 2 1

This book is lovingly dedicated to the real Whitney.

Thank you for allowing us to name a character after you—even when I told you what we were going to put her through.

You were the first of the Powell girls to take lessons from me, and we shared so many amazing times together. I have been blessed to know you all these years.

You. Are. A. Joy.

We've shared laughter, tears, FaceTime calls, chats, and lots of music.

Remember how very much I love you.

Remember I'm here for you.

And remember that our God loves you more than anything and has blessed you with amazing talent. Keep using it for Him. Always.

Put Him first, and everything else will fall into place.

I'm praying for you, and I adore you.

—Kim

And to Havyn and Madysen, Tracie and I hope you have enjoyed having your namesake characters. I can't wait to hear all about what you are up to next. If the two of you ever take up working on a farm with chickens and sheep, I'm going to laugh hysterically. Just make sure you tell me all the stories.

You two are so precious, and I love having you in my life. Give each other a hug from me and Tracie, and give your parents hugs too!

Dear Reader

Several years ago, Tracie and I were having a book signing and fund-raising event for the scholarship fund in Cassidy Hale's honor with the launch of our HEART OF ALASKA series' *In the Shadow of Denali*. Music students of mine—the Powell girls—came to meet their beloved favorite author, Tracie Peterson. The girls' mom—Monica—and I are dear friends, and she's quite a fan as well. The excitement as the foursome walked into the event was contagious. Even though the girls knew me really well, had spent hours at my home, and understood that I had written several books already with Tracie, the joy of getting to meet her in person put them over the moon and in total fan mode. Giggles and smiles and chatter filled the air.

It was at that event that Tracie looked at me and said, "Books need to be written about three precocious, musical, redheaded sisters."

THE TREASURES OF NOME series was born that day.

The three main characters throughout this series are named after my precious girls. (I will always claim them as mine—once a student of mine, *always* one of my kids.) Whitney, Havyn, and Madysen. And while we might have used a few character traits of the real girls, the Powell sisters in our series are purely fictitious. I'm truly thankful that the real sisters haven't had to endure all the craziness we threw at the characters in our books.

Tracie and I have loved sharing these girls, the chicken stories, the sled dogs, the chaos with the sheep, the cheese making, and all the other adventures in this series with you.

For those of you who have read Jack London's *Call of the Wild* or have seen the movie, you know the command *mush* is used to get the dogs to go. Most likely this is the English derivation from the French-Canadian *marche*, which meant "go."

In this book, you will find these terms:

Let's go simply means "go." (The most common terms used are *hike*, *let's go*, and *all right*, which you might remember me using in *Race Against Time*.)

Haw means "turn left."

Gee means "turn right."

Whoa means "slow down and come to a stop."

Because I have spent so much time with real-life dog-sled pros while we lived in Alaska and during research trips there, I want to honor the knowledge they've poured into me and respect the amazing sport.

The Grand Nome Hotel and Golden Palace Restaurant in this book are fictitious. I know how many of you love the historical landmarks we use, but in this instance we needed to create something for the purposes of the story.

You will also notice that there are two different terms used for the native people. *Inupiat* is plural, *Inupiaq* is singular. There you have it, your language lesson for the day.

Lastly, I wanted to tell you about something that a lot of people don't know. Are you ready?

The northern lights—auroras—make noise.

This is shown in *Ever Constant*, and I wanted to assure you that, yes, it is true!

I've heard them many times myself, but it's not loud. In fact, the best way to truly experience them is to be out away from everything else. Their sound has been described as crackling, the bursting of soap bubbles, and sputtering. Sometimes you have to concentrate on listening to actually hear them.

Check out the Note from the Authors at the end of the book for some fun facts and links. And make sure you join us for our next series, which takes place in Kalispell, Montana.

As always, we couldn't do what we do without YOU, our readers.

Enjoy the journey,

Kim and Tracie

Prologue

Cripple Creek, Colorado—1889

Flurries of snow drifted down from the dark and cloudy sky. Whitney Powell shivered and lifted her face to the heavens as she stopped in the middle of the quiet street. Mama would scold her for being out in the wee hours of the morning, but it was her mother's tears that woke her.

Daddy wasn't home. *Again.* Which meant one thing. Whitney wanted to growl out her anger and throw something. Really hard. She'd been old enough to understand what was going on for a couple of years now. No matter how much her parents tried to hide it.

Lifting her chin, she clenched her jaw against the chill in the wind and shoved her hands into her coat pockets. She had to fix Mama's tears. Havyn and Madysen were too young. So even if she had to drag her good-for-nothin' father back from the saloon—again—at least he would be home.

She cringed. Good for nothin'? What a horrible thought!

What would Mama say? How often had she drilled into her that thoughts were just as important as the words that came out of her mouth? Reminded her that God knew every one of them?

No doubt about it, their mother would be crushed. And she'd be so embarrassed if she found out that her oldest daughter had gone to Saloon Row to haul her father home. More than once.

Mama was the best lady in the world. *And* the most talented. If only she could stand up for herself. She always saw the good in everyone, believed in them, cheered them on, and recognized what she called their *potential*.

Why couldn't she see that people took advantage of her goodwill?

No matter how many times Mama had been hurt, she'd still forgive.

Whitney gritted her teeth. In all her ten years, she'd never met anyone on earth as good as her mama. If only *she* could be as kind and generous. No matter how much she tried to mimic her mother's behavior, she couldn't do it. Mama's patience and goodness rivaled that of any saint. Granddad said so himself.

"Maybe by the time I'm all grown up I can be like Mama." Her words puffed from her mouth in the icy air.

For now, as the oldest daughter, it fell to her to take care of their mother when their father wasn't capable of doing it. She'd gone to get him four times now. Four. She'd had to scrape up all her courage to go to the saloons that first time, but she'd done it. Because she loved her Mama and couldn't watch her suffer and worry.

She shook her head and continued walking toward Saloon Row. The still of the evening was disrupted by sounds of the establishments ahead. The noise crescendoed with every few steps.

How many more times would she have to do this? How long before someone found out? She'd thought about asking Granddad for help. Other than her sisters, he was her best friend. But he already didn't think too well of Daddy. . . .

The wind bit at her face while the scent of logs burning in stoves filled her nose.

Music from the saloons drifted toward her, and she flinched. It was nothing like the beautiful music they played and sang at home. This was harsh, raucous, and out of tune. How could people even stand it? It hurt her ears. The closer she got, the more she hated the sound, the noise, the smells. Oh, to curl up in her bed like her younger sisters and go to sleep as if she didn't have the weight of the world on her shoulders. All because Daddy couldn't control himself.

Two men wobbled down the street toward her, then one of them doubled over and got sick in the middle of the road. She covered her face with her scarf and stepped several paces around them. Why did they *do* that to themselves? Disgusting.

Picking up her stride, she kept her chin down. There were things here that she didn't want to see.

Not again.

Questions peppered her brain. She wouldn't allow them entry. Best to think about music. Mama. Havyn and Madysen.

Wait a minute . . . the hairs on the back of her neck prickled and a shiver raced up her spine. A lump in the street—no, not a lump. A man.

For a moment, she couldn't take another step. Could barely breathe. No. Please. That scrawny heap couldn't be her father. But . . . the blue coat.

She'd recognize the coat anywhere. Mama made it for him last Christmas.

With a deep breath, she moved forward. At least she could be thankful he wasn't *inside* one of the saloons. She hated going in them. The adults always tried to shoo her out, but her presence made it easier to get her dad out the door. No one wanted a little girl inside.

The closer her feet brought her to the telltale form, the more she wanted to run away. But then she was standing beside him. Daddy wasn't moving. Was he even breathing?

She knelt down beside him and poked at his shoulder. Hard.

Nothing happened.

When she touched his face, it was cold. Her stomach revolted and her heart sank.

Oh, Daddy . . .

Shaking her head, she closed her eyes and took several deep breaths. A sharp clenching in her chest made her gasp for air. She fought the tears that threatened to flood her eyes and race down her face. He wouldn't leave them . . . would he?

As much as she detested his actions, he was still her daddy.

She leaned her ear close to his face. He stunk. It made her stomach turn again.

She couldn't hear any breath.

She poked him again. Harder. And again. Even harder.

"Daddy?" She shook him with all she had.

No response.

She touched his face again. Cold. But it was snowing outside, and the temperature was frigid. Maybe he was passed out. He did that at home all the time lately.

Sitting down beside him, she shook him and poked him.

Over and over. If he was dead . . . what would they do? Mama and Havyn and Madysen would cry. So would she.

What would become of them?

The few wonderful memories she had with her dad began to play in her mind. The way his eyes crinkled when he laughed. Playing outside in the snow. Him chasing her around the house until she crumpled on the floor, giggling.

She shoved him again. "Wake up! Havyn and Maddy need some good memories too." With her other hand, she swiped at her hair.

If he was dead . . . she'd never have to come find him again. He'd never come home drunk. Never make Mama cry.

No. He couldn't get out of his responsibilities that easily. *Someone* had to take care of them. He'd promised he'd stop. Get cleaned up. Be the husband and father they needed.

A pounding started in her ears as heat rushed to her cheeks. Every ugly thing she'd ever wanted to say to him threatened to spew from her mouth as she pushed and shoved, poked and prodded.

But after several minutes, she slumped down. Not a moan or a sound came from him. Swallowing against the tears, she swiped at her cheeks.

It was no use. He was dead. Gone.

Glancing from side to side, she searched the street. Not a soul around that she knew. No one she could trust to help.

What would she tell Mama? How could she fix *this*?

The wind howled, and her hair flew in her face again. The strands, wet from the snow, stuck to her nose.

She *couldn't* fix this. She couldn't even get him home. It was one thing to drag her drunken father home when he had use of his legs, but when he was dead weight?

The tears stung her cheeks as they escaped, and the wind

threatened to freeze them on her skin. As much as she wanted
to be strong, all she wanted now was Granddad. Whenever
she couldn't turn to Mama, he was her rock.

But how could she leave her dad in the street to go get
Granddad? What would happen to Daddy if she left him
there? Would anyone care? Would he get run over by a horse?

How could Daddy do this to them?

For several minutes, she allowed the tears to flow. Then she
swiped at them again, her wool coat scratching and rubbing
her cheeks raw. Why couldn't he do what he was supposed
to do so that she could be a kid? But *no* . . . here she was in
the middle of the street crying over his sorry form. Mama
would tell her not to be angry with him. Again. But she was.

She was furious!

Whitney surged to her feet and glared down at her father.
Her hands fisted at her sides. "I *hate* you. Hate you for leaving us. Hate you for making Mama cry." She lifted her chin.
"But I won't cry for you. Never again." She made the meanest
face she could and forced it at him. Too bad he couldn't see it.

"Whitney? What are you doing out here?"

She whirled around.

Granddad!

"Whoa, young lady. What's got you all fired up?" He held
his hands in front of him.

She jabbed a finger toward her father. "He's gone and done
it. He's dead. Left us. What're we gonna do now?"

Granddad furrowed his brow and stepped closer. Tilting
his head, he placed a hand on her shoulder.

The touch melted the edges of her fury.

"I don't know for sure if he's dead, Whit. Why don't you
let me check?" His soft words washed over her, cooling the
fire in her heart.

Her shoulders slumped, and she dove toward him, wrapping her arms around his waist. She didn't want her dad to be dead. She didn't! But he made her so mad. How could he do this to them?

A long sigh escaped her grandfather as he embraced her. "I'm sorry, Whit. You should never have to see anything like this." His arms tightened around her, and then he pulled back, his hands on her shoulders. "Let me check on him, and then we'll talk about it, all right?"

She sniffed and lifted her chin to give a slight nod.

Granddad put a hand over her dad's mouth and nose for several moments. He turned back to her. "Your dad's not dead, honey. He's still breathing."

Thank You, God.

But as soon as the prayer whipped through her mind, she shook her head and pressed her lips together. She'd have to deal with this again. What about poor Mama?

"Let's get him home." Granddad grunted as he picked up her father and tossed him over his shoulder like a sack of grain.

They walked in silence for several minutes.

"Wanna tell me why you were out there in the middle of the night?" His tone wasn't scolding, but she could tell by the way his eyebrows drew together that he'd been unhappy to find her there. Would she get in trouble for going to the saloons?

"Mama was crying because Daddy wasn't home."

"Ah, I see. So you thought you should just wander out into the middle of town looking for him?"

The truth was the best way to go. "I've gone to get Daddy a few times. I don't see why I should get in trouble for that. *He's* the one who causes all the problems." She dared a look up at her grandfather.

His eyebrows raised. "Young lady, that's no way to talk about your father. . . ." His face pinched and he clenched his jaw several times. A long breath came out before his next words. "And I wasn't saying you were in trouble, though you should never leave the house unaccompanied—especially in the middle of the night." The words were hushed. Sad.

"But . . . what else was I supposed to do?" She crossed her arms over her chest and frowned. "Besides, I've heard what you've said about him to Mama—"

"What were you doing listening in on our conversations? Those words weren't meant for your ears. And besides, that's no excuse for you talking about him that way."

Now he was scolding.

She bit her lip. Caught. Heat rose into her cheeks. "I'm sorry, Granddad. But someone has to take care of Mama. That's why I was up. If Daddy isn't home, I always listen for her . . . to make sure she's all right."

His lips pinched together. Several moments passed before he continued. "Your mother would be heartbroken to hear you say those things about your father. And to find out that you've been sneaking out in the middle of the night to bring your dad home." He huffed and shifted her dad's limp form on his shoulder. "I'm sorry, Whitney. So sorry that you've had to do this. This is all my fault."

She had to strain to hear his last faint words. "Why is it *your* fault, Granddad?"

He shook his head as they trudged up the hill to their little house, and his breaths came faster. "I should have taken care of this long ago."

"Taken care of what?" Her heart pounded in her chest. "Could you have stopped Daddy from drinking? From it making him sick all the time?"

18

Then why hadn't he done so? Why had he let them be hurt this way?

"No. I've tried to get him to stop, but to no avail. Your mother has tried too. This is something only your dad can stop."

"So what should *you* have taken care of?" It made little sense.

Granddad turned to her and stopped. He took several moments to catch his breath. He smiled, but not really. It wasn't a smile that warmed her or made her want to smile back. Instead, she wanted to cry. "It doesn't matter now, Whitney. Your dad drinks until he's sick—"

"But why?"

Granddad sighed. "The one thing I can gather is that it helps him to forget."

"Forget *what*? He doesn't want to forget *us*, does he?" Tears stung the corners of her eyes, but she refused to let them out. Fine! If Dad didn't love them, she wouldn't love *him*. She didn't want his love. Let him forget her. She didn't care.

The tears almost escaped. Almost.

"No, sweetheart. He'd never want to forget you." Granddad started back up the hill. "But a lot of adults need to forget the bad things that have happened to them, and the bad things they've done."

"Like God forgets?"

Granddad's face scrunched up and then relaxed. "Yes. We wish we could forgive like God does. But we have a hard time doing it, don't we?"

As they walked the rest of the way up to the house, Whitney couldn't get Granddad's words out of her head. If only she could forget all the bad things she'd done too. All the times she'd been mean to her sisters. Or selfish. Or the times she'd lied. Mama said Jesus forgave her when she apologized to Him. But those bad actions came back to haunt her.

A lot.

Why couldn't she be better? Like her mother.

A few Sundays ago, the reverend talked about forgiveness and how God chose to forget their sins, to put those sins as far away as the east from the west. How could He do that?

God, I sure hope You forget all my bad deeds.

Maybe God could forget her daddy's too? And forgive him? Make him do better?

Jesus died for everyone's sins. God loved all of them the same no matter what they'd done.

She sniffed and winced. She was supposed to forgive Daddy like God did. It was a good thing her dad wasn't dead. Now she had to find some way to help him forget so he didn't need to go out drinking.

Mama made certain to tell them every day that Daddy loved them. She promised it was true. That should be reason enough for him to give up his drinking. Shouldn't it?

If he could stop, then she could forgive him. God would help her.

Then Mama wouldn't cry anymore.

And then they could be a *proper* family.

That ate every meal together around the dinner table.

Talked about their days.

Laughed together.

Made memories together.

Went to church together.

Gathered around the piano to play music and sing.

Had picnics in the meadow on red-and-white checkered cloths.

The pictures in her mind were so vivid that she smiled.

"Whitney?" Granddad's voice broke through her thoughts. "It's freezing out here, honey. Let's get inside."

"Yes, sir." As she walked into the tiny cabin they called home, she let the remnants of the pictures cement into her mind. She turned to close the door and watched as the snow laid a fresh white coating on everything.

Clean. Bright.

New.

Tomorrow could be the start of something new for them. It could.

And she couldn't wait.

ONE

Sixteen Years Later
Monday, January 9, 1905—Nome, Alaska

Snow glimmered in the moonlight. A beautiful start to another morning in Nome. Whitney whistled a lively tune as the sled swished and shushed over the snow. Her dogs were in fine form, obeying every command with precision and executing each turn in perfect unity. Not a tangled line or misbehaving pup. By the time the sun crested the horizon, there wasn't a cloud in the sky.

Oh, for more perfect days like thi—

She grimaced.

The ache started in the back of her neck and radiated up into her head. She lifted a hand to her neck and rubbed. But once this pain started, it was hard to get rid of. What came next was usually much worse.

When would these blasted headaches let up? They'd tormented her for months.

Ever since—

No. She wouldn't think about it. She'd gotten away from him. That's what mattered.

"Whoa!" Her dogs responded, coming to a stop.

She reached into her pocket and pulled out the bottle of tonic. Dr. Cameron gave it to her months ago because of the blow to her head. Thank heaven it helped ease her discomfort. A sip here and there was all it took.

She took a sip, replaced the bottle in her pocket, then urged the dogs back into motion. The pain lessened enough that she could make a mental list of everything she needed to accomplish today.

Lists kept her on track. Helped her to focus.

Life on the farm moved at a rapid pace, thank goodness. It kept her mind occupied, her hands busy. Between the cows, dogs, sheep, and chickens, she and her family had their work cut out for them. Havyn and Madysen had found good men to marry, men who wanted to help run the farm. Which she and her sisters needed. There was no way they would have been able to keep up by themselves.

Especially with Granddad still laid up after the bouts of apoplexy.

His movement had improved with exercises, but this past week he'd looked so weary. Maybe the winter doldrums were taking effect. It was, after all, the dead of winter. Or maybe he'd pushed himself too hard and too long over the past few weeks. He'd been determined to get up and walking soon.

Whatever it was, there had to be a way to lift his spirits. Lift *all* of their spirits. Maybe they should spend a bit more time around the piano in the evenings, on nights they weren't at the Roadhouse.

Just the thought of playing with Havyn and Madysen brought a smile to her face.

With Maddy on cello and Havyn on the violin, they made quite the trio. But it was when they sang together that everything was the way it should be. There was something wonderful about singing tight harmonies with her sisters. With letting their voices soar.

As much as she was a mother hen to her younger sisters—even more so since Mama's passing last year—the way they'd come around her after she'd been attacked showed her how much she needed them too. Whitney didn't want to face a day without either of them. No matter how much they might get on one another's nerves.

As her sled crested the hill, she caught sight of the farm. The expansive log-and-stone home Granddad built had smoke billowing from the chimney. The barns were alive with plenty of activity as the workers milked the herd. The usual cacophony of chickens chattering drifted on the air.

The sled glided over the snow as the dogs brought her back to the kennel area, their delight clear in their wagging tails and lolling tongues. Whitney hopped off the sled and worked with deft fingers in the bitter cold to unhook her team and get the dogs rubbed down and fed. Her mind sped through her responsibilities. Surely she had *some* time to shut her eyes against the pain. But no. Next came helping with breakfast, and then, since it was Monday, it was her turn to work with Granddad on his exercises.

She hesitated. Maybe Granddad needed something other than the same ol' things he did every day. What if she were to read to him . . . or perhaps wheel him into the gathering room by the roaring fire and play the piano for him?

Of course! That was it. He'd love that. And it would be a pleasant change of pace for him. A break from the strenuous routine of stretches he did every day.

Ohhh . . .

Why wouldn't the pain in her head stop? What she needed

was a hot bath. So hot that it could melt the pain. But there were too many things on her list to do before she could even think about relaxing.

The morning meal passed in a flurry of pancakes, eggs, and fried ham steaks. All the noise and laughter increased the stabbing pain in her head. It took every ounce of her self-control to not let it show. She scraped plates into the bucket they took out to the animals. She rubbed her forehead.

Relax. Breathe. So much left to do.

But the throbbing didn't lessen.

These darned headaches seemed to come more often. Maybe she needed to see Dr. Cameron. Find out if something was really wron—

"Whit . . . another one?" Havyn placed a hand on her shoulder.

With a sigh, she glanced at her sister. The child within her was beginning to show. "Yes. But don't worry. You've got enough on your plate. I'll make it through. I always do."

Hands on her hips, Havyn quirked an eyebrow at her. "You might be the oldest and think you can still boss us around, but I most certainly *will* worry. When one of us is hurting, the rest of us hurt." She grabbed the wooden spoon out of Whitney's hand and tilted her head. "Let me finish this and take it out. Everyone else has already gone out for the rest of the chores, so you go ahead and spend some time with Granddad. I think your idea of playing music for him will help you both. Especially with the house being quiet for a bit."

Since when did Havyn give her orders? Still, her fingers itched to play some relaxing music on the piano. She'd give in.

This time.

"All right. But don't think you've won."

Havyn's wide eyes blinked at her. "Oh, never."

"I can hear the sarcasm, sis."

"Good." Havyn gave her a little pat. "Now go on."

Whitney removed her apron and hung it up before heading into their large parlor. The piano gleamed in the lantern's light. The dark wood drew her. Mama had them polish it with oil and beeswax twice a week without fail. Running her hand over the smooth surface, she allowed the memories to assail her senses. All those times they'd gathered around it, the times Mama taught them at it, the times she accompanied them as they sang . . .

Oh, to see Mama at the piano again.

Stop it. Sadness wouldn't help. Not her or Grandad. Whitney went to the cabinet in the corner to pull out the music to Chopin's *Fantaisie-Impromptu.*

Mama's favorite piece.

How Whitney had loved to sit on the floor and watch mother's fingers fly over the keys as she played this piece. For years, Mama had wanted Whitney to learn it. But the technical piece intimidated her when she was younger . . . and there was something special about watching someone else play such a phenomenal creation.

Whitney set the music on the grand piano and opened the lid. She should have learned it at Mama's side—

No. Stay positive.

She could work on it for Granddad. It was his favorite too. And maybe, just maybe, they could comfort each other with the music. Be reminded of the beauty his daughter, her mother, gave them.

With a few deep breaths, Whitney examined the opening of the piece. The part that amazed her and daunted her the most. The triplet pattern in the left hand was contrary to the rhythm of the sixteenth notes in the right. Mama always called it three against four. Told her that the way to conquer it was for each hand to learn how to play independent of the other.

"*You have to master it hands separately, my dear.*" Mama's voice was so clear in her mind. Almost as if Whitney could conjure her up beside her. "*Then let them come together. They will know the rhythm. They will know what to do. But only after you've practiced it hundreds of times hands separately.*"

The emphasis on the words brought a smile to Whitney's face. How many times had her mother drilled into them, "*Count. One and two and three and four and . . . watch those scales, tuck that thumb . . . hands together, hands separately!*"

Whitney sat and practiced the first couple of pages. Hands separately, she played each part and paid careful attention to the fingering and rhythm. She knew what the song sounded like, so it was easy to imagine how it would be all together. But this would take a good deal of practice.

The clock chimed and she glanced up. Maybe she should just bring Granddad in here and tell him she would learn the piece for him. He loved to hear her and her sisters practice, no matter how many mistakes they made.

She got up from the piano bench and headed down the hall to Granddad's room. The past year had been hard on the whole family, but they'd come through it. Together. Music was one way they accomplished that.

She opened the door to their grandfather's bedroom. Light spilled in from the eastern window and blinded her for a brief moment. A sharp pain started at her right temple and shot across to the left. Blast these headaches!

She covered her eyes for a second and hoped Granddad

hadn't noticed. He was a worrier now that he was laid up all the time. She moved her hand and then squinted into the room. "Granddad? How about we take a little break from the exercises and I'll play some musi—"

She gasped.

Granddad lay on the floor. His form awkward and unmoving.

"Granddad!" She rushed to his side. "Did you fall? Let me help you get back into bed."

But as she tugged at his shoulders, there was no response.

She put a hand to his face, then yanked it back at the cold that greeted her fingertips. She rubbed her hand on her leg to rid herself of the offensive feeling.

No. It couldn't be.

Forcing her trembling fingers forward, she held them over his nose and mouth, counted to one hundred.

No breath escaped.

The gray pallor in his skin made her want to lose her breakfast.

No.

With a hand to her forehead again, she closed her eyes. This couldn't be happening! Not again. Not now. Her headache must have her imagining things. Granddad was indestructible. He'd survived *two* bouts of apoplexy!

She opened her eyes and stared at his form on the floor.

No nightmare.

It was real.

As she knelt beside Granddad, time stood still.

She couldn't breathe. Couldn't utter a sound.

The ticking of the clock on the dresser suddenly broke through the cloud in her mind.

Tick, tock. Tick, tock. Tick, tock.

Each sound grew louder and louder until she put her hands on the side of her head. With a gulp of air, she collapsed on her grandfather's stiff chest and sobbed.

He'd always been there. Always. Ever since Dad died—well, left—Granddad had been a father figure to her. Besides Mama, he'd been the one to understand her the most. Something she desperately needed—because she wasn't merciful like Maddy, nor fun loving like Havyn. She was just like him. He'd said so on hundreds of occasions.

He'd *always* been there.

But . . . he wouldn't be with them any longer.

Granddad . . . was dead.

Tears clogged her throat and blurred her vision. It was too much. The throbbing in her head grew as she wailed out her anguish into Granddad's shirt. But what was a little more pain in the face of another horrific loss?

The clock ticked the minutes away until her nose was stuffed and her tears dried up. Straightening and swiping at her eyes, she stared down at her grandfather.

No. *No!* This wasn't happening!

She looked up at the ceiling. "Why, God? Why would you do this to us? Do you *hate* us? Want to rip away everyone we love? Don't you know how much we need him? Especially with Mama gone. How are we supposed to go on?"

Heat rose within her. Choking her. This was *wrong!* She jumped to her feet. "Or are you punishing me?" She spat out the words. "What? I haven't had enough faith? Haven't been good enough? I'm too strong-willed? I let my temper get the best of me too many times? *Why?*"

Her fury faded into silence. No answer. No sense of God. There was only . . .

Nothing.

The same silence, the same void that, for too long now, had met her attempts to pray or to sense God. It was almost as if He were dead too.

And if He was, so what? What good had He been to them?

He'd allowed their father to be a drunk. To leave them and pretend he was dead. Sure, it was at Granddad's urging, since their father had already started another family. An idea her grandfather probably got from her that night when she *thought* Dad was dead.

But Dad had agreed. Had gone through with it. Left them.

Then God had allowed Mama to die.

And now Granddad.

He'd allowed Garrett Sinclair to *attack* her.

Where were you, God? Why didn't you help?

Enough.

She wiped her face with the back of her hand again and straightened her shoulders. No time now for tears. Only the tasks ahead of her . . .

Tell her family. Send for the doctor. Send for their pastor. Plan another funeral.

In the dead of winter.

Her heart sped up. She couldn't breathe. How was she going to do all this? *How?*

She pulled the bottle from her pocket and took a sip, closing her eyes as the burn hit the back of her throat. Her pain didn't fade, but as the warmth eased through her, she seemed to float above the anxiety that had become her daily companion. Ever since that awful day.

The day Sinclair attack—

No. Don't think about that.

Another small sip, another spreading burn, and her thoughts settled. Focus on one task at a time.

One, tell the family.

She tugged on the collar of her blouse and forced herself to look back to Granddad's still form.

Her heart broke, and a cry almost escaped her. Oh, to sit with him and have one more conversation. To tell him what was going on with her. The truth, this time. He would understand.

But . . . she hadn't made her peace with him. Oh, they'd acted as if nothing was different, but only because they were both too stubborn to confront the situation. Not after he'd shared the truth with them about her father. Not after he'd invited Dad's other family *here*. To live with them, the daughters her father abandoned.

The night they arrived was the same night that Garrett had put his hands on her.

Oh, Granddad, how could you leave me?

She sank to the edge of his bed. "I wasn't angry at what you did. Dad deserved it. And really, you saved us. But why? Why did you keep it a secret? From *me*? Didn't you think I could handle it?"

With a shake of her head, she banished the thoughts. Granddad knew what she'd seen as a child. What she'd done. What she'd endured.

Her sisters? They would never understand. They'd been so young. And they had been much more willing to show forgiveness. What would they think of her if they knew the truth of what was in her heart?

She stiffened. They wouldn't. She'd make sure of that. It was her job now to keep them together. Keep things running.

She owed that much to Granddad.

Her fingers traced the outline of the bottle in her hand. At least she could count on this to help. To give her relief.

She lifted it, took one more swallow, then put on the cap and tucked it away. She stood and walked to the door. Havyn and Madysen would be devastated, but John and Daniel would console them. Help them get through.

Who would help *her*?

She closed her eyes again and faced the stark truth.

No one. She really was alone now.

Her hand went to the doorjamb, gripped it to steady herself.

Focus. Focus on what needs to be done . . .

Tell her family.

Call for the pastor and the doctor.

Tell the workers.

Adjust schedules.

Start making funeral arrangements.

The list grew in her mind as she walked toward Granddad's study. The locked cabinet in the corner called to her. She was the only one who had a key to it now. Granddad's key. No one had even asked about it because there was no reason to.

No one else ever needed the relief she did.

She shut the door behind her and leaned against it. Granddad didn't need his whiskey anymore. It was there for her now. She almost smiled. Granddad *was* still taking care of her.

It wouldn't hurt to refill her bottle one more time. She rarely drank it anyway. Only when anxiety or pain threatened to overtake her.

Striding toward the cabinet, she pulled in a deep breath.

As she unlocked the cabinet, Granddad's words from long ago, when he tried to explain why Dad drank, rang in her ears. *"A lot of adults need to forget the bad things that have happened to them, and the bad things they've done."*

She nodded. She understood now.

Not that she was like her dad. Of course not! She used the tonic for medicine. Dr. Cameron had told her it was all right. The original tonic he'd given her had been more whiskey than anything else. He'd admitted as much.

She wasn't doing anything out of order.

She poured the amber liquid into the dark glass bottle and replaced the corks. There. That should help her through the next few months. Just enough to take the edge off of everything she had to face.

Is it enough?

She stopped. Stared at the bottle. Of course it was. She was being silly.

Before she could change her mind, she placed the whiskey bottle back into the cabinet, closed the door, and slid the key into the lock.

Her head twinged.

She couldn't avoid it any longer. She had to tell her family about Granddad.

Go ahead. Lock the cabinet.

But her hand wouldn't cooperate. It just held the key. And shook. Maybe she should take Granddad's large whiskey bottle back to her room—

No. There was enough in her pocket.

Setting her jaw, she turned the key. With the click of the lock, she jumped. Blinked her eyes. Felt a little like she was waking up from a deep sleep.

Shaking off the feeling, she went to grab her coat and boots. Then stopped. Why was she so jittery?

Then again, why *wouldn't* she be, considering what she was about to do?

Her trembling hand slipped into her pocket, drew out the bottle, and raised it for a sip. Just one, to steady up.

Her nerves calmed with the warmth of the liquid, and she patted the bottle. Her companion and help in facing what was to come. As she passed through the kitchen, she tore a leaf off the mint plant and shoved it into her mouth to chew on. A habit she'd picked up from her grandfather.

Oh, Granddad . . . how will we make it without you?

───────

Dr. Peter Cameron pushed his horse as fast as he dared over the snow-covered road leading to the Bundrant farm.

How could one family endure so much loss and hardship? So much unexpected and unsettling change. The Bundrant family never seemed to get a break.

Especially Whitney.

Ever since he'd met the eldest Powell daughter, he'd been impressed. And just a little concerned. Unless he was misreading her, she was keeping something hidden behind those deep brown eyes of hers. As much as he'd tried, he hadn't been able to break through the wall she kept around herself.

But she seemed to trust him. A rarity, he'd learned, for anyone but family. Because Miss Whitney Powell kept to herself.

Especially where Mr. Sinclair's attack on her was concerned.

At least she spoke to him as her doctor. That was a good start.

He'd spent a lot of time at the Bundrant farm checking on Chuck and getting to know the family. Christmas had passed in quiet apprehension while the family seemed to hold their collective breath, awaiting the next tragedy.

Now it had arrived.

He let out a long breath and watched it float behind him in a frozen mist. If the news from the milker was correct, they'd just lost their beloved patriarch. *Lord, how will they ever endure* this *tribulation?*

As he rode up to the house, Whitney was outside the door. Without a coat, gloves, or scarf. She stood there, stiff.

Her mussed, dark-red hair hung in a mass of curls around her shoulders and down her back. Her cheeks were ruddy and tear stained. But it was the look in her eyes that threatened to undo him.

Never had he seen such anguish and anger in one person.

"He's gone, Dr. Cameron."

Her clipped words and clenched jaw struck him to the core. How he longed to comfort her, to reach out and hold her close, but he knew better. After all these months, all the trauma, all the struggle, she would withdraw again. Of that, he was certain.

Would she be able to get past this and heal?

"I'm so sorry, Miss Powell."

She sniffed. "Thank you for coming. I'll take you to him."

As she led him through the familiar home and down the hallway to Chuck Bundrant's room, he caught a glimpse of the rest of the family gathered in the room with the piano. Their voices were soft, as were their sobs and sniffs.

His steps echoed on the wood floor. The hall stretched out before him. And then he saw Chuck.

"I didn't move him—"

How was Whitney keeping her words so calm and controlled?

"—because I thought you might be able to save him at first, and I didn't want to hurt him if he broke any bones when he fell. Then . . . well I wouldn't let anyone else touch him." She choked on the last word, then the stoic expression was back in place.

This woman was a force to be reckoned with.

She cleared her throat. "Do you need my help to move him back to the bed?"

Peter set his black bag down and shook his head. "No. I can manage." He'd been told that Chuck had been a robust and strong man before his bouts with apoplexy. The last year had taken a devastating toll. The man before him was thin, his skin sagging.

Peter leaned down and lifted the older man into his arms. A man who had lived a long life. Worked hard. Provided for his family. A man who had hoped to see many years to come. A man who told him just a few days ago that he was ready to put his efforts into walking again.

And yet, there was hope. Chuck had been taken from this life of suffering and gathered into the arms of his Savior.

No matter how many times Peter faced death, he never got used to it. This time, the loss lodged a lump in the back of his throat. How many had he not been able to save?

Why God?

Why did he keep failing?

"Failure is just the first step to surrender." Chuck had told him that. He'd shared hours of wisdom with Peter. Hadn't tried to hide his failings. Yearned to be a better man.

It had challenged Peter to do the same.

Why did You take this man, Lord?

He shook his head. It wasn't his place to question. Not now.

He laid a blanket over Chuck. Rigor mortis had set in, so the man had been dead for some time.

Peter looked at Whitney. "When did you find him?"

"About an hour and a half ago."

"He didn't have breakfast with the family this morning?"

"No." She lifted her chin. Did she think he was criticizing

her? "Granddad was awake when I went out at five thirty, but he asked to have more time to rest because he didn't sleep well last night." She pointed to the box in the chair. "Apparently, he stayed up writing his thoughts. I found the stack of paper in the bed. So I went out to run my dogs and then the rest of us had breakfast. Everyone else went back out to work, but it was my morning to help Granddad with his exercises. Since he'd seemed so weary, I thought I would bring him over to the fireplace and play for him. . . . But when I came to wake him, I found him on the floor."

She related it with such control. "Was he breathing at that point?"

She bit her lip. Controlled, yes. But there were deep emotions there. *Lord, help her.*

"No. His skin was already cold to the touch. I held my hand over his nose and mouth for more than a minute, hoping that he'd just fallen and I would feel him breathe. But he was already gone."

He dipped his chin. "I'm sorry you had to discover him like this."

She winced. "I'm glad I found him rather than my sisters. This is devastating to them."

He met her eyes. "What about you? You were so close to your grandfather."

Her shoulders lifted a bit. "I'm fine. Things have to be taken care of."

It wasn't healthy for her to keep everything bottled up—not even for an expert like her. Still now was not the time to probe deeper. But he would. Eventually. "Would you get John and Daniel for me? Your sisters too . . . there's a lot we need to discuss."

"All right." She left the room, and Peter stared down at

the man who'd built this farm from nothing. "I'm sorry I couldn't give you your wish to walk again, Chuck. But I'm grateful for the time I've known you." He lifted the blanket to cover Chuck's face.

On second thought, maybe he should go speak with them instead of asking them to join him in here. With quick steps he made his way to the large family gathering room.

The family stood as he entered.

"Please take your seats. I realized it would be easier if I came to you."

John reached out a hand. "Thank you for coming, Peter."

"Yes, thank you." Daniel offered his hand as well.

"I'm sorry for your loss. Chuck was a good man. He taught me a lot." Peter waited as they all took their seats. With a deep breath, he dove in. "I will prepare the body for burial today, but as you know, it's next to impossible to dig graves in the winter. You are probably aware that in town they store the coffins until the thaw. Since you have your own family cemetery here on the farm, Chuck won't need to be taken into town, but we need to find a place to store him where wild animals won't pick up the scent and try to get into the coffin. Is there a place here where it will stay cold, but also be protected from wolves and such?"

The ladies looked at each other with wide eyes. He hated having to discuss such delicate matters in front of them, but it was necessary. And they understood the harsh life in Alaska better than anyone else he knew.

Daniel lifted a hand and pointed to the fireplace. "You know, when I was in the Yukon, we often built huge fires to thaw out portions of land where we needed to dig for gold. It worked, but it took time. Maybe we could do that so we could give Chuck a proper burial sooner rather than later."

John patted his brother-in-law's shoulder. "I think we should do it."

"What about a coffin?" Havyn wiped at her eyes. "Do we need to go into town and purchase one?"

Shuffling sounded near the door.

"That won't be necessary."

All eyes shifted to find Christopher Powell standing there, his hat in his hands. "It would be an honor for me to build Chuck's coffin. I can start on it right away. If you will allow."

Peter glanced back to the family and then to Whitney. Her furrowed brow and the sparks in her eyes gave away her anger that their father had come. How long would she hold him at arm's length? While Peter understood the struggle and the painful history, the man was still her father. And she desperately needed him—even if she didn't realize it.

Madysen sprang up from the couch and went over to greet her father. "Would you? I know Granddad would appreciate that. As we all would." She glanced back at everyone, her eyes pleading.

"I could get it done by tomorrow." Christopher looked down at his hat. "I owe the man my life."

As the family stood and went to the man, the conversation stayed hushed as they expressed gratitude and sorrow.

Everyone except Whitney.

She hung back from the huddle of her family and watched. Then without a word . . .

She turned on her heel and raced out the door.

Two

So good ol' Chuck was dead. Very interesting. The question was, how could he use this to his advantage?

Judas paced his office. All these years, he'd worked to get himself into the family's good graces. They trusted him. Relied on him. But it hadn't gotten him any closer to acquiring Chuck's land. Or finding out where the man's gold came from. Gold that Chuck seemed to have in abundant supply. . . .

Out of everyone in this town, Chuck had been one of the few Judas couldn't control. He had nothing on the man. During Chuck's apoplexy recovery, when the family didn't know about their plentiful resources, Judas thought he'd wriggled his way in . . . but no. They paid their debt off to him as soon as Chuck could communicate.

Well, things were bound to change now.

A knock at his door brought his attention up.

The door opened, and his secretary nodded. "Mr. Davis is here to see you, sir."

"Show him in." Lifting his chin, he straightened his waistcoat and tie. It was a good thing the lawyer came as quick as he did.

"Mr. Reynolds." The mouse of a man entered and skittered into a chair. "I received your message."

Judas walked back behind his desk and took a seat. "You're the family lawyer for Mr. Bundrant?"

The man rolled his eyes. "You know I am. And I'm quite certain you've been informed of his death. Otherwise, you wouldn't have sent for me."

"That's indeed why I asked you here." He took his time and folded his hands on the desk in front of him. "Let me remind you of the debts that you owe, Mr. Davis. Debts in which you are delinquent because I hear you have a bit of a gambling problem. . . ." He let the words strike their mark.

Samuel Davis squirmed in his chair and looked everywhere but at Judas. "What do you want to know?" He stuck a finger in between his lips and began chewing on the nail.

"The terms of Chuck's will. How much is his fortune, and where is it?"

Davis shrugged and shifted in the chair. Was the man sitting on a tack? "I don't know the total of his fortune. He didn't put any of that into writing, and he definitely didn't put it in the bank. But I can tell you he split his property and everything he had between his three granddaughters. Originally, it was between his daughter and the granddaughters, but after Melissa died, he asked me to update the will, which I did. That's all I know."

Worthless fool. "I find that hard to believe."

Davis held out both his hands. "I promise. That's all I know. I've only seen Chuck once in the past year. You know how secretive he was."

Leaning back in his chair, Judas examined the man. "Fine. You can go. But not a word of this to anyone."

Davis stood and rushed out of the room. Judas would

have to deal with the debts later. For now, he might still have a use for the lawyer.

Sad, really. The man had once been quite the upstanding citizen. Now look at him.

His secretary stood in the doorway. "Anything else, Mr. Reynolds?"

With a tap to his desk, he looked up. "Yes, arrange with the hothouse to deliver several bouquets out to the Bundrant farm. One for each of the ladies. Make sure there's a personal card with each one that expresses my deepest condolences and sympathy. That if they need anything—anything at all—they need but ask."

"Right away, sir." She pulled the door closed as she left.

He turned his chair to stare out the window. What he needed was leverage. For all that Chuck kept things close to the vest, Judas had managed to wriggle his way into the man's good graces. The whole family considered him a close friend. Truth be told, his relationship with Chuck had been the longest-standing so-called friendship he'd ever managed. Probably because he had no use for anyone once he'd attained what he wanted from them. Easy enough to make useless people disappear over the years, and no one was the wiser.

But Bundrant had managed to keep him at a distance where his finances were concerned. Judas hadn't been deterred. Indeed, he'd risen to the challenge of capturing Chuck's fortune. Nothing like a good contest to get the blood flowing.

But things had changed the past year. Havyn married John Roselli, whose grandfather had been close friends with Chuck. John seemed as righteous as they came. Then Madysen married Daniel Beaufort. While Beaufort had a past, he'd shown that he'd changed. Of course, Daniel's father owed Judas a great deal of money, but that didn't help him get his hands on the Bundrant farm.

Then there was the eldest Powell sister . . . Whitney. Still unmarried.

A thought about how he might use her had flitted through his mind once before, but he'd brushed it off after watching her reaction to Sinclair. Now? Maybe it was a good time to revisit the idea.

There was a good deal of age difference between him and Whitney . . . but that didn't matter in this day and age. Besides, she trusted him. After all, he came to her rescue in the Sinclair incident. He'd stepped in when Sinclair spread rumors about Whitney after he attacked her, making the man admit, in front of the entire town on multiple occasions, that he'd lied. So Whitney owed Judas for restoring her reputation. Now that enough time had passed, he could remind her that he was her knight in shining armor.

He allowed a smile. It was about time he settled down and took a wife. Whitney was no-nonsense. Business minded. Not to mention beautiful. The choice couldn't be a better one.

He'd always wanted a son to carry on his name. To be remembered.

Maybe it was a good time to pursue more of a political career. With an upstanding bride by his side, he couldn't lose. Not that anyone in this town would ever go against him.

Standing up, he reached for his hat and coat.

Time to put the plan into motion.

After all, it was only right for him to call on the Bundrant family and express his deep sorrow in person.

Whitney climbed the small hill to the fenced-off family cemetery. Funny, when Granddad first worked on the area and told the family his plans for a cemetery, they thought it would be years before any of them would have need of it. Then life dealt them the blow of losing Mama.

With slow steps, she crested the hill and stared at the wooden cross in the center. The snow was deep. None of them had been up here for several weeks. There was a good chance she wouldn't even be able to open the gate. But she could climb the fence, if need be.

Frozen in place, she continued to stare. This was not how life was supposed to go.

A tear slipped out and rolled its way down her cheek, making her feel the sting of the frigid temperature.

The cold forced her forward with a shiver as she wiped at the frozen streaks on her cheek with her mitten.

Over the fence and through the deep snow, she trudged toward that cross marking where they'd buried their mother just a few short months ago.

"Mama . . ." The name escaped on a whisper. Several heartbeats passed as she wrestled with her heart and mind. "I never understood why people spoke to the dead, but I guess it makes sense now. Makes it feel like maybe you're not gone. Not really. Just for a little bit."

The wind whipped her scarf into her face. She tugged her hat down a little lower and crossed her arms over her chest. "I feel like I've been wandering around in a fog without you. Didn't realize how much I needed you until you weren't here anymore." Her throat threatened to close with the words. She shut her eyes and forced herself to stand tall.

She was supposed to be the strong one, wasn't she? "The thing is, Mama . . . you were the one who held us together.

You were the strong one. When I was young, I thought I had to fix things, but all along, you carried the load. So much more than any of us ever imagined. You protected us from the harsh realities of mining life. You did what you could to shelter us from the truth of what Daddy was—always talking about him in a positive way and telling us how much he loved us. No matter how many times he failed you . . . hurt you, you never spoke ill of him. For many years, I thought that made you weak. And that you allowed people to take advantage of you. But I was wrong."

She choked back a sob. "There were so many things I was wrong about. I'm sorry, Mama. I never thanked you properly for everything you did for me. For all of us. And now that Granddad's gone, I'm afraid I'm not good enough to fill either of your shoes. I feel lost."

Admitting it out loud made the burden on her shoulders lighter . . . but the ache worse.

She couldn't fault Mama for loving her dad. For seeing the good in him. That took a special person, someone who had an enormous heart and offered grace and forgiveness. Things *she* didn't excel at.

Many days, she'd pleaded with God to make her more compassionate and fun loving like Havyn. More merciful and positive like Madysen. More gracious like Mama.

But she was simply Whitney. Strong-willed. Stubborn. Hard. Broken and lost.

Where did that leave her? Havyn and Madysen were both married. She wouldn't change that for anything. John and Daniel were great men. She loved having brothers now too. But Dad had come back, bringing Eli and Bethany—his new family—and the distance in her heart grew.

Oh, her sisters never left her out of anything. But Whit

hadn't shared with them what was going on in her heart and mind the past few months. They thought her quiet moods were because of the attack.

But she had much more to heal from than just Garrett Sinclair. Admitting it felt wrong. Like she was betraying herself. But she was too weary to try to cover it up anymore.

Tears dripped down her face. "Oh, Mama . . . I wish you were here." A sob caught in her throat.

The snow crunched behind her, and she swallowed against the overwhelming grief, swiping at her cheeks. Whitney turned to see Ruth headed her way.

At least she didn't dislike Ruth anymore. What had started out as an awkward relationship between them, since she was Dad's new wife's sister, had turned into a timid friendship.

"Hi." Ruth's cheeks were pink. It made her look young and vibrant. She stayed outside the fence and leaned over it. "I'm so sorry to hear about Chuck."

Whitney took one last glance at the cross.

"I'm sorry, Whitney. I didn't mean to intrude. I'll head back and wait for you back at the house. Or maybe I'll go visit your dogs—"

She held up a hand. "No reason to apologize. I'll walk back with you." Whitney climbed back over the fence and forced every bit of emotion back into her heart. She was the strong one. Right? "It's hard to believe. I don't know if I've been able to process it yet. That's why I came up here to talk to Mama. Which probably sounds silly, but I miss her more than I can say."

Ruth stepped forward and wrapped her in a hug.

It wasn't as good as being hugged by her mother, but it soothed the cracked places in her heart she hadn't even realized were there. But she couldn't give them attention. Pulling back, she stiffened her shoulders and put on the mask she'd become all too accustomed to wearing.

"Pastor Wilson and Mr. Norris brought me out since Chris was already here. He came early to finish the coffin for Chuck." Ruth linked arms with her. "I know they are here to help with the plans for the funeral. But I wanted to tell you . . . anything you need me to do, I'm here. Just say the word."

"Thank you." The words were easy enough to say, but they were empty.

They hiked through the snow down the hill toward the house. Smoke puffed from the large chimney in the center of their home. The place that Granddad had designed and built for them. It was the most amazing house. Had she ever told him how much it meant to her? How much *he* meant to her?

"Losing your grandfather so soon after your mother must be devastating. How are doing? Have you eaten? Slept?"

Whitney waved her off. "I'm doing all right." A tiny part of her ached to talk about it, longed to tear down the walls around her heart and be seen, but she wasn't ready. Not yet. Maybe not ever. "How's the search for Stan going?" Ruth's husband had been missing for a long time.

Ruth shook her head. "Whitney Powell. You're trying to change the subject." The look in her eyes was full of compassion. "But I won't push. Whenever you need to talk, I'll be here. It's a promise."

"I appreciate that. I do." But she had to get the conversation off of her. "And Stan? Any news?"

"No news. Sadly. Every time we think there's a lead or some bit of news, it goes nowhere. Chris is trying to keep my spirits up, but I've resigned myself to hearing the news that Stan is gone." She sighed. "I guess it's easier to guard my hopes and my heart. The longer he's gone, the more I have to face that reality. One day, I'll have to tell my children, and that's the day I don't look forward to."

"I'm sorry, Ruth. Truly, I am. I know you must miss your children something fierce." The woman had left them with her mother back in Colorado while she came to Alaska to find her husband. How she handled the separation was beyond Whitney's comprehension.

"You understand loss and heartache better than anyone else. Time away from my children is much harder than I imagined, even though I know they are in excellent hands with my mother. But I haven't heard their voices in far too long . . . haven't been able to hug them. Watch them grow." She put a hand to her throat. "It's even harder to have no news on Stan. I don't know why . . . but I thought if I came up here that I could help find him. That I would know where he was, that I could *feel* him somehow. But instead . . . I feel nothing. And it's heartbreaking. Does that even make sense?"

Whitney pressed her lips together. "It does."

"I don't mean to burden you with more, Whitney. Please forgive me. You of all people understand the constant bad news. How it's easier to steel yourself for the next blow. You must have felt like you were walking on eggshells for months now. Waiting for something else to happen."

Amazing how Ruth could put it into words. "It's been the hardest year of my life."

"Just remember that you have a friend here, all right? I know you have your sisters, but I've seen how difficult it has been for you to be strong and be the oldest while the others are married. It must be lonely for you."

Lonely was never a word that she would have used to describe herself. Never.

A loving family with lots of laughter and music had

surrounded her for her whole life. There were moments she ached to have time to herself, so she could get her thoughts straight. But now . . . now she wished it back. For her family to be intact again. For Madysen to be twirling around the parlor with some fanciful idea in her head, excited to share the joy. For Havyn to come in and chatter with one of her chicken stories. For Mama to play the piano and try to wrangle them into practicing at the same tempo.

For Granddad to be sitting in his chair, his face beaming, clapping his hands and telling them that his girls were the most talented in the world.

Why hadn't she treasured and appreciated those times while she had them? Why couldn't she understand this big hole left behind? Nothing seemed right. Or normal. Or okay.

"Whitney?" Ruth's voice stopped her in her tracks. "Are you all right?"

They were already back to the house. Funny, she hadn't even paid attention to where she was walking. "I'm fine."

"I'm having trouble believing that." Ruth reached for Whitney's hands. Then she squeezed them. "You've endured a horrible loss. It's perfectly acceptable for you to say that you are struggling. You don't always have to be the strong one. Let those of us who love you help to carry the load."

Ruth sounded so much like Mama. Her words struck Whitney's heart and made her want to crumple into the snow and cry. But she couldn't do that. Not with everything to be done. "I appreciate that, Ruth. I do." She knew her words sounded cold, but that was all she could offer at the moment.

"Miss Powell . . . Whitney."

She lifted her chin and looked toward the door. Pastor Wilson stood there, his eyes full of compassion. "Thank you for coming, Pastor."

He held out a hand to her. "We've gathered in the parlor to discuss the arrangements for Chuck. Will you join us?"

"Of course." The expression in his eyes pierced her chest like a knife. The man had journeyed with them through too much this past year.

She looked away, needing no more reminders of all she had lost.

They followed the pastor into the parlor after shedding their coats and gloves. Whitney steeled herself for the conversation to come.

She looked around the room to each face. Havyn and John, Madysen and Daniel, Pastor Wilson, Mr. Norris, Chris—her dad—and two of his other kids.

Havyn scooted closer to John and patted the settee next to her. "Here, Whit."

Taking the seat, she turned to their pastor. "I know you are very busy, but we appreciate you taking the time to come out and help us with this. Granddad was quite specific about what he wanted."

The pastor chuckled. "Chuck was indeed specific. That's why we came as quick as we could. Mr. Norris has offered his Roadhouse to have a service since so many in town would like to be present. Things can be done a little different since it's the middle of winter. We can do the service at the Roadhouse and then if people want to come out here for the burial they can, but most people won't expect a burial to be happening anyway."

"We're going to start the fires as soon as we are done here, and Amka has taken it upon herself to arrange for the grave to be dug. It will have to be done in layers as the fire thaws the ground, but Inuksuk and Yutu have assured me they will get it taken care of so we don't have to worry about it." John leaned forward and put his elbows on his knees. "We know that Chuck wished to be buried immediately. But this will have to do."

"Will tomorrow after lunch work for the service in town?"

Madysen lifted her hand and piped up. "That won't interfere with your business, Mr. Norris?"

"Not at all. I will close tomorrow morning and set up the room. There will be plenty of time to reopen for dinner." The owner of the Roadhouse had been lavish with his generosity to them over the years. As Whitney watched the man's face, she realized his eyes shone with unshed tears. He'd been friends with her grandfather for many years.

"Your goodness to our family is overwhelming, Mr. Norris. Thank you." Whitney tipped her chin toward him but couldn't meet his eyes. The numbness inside her grew.

"It's the least I can do for Chuck."

Pastor Wilson clasped his hands behind his back and cleared his throat. "I have notes from Chuck about his wishes. He wants several hymns to be sung and for the Gospel to be shared. In his words, 'I don't want sad and dreary. I want joyful. People celebrating with me that I'm in heaven.' Now, I know that is hard to even imagine for us. It's extremely difficult for those left behind to embrace joy in the midst of their grief. That's why I'd like to ask if there's anything you ladies would like me to include? Any wishes that you have?"

"Granddad asked if we would sing at his funeral." Havyn's words sounded as if they were choked. She caught Whitney's gaze. "But I don't know if we can do that. Can we?"

She'd forgotten about Granddad's request.

Madysen chimed in. "I will probably cry my way through it, but I think we should. It was what he wanted. What do you think, Whit?"

As much as it hurt to even think about, Whitney straightened her shoulders. "Since it was Granddad's wish, I think it's the best way we can honor him. It's what we should do." Easy enough to say, but doing it would be another thing altogether. The mask and the numbness would have to stay in place.

For as long as it took to make it through.

Riding out to the Bundrant farm, Peter prayed for each member of the family. Havyn and John had become good friends to him, and he had the opportunity to be their doctor as they awaited their first child. Always an exciting time.

Madysen and Daniel were just as much a joy to know. Maddy would have made an exceptional nurse as much as she loved to rescue people and animals alike.

Then there was Whitney. She had been heavy on his heart for months now. He always prayed for his patients, but for some reason the good Lord seemed to bring her to mind more often than any other.

It was amazing how much she'd endured, and yet she kept on going. Perhaps he could get her to open up and that might help her heal. *Lord, please show me how to help her.*

The frigid air cleansed his lungs as he prayed. The farm came into view, and he slowed his horse. Several other horses were hitched to the post. Probably the pastor helping to make arrangements. But then a flash of cinnamon-red hair caught his attention. Whitney was out with her dogs. He took a second glance. Her hair was the most beautiful shade of red.

Instead of going inside, he headed toward her. Alone with her, he could assess how she was *really* doing.

"Good morning, Miss Powell." He always made a point of letting her know he was approaching. After a physical attack, many women couldn't bear to be surprised by a man's presence.

Her head snapped up. "Good morning, *doctor*. Didn't I ask you to call me Whitney?"

He grinned and removed his hat. "As long as you call me Peter."

One eyebrow quirked up at him as she crossed her arms over her chest. "You first."

"All right. Good morning, Whitney."

"Good morning, Peter." No smile, but neither did she frown. That was better than nothing.

"How are you holding up?" Best to just dive in. Whitney wasn't a fan of chitchat.

She blinked several times. "I'm fine."

"Care to elaborate on that?"

She flung her hands out and huffed. "What do you want me to say? That I'm devastated my granddad is gone? That life won't be the same . . . ever? That I haven't even dealt with the loss of my mother, or both of my sisters getting married, or my long-thought-dead father coming back to life with a whole new family?" Her eyes widened as if she was waiting for some kind of answer from him. "I'm *fine*. See?" Walking past him, she grabbed a bucket with more force than was necessary and growled at him.

"Yeah. Sure. You're fine." He tried hard to keep a neutral expression on his face, but he doubted it was possible as the sarcastic words slipped out. At least she was talking to him.

"You just won't leave me be, will you?"

"Nope." He shoved his hands in his pockets. "Not only am I your physician, Whitney, but I'd like to think that I'm your friend as well. And I can't be good at either one if I leave you be." This could lead to treacherous waters if he wasn't careful. Charlotte used to tell him that his Achilles' heel was the investment he put into his patients. A double-edged sword—because he cared so much, which was necessary in a doctor, but it cost him greatly.

Charlotte. His heart twinged. She'd waited while he finished medical school. Helped him study. Was the one who understood what made him push himself to be the best doctor he could be.

"Well, as soon as you share what put that look on your face, I'll spill the beans about everything I'm feeling."

He looked up.

Whitney's hands were on her hips. And she dared him with her eyes.

How long had he been standing there thinking of Charlotte? "I'm here to check on *you*."

"That's an excuse, Peter. You just said you thought you were my friend. Last time I checked, friendships went both ways." Her cheeks flushed and her eyes sparked.

But he saw through them to the fragile veil that was her shield for now. Deflection. Redirecting attention off of her. Somehow he needed to help her protect that, or she might very well fall apart. And he didn't want that. "I am your friend. And you're correct. It goes both ways." Honesty was always the best policy. "I was remembering someone . . . I lost."

Her gaze shot down to the ground, and she toed the snow with her boot. "I'm sorry. Sometimes I forget others have lost people too. How incredibly selfish of me . . ." She shook her head and walked toward him. "I didn't mean to lash out at you. You've done nothing but help during some really troublesome times." The strong façade was back up. Appearing in control of her emotions again, Whitney stared at him. "Thank you for checking on me. I admit I was a bit overwhelmed talking about the funeral, so I came out here to have some time to myself."

"Totally understandable that you wanted time." He put his hat back on his head. "I didn't mean to intrude. I'll head back to the house and see if there's anything I can do."

"I said I *thought* I needed time to myself. But then I realized that I would spend a lot more time by myself from now on. Makes me feel alone. And I don't quite know how to deal with that."

Look at that, she was opening up after all.

He kept his voice casual. "Grief is tricky that way. You won't know how to feel for quite a while."

She nodded. Stared away toward the horizon.

The silence stretched. Not one to fill empty space with shallow words, Peter weighed his options. "You're not alone, Whitney. Remember that." Turning on his heel, he tossed over his shoulder. "It was good to see you. I'm praying for you."

"Wait."

He stopped and looked back.

"The funeral is tomorrow at the Roadhouse." Her words were hushed. Defeated. "After lunch."

He stepped closer to her.

She knelt down and petted one of her dogs. "Will you come?"

"Of course. I'll be there."

Her chin dipped in a slight nod, and then she walked past him one more time. "Thank you. I better go check on my family now."

As her words washed over him, so did her breath.

Peter let her retreat. It was her safety net. But the whiff of whiskey couldn't be denied. One day soon, he'd have to ask her about it. And it might very well be the end of their friendship.

A thought that hurt more than he wanted to admit.

THREE

Watching Whitney stand beside her sisters, Peter couldn't ignore the niggle at the back of his brain. The liquor he'd smelled on her yesterday hadn't been a figment of his imagination. Normally she smelled of mint. A scent that now always reminded him of her. She'd mentioned to him how she liked to chew on the leaves—especially when she was mucking the dogs' kennels. Made complete sense. But it wasn't mint yesterday. He knew what he'd smelled. If he didn't speak to her about it, who would? No one else probably even knew. Why hadn't she talked to him about needing more tonic? The pain had obviously continued, and he didn't blame her for doing whatever she could to keep going. That was who she was. Strong, capable, independent. But if the stoic look on her face was any indication, she would continue to run herself ragged and treat herself with alcohol, and things could spiral out of control.

The funeral service had been beautiful, but it had taken its toll. The dark circles under her eyes and the slouch to her shoulders made him want to take her home immediately and insist that she get some rest.

But she would refuse. Every fiber of his being could predict it.

It had been months since he'd given her the tonic, but the consequences of the attack were more than just physical. She'd dealt with anxiety and fear since that day. Things that Whitney attested to being new and strange to her. And she'd made him promise that he wouldn't tell her family.

Rumors had flown throughout Nome that Whitney was a loose woman. Until Sinclair changed his story and made a public declaration of her innocence in the matter. The apology had, no doubt, been forced by the man's employer. *Judas.* Which didn't matter—at least her reputation had been restored.

Then Sinclair disappeared.

No one missed the man. But Whitney had once mentioned her fear of him returning.

Even though she never gave details of the attack, it hadn't been hard to put two and two together.

The physical attack and emotional consequences would be difficult to heal from even if that was all Miss Powell had to deal with. But when compounded with every other trial her family had encountered in the past year, she was on the verge of breaking. She'd never admit it, but he could see it. Almost as if she stood on the brink of a precipice and it wouldn't take much to push her over the edge. If she continued to keep things bottled up and turn to the "tonic" for help, the results could be catastrophic.

He'd just have to stay attentive to Whitney's demeanor, actions, and health.

So far, she'd been honest with him when he'd checked on

her. At her last visit, she hadn't mentioned needing the tonic any longer . . . but would she use this latest grief and loss to shut everyone out, including him? If not, would confronting her about what he suspected push her away?

He shook away the questions and focused on the here and now.

The Roadhouse hummed with quiet chatter. The service had been beautiful. The girls sang "Rock of Ages" to close the service in the most beautiful performance he'd ever heard. Their harmonies were glorious. Their voices strong. Even though each one of them had tears glistening in her eyes.

It appeared the entire town of Nome had shown up for the service.

Peter stood in line to speak to the family, listening to the praise and memories of Chuck Bundrant.

Before Peter reached the family, Whitney excused herself and went out the side door.

Odd. Or maybe not so much. Grief could make it difficult to be around crowds of people.

For several moments, he watched the door she'd used as an exit and debated with himself. But when she didn't return, he followed her in the direction of her retreat.

Bright sunlight blinded him for a moment, and he put a hand over his eyes to adjust. The snow shimmered like diamonds. He searched the area around the building and then spotted her. With her arms crossed over her middle, her chin was dipped low. She'd taken out the ribbon that had tamed her curly hair, and it hung from her fingertips. As her curls swayed in the bone-chilling wind, she lifted a hand to rub one of her temples.

Oh no. Another headache. There had to be something else he could do to help relieve her misery. When he got back to his office, he'd have to search every medical text he owned. One more time.

Taking long strides toward her, he didn't try to quiet his steps. Just so she'd have warning that he was approaching.

She turned and tucked something in her pocket.

Oh, Whitney. Not the tonic again. How much of a habit had this become? How did she have any left . . . or was she refilling the same bottle when it emptied?

The desire to confront her fought with his compassion. Perhaps now was not the time.

Lord, I need Your divine wisdom here. Please help me understand when I need to bring up this topic with Whitney. I want her to trust me so she knows my concern is genuine and for her benefit.

"Hi." Her voice cracked. Though he'd seen her eyes appear to be teary a few times, she hadn't sobbed like her sisters. "Thank you for coming."

He'd expected her to keep control of her emotions, because she was the constant strength for her sisters. But she needed a good cry. To grieve. If only he knew the solution. "I wanted to offer my condolences."

"You already did back at the house. But I appreciate it nonetheless." The hankie in her hand twisted with the ribbon between her fingers.

"I realize you probably would like some time to yourself, and I won't stay, but I know you prefer talking one-on-one."

A sad smile lifted her lips, but she wouldn't make eye contact. "You do seem to understand me, Peter Cameron."

That was encouraging. "I think it would be good if we made an appointment later this week for me to assess how your head injury is healing. I want to make sure you aren't having any adverse reactions in your vision or hearing. Those are the most common side effects that people ignore, not realizing more damage was done than originally thought. I don't wish to miss anything." Maybe appealing to her logic would get her to acquiesce.

"I'm fine. But I appreciate your concern." Wrapping the ribbon around her fingers, she stared at the ground.

"You're not fine. You're in pain. Another headache?" He inched closer, as if he was approaching a timid animal.

Her shoulders drooped as she let out a long breath. "I didn't want anyone to notice."

"It's my job to notice these things." Another step. Keeping his eyes on her face, he hoped she wouldn't flee again.

She whipped around to face him, her eyes narrowed. "I don't care." Clamping her lips shut, she softened as tears filled her eyes. "I'm sorry. I don't mean to snap. But my family doesn't need anything else to worry about. They need to grieve, and it's *my job* to take care of them now."

Of course she would take the responsibility of the world on her shoulders. "All right. I won't push for now. But I'm here if you want to talk to someone. I understand and I won't judge. I do need to see you within the next month. Agreed?"

She shrugged. "If it will keep you from nagging me."

"Is the good doctor nagging you?" Judas Reynolds's smooth voice behind him made Peter frown. He turned.

Havyn and Madysen walked on either side of the man.

Peter forced a smile. "Only doing my duty as her physician."

"Of course, of course." Judas patted Peter's back, then he walked past him to Whitney.

"Judas wanted to check on you, Whit, and so did we." Havyn stopped beside Peter. "Thank you for coming, Dr.

Cameron. We are indebted to you for your impeccable care of Granddad."

Madysen stepped over to her eldest sister and linked arms with her before kissing her on the cheek. "We didn't want you to be alone."

"As you can see, I'm not alone. I'm fine." The words were stiff. Without emotion. Poor Whitney.

Madysen patted her arm. "Well, I know Judas wanted to speak with you, so we will head back inside."

John appeared beside Peter as he tried to keep an eye on Whitney. What was Judas up to? The man offered Whitney an arm and she took it.

John stepped into Peter's line of sight. "Could I ask you a question?"

"Of course." He moved his eyes to John, but kept his ears attuned to the other conversation happening.

John was simply worried about a toenail he'd lost after a calf stepped on it last week. He said that Havyn made him promise to talk to Peter about it, but he hadn't wanted to be a bother.

While Peter gave John instructions on what to do, he overheard Judas remind Whitney that he was there for her. That he'd helped restore her reputation and wanted her to know that he would forever be her champion. The man was laying it on pretty thick. Especially when he shared that Whitney had always held his attention and admiration.

Peter wanted to interrupt, but that would be rude. John was talking now about his nervousness about the coming baby. After giving the father-to-be some encouragement and words of affirmation, he snuck a glance back at Judas. The man was looking down on Whitney, his expression far too intimate.

The man was attempting to woo Whitney. Good grief.

Well, the rest of the town, and the entire Bundrant clan, may think the man hung the moon, but he knew better. Judas was never there for anyone but himself. He wanted to be in charge. To own and run the town.

How the man had besotted so many people was beyond Peter, but at least *he* was wise to the truth. Years ago, when he was young and just out of medical school, he'd met a man just like Judas. Sadly, Peter had been hoodwinked by the fraud, like the rest of the town. But lesson learned. From the moment he'd met Judas Reynolds, he knew. What he was going to do about it at this point was yet to be seen. Best to observe and watch and pray for the right words when the time came to say something.

As he watched Judas walk Whitney back to the Roadhouse, a sinking feeling filled his gut. How could he protect Whitney—and Nome for that matter—from a powerful man like Reynolds?

Everything passed in a blur. Like it had all been some sort of play and she wasn't actually living it. It wasn't until Judas came out to chat with her that Whitney saw through the fog.

Not that him speaking with her was so jolting. It was the way he'd looked at her. Different than ever before. And it was the first time she'd really studied the man's eyes. Judas Reynolds had been a part of their lives since they'd come to Nome. He had been a dear friend of the family, someone they knew they could rely on, no matter what. He'd helped them time and again, and Granddad had trusted him.

But today . . .

His gaze had penetrated her grief, and she'd noticed the

icy blue of his eyes. She'd always thought him to be a handsome man. Even had remarked with her sisters about how striking his eyes were. But she'd never felt so . . . connected to him.

She rubbed at her eyes as the sleigh reached their home. She was being ridiculous. Grief did weird things to people.

Climbing down, she told her family that she needed some time alone and was going to Granddad's room. She hated abandoning her sisters, but if she didn't get a few moments of silence, her head might explode.

They hadn't expected half the town to come out to the burial. It was amazing that Amka's brothers had been able to dig the grave to the depth they had. But it was all over now.

Thank God.

Granddad was buried. A cross had been placed.

Now they just had to find a way to go on without him. And without Mama.

She took off her snow-covered boots in the coatroom Granddad had built into the entry, shed her hat, coat, and gloves, and then went down the hallway toward his room.

The doorknob squeaked as she turned it. She held her breath and pushed the door open slowly. Was she ready to see the room empty of her grandfather's presence?

The winter sunshine spilled through the window and pooled on the floor almost exactly where she'd found him. As she closed her eyes, she could still see him there. Crumpled and lifeless.

She forced herself to look again, but he wasn't there.

Closing the door behind her, she took a deep breath. Wished she could cry her heart out like that first day. But the tears wouldn't come. All her life she'd had to be strong, and she'd convinced herself that tears didn't fit that. Now, when she needed the release more than anything, she was numb. Empty.

She'd promised her mother she would always look out for Havyn and Madysen. Was she feeling this way because her sisters were both married now? Daniel and John did a fabulous job of taking care of their wives. No one had shunned or ignored Whitney. And it wasn't like she didn't feel like part of the family, but . . .

What was her place now? Her sisters didn't need her to mother-hen them. She couldn't take Mama's place in their lives. Couldn't fill the enormous shoes their grandfather left.

The plain and simple truth was . . .

She *had* no place.

There was no one to care for her needs except herself.

Or was there?

Judas's warm expression this afternoon came to mind.

Foolish thought. Now was not the time to be dreaming of romantic notions.

Over the years, he'd shown them many kindnesses. A lot of compassion. Grace by the bucketload. For instance, when Maddy stole the sheep.

Or when Mama was sick and he paid for the passage for two so Madysen could take Mama to Seattle.

Instance after instance came swirling back. Judas had become like part of the family.

The door gave its telltale squeak, and Whitney turned to see her sisters peeking in.

"It's all right. Come on in." She held out her arms, and they embraced in a group hug.

"You all right?" Maddy stroked her shoulder.

"Yes. It's simply been an exhausting day. All the way around." She snuck a glance back at the spot on the floor where she'd found Granddad. Swallowed against the lump in her throat. She wanted to sob on his chest like that morning. But he was gone.

"I'm so sorry you had to be the one to find him, Whit. I know that couldn't have been easy." Havyn sat on the edge of their grandfather's bed and put a hankie to her eyes.

"I'm glad it was me so that you two didn't have to go through that." She'd been trying to shield her younger sisters from the pain of life ever since she'd first dragged their father home from Saloon Row. It was a vow she'd made to herself as a little girl. No one should have to endure the pain and heartache she did. Especially her family. "In particular you, Havyn. In your delicate condition, that wouldn't have been good."

Havyn put a hand to her waist. "I wouldn't say that I'm delicate, but I sure do seem to cry at the drop of a hat nowadays." Tears streamed down her face. "See? I can't seem to stop them."

If only *she* had that problem. Maybe she wouldn't feel like she was hollow one minute and then like a volcano ready to erupt the next.

Maddy sat by Havyn on the bed. "We came in here to tell you Mr. Davis—Granddad's lawyer—approached Havyn and John after the funeral. He asked if we would come by his office on Friday for the reading of Granddad's will."

Why did that feel so final? She said as much to her sisters. "I guess there's no getting around it. We have to move forward. It's not like the world will stop spinning just because we want to grieve for a little longer."

"Or pretend none of this happened." Havyn burst into tears again.

Maddy wrapped an arm around Havyn's shoulders. "There

are still mornings that I wake up and forget that Mama is gone. I keep thinking I'll hear her singing in the kitchen. Or telling me to tune my cello."

Whitney sat on the other side of Havyn and held out her hands to her sisters. "We'll get through this together. We have to think about what Granddad would want us to do with his farm. How we can honor him and the legacy he left to us."

Maddy squeezed her hand. "He'd want us to run the farm together as a family, give glory to God, and be happy."

Havyn straightened her shoulders and sniffed. "I agree. And Mama would want us to stay close to God and each other." She looked back and forth between Whitney and Madysen. "I know you already know this, but I can't tell you how important it is that you both are with me during this time. I wouldn't want to be anywhere else, and I would hate for either of you to leave. First and foremost because I love you both so much, but even more so as I'm facing the birth of my first child. Which, I have to say, scares me more than I'd like to admit."

Maddy laid her head on Havyn's shoulder. "We will be here for you no matter what! Every second. Right, Whit?"

Forcing a slight smile, she nodded. "Of course. Every step of the way, we'll be by your side. Just let us know what you need." She could be strong. Keep up the façade. They needed her.

At least for now.

———

Madysen closed the door to their grandfather's room and walked to the kitchen. She'd offered to get some sandwiches together. Even though none of the sisters had much of an appetite, the men had to be hungry.

Havyn was beginning to show that she was with child, and Maddy's heart soared. Hopefully, she wouldn't have to wait too long before she could share that same joy.

But what would that do to Whit? Her heart sank.

Something wasn't right with their older sister. Hadn't been right for some time now.

True, they'd all taken an enormous hit when they lost Mama. But it affected Whitney the most, even though she wouldn't admit it at the time. But she'd closed off more since then. Walled off her heart and became more stoic than ever. Even more reluctant to allow anyone in than before. Poured herself out for everyone else. For a while, Madysen had chalked it up to their grief. That it was how Whit was coping. But Madysen's heart had begun to clench every time she noticed one of the signs. This wasn't the sister she knew. Something had to be done about it.

Then that horrible Sinclair fellow put her into a downward spiral toward melancholy. Something that none of the Powell women had ever been prone to.

They'd walked on eggshells for a while, not wanting to make things worse. Then there were the headaches.

Those terrible pains still seemed to plague her sister on too regular of a basis. But Whitney refused help or attention. Dr. Cameron had seen her many times but hadn't expressed any serious concern for a while now.

Madysen bit her lip. Was she overprotective? Mama would tell her that worry was a sin. That she should cast her cares upon the Lord just like 1 Peter chapter 5 instructed. But what would Mama *do* in this kind of situation? They'd never dealt with anything like this. No one had ever injured any of them before. Their lives had been protected, even though they'd lived in some rowdy places.

Granddad had made sure that "his girls" were taken care of. Tears pricked her eyes for the umpteenth time. Daniel and John would do an amazing job taking care of them all, of that she was certain. But it was different. Granddad couldn't be replaced. He was one of a kind. At least she could rejoice that he was in heaven.

Footsteps sounded in the hall, and Havyn joined her in the kitchen. "Whitney is going to check on the dogs and then go to bed. I think another headache is coming on."

With a glance out the window, she saw Whitney walking toward the dog pens. "I'm concerned about the headaches, Havyn. Do you think she's having more of them now?"

"I'm not sure. I haven't been keeping track." Her sister's brow crinkled in the middle. "But you know Whit. She keeps to herself since she's the one who was always looking out for us."

"But it's exacerbated now. Maybe we need to show her that she doesn't have to carry the burden by herself. You know, show her how much we care and want her to be a part of everything. It can't be easy for her with the changes that have happened. I can't imagine how I would feel if I were the one unmarried and the oldest." She bit her lip. It wasn't something any of them had said out loud, but Madysen had thought about it several times.

"You're right." Havyn sliced through a loaf of fresh bread. "I hadn't thought about how our happy changes could affect her negatively. I always thought that it was nice to have some joy in the midst of our troubles, but maybe not so much for everyone."

"Do you think she's lonely?"

"As much as she tries to have time to herself? I don't think that's ever been a problem." Havyn slipped a bite of bread into her mouth. "How could anyone feel lonely in the middle of this family?"

Maddy wanted to agree with her sister, but as her gaze went back out the window, she watched Whitney walk across the farm, her shoulders slumped, her steps slow.

Could they be wrong?

FOUR

The stack of mail on his desk beckoned, but Judas paced the room instead. All because of the handwriting on the top envelope.

Why would the imbecile decide to write to him now? It had been . . . years. Decades, to be honest.

That life was far behind Judas. He'd left it as soon as Olivia informed him that God "told" her not to marry him. *God*.

As if her revelation would make him change directions and follow in his father's and grandfather's footsteps as a traveling preacher.

His nostrils flared. Narrowing his eyes, he placed his hands on his hips and stomped over to the desk. Ripping open the letter, he pursed his lips and tried to push thoughts of Olivia back to where they belonged—where *she* belonged—the cellar. Locked up tight. If only he could banish her completely from his mind.

With one hand he slammed the torn envelope to his desk while he flicked open the folded page with the other.

Judas,

I know you asked for me to never communicate with you again, but the good Lord has placed you on my heart. It is a heavy burden that will not go away. And even as I have tried to abide by your wishes, I have been tortured by my neglect of you. Ever since the passing of Ananias, I knew that it would fall to me to bring you back into the fold.

Time is running out for you. The urgency that has filled my very being will not rest until I see you again. Please let me know when I am welcome. I will make plans to journey north later this summer and perhaps stay for the winter.

I will not accept a negative response. My congregation is aware, and they have been praying for you daily. They are also raising money for the long journey. You are loved and not forgotten.

In Christ's Love,
Cain

Time was running out for *him*? Oh, to be so naïve and brainwashed into thinking such morbid thoughts. Who did Cain think he was to make such demands?

Ridiculous. The man would never raise enough funds with that ridiculously tiny church of his. There was nothing to worry about.

Judas stuffed the letter back into the mangled envelope.

Cain was full of bluster. His words would never amount to anything.

Just like the man himself.

Mr. Davis's office was comfortable enough, but Whitney still wanted to squirm. She didn't want to be here. Didn't want it all to be over. It was bad enough that they'd buried Granddad two days ago. Couldn't they pretend none of this happened and just continue on as normal? Why did reading the will have to be taken care of now?

"Good morning, ladies. I appreciate you coming." Mr. Davis nodded at each of them. "Thank you for coming here as well, Mr. Roselli and Mr. Beaufort."

Daniel and John stood behind the chairs where their wives sat.

No one stood behind her chair.

The reality glared at her and made the expanse of the room widen in her mind. She was alone.

She straightened her shoulders. There was nothing wrong with her. She was fine.

"As you know, your grandfather changed his will after each one of you married. To make things clear, the entire estate is divided equally between Chuck Bundrant's three grand-daughters. But to ensure that things cannot be legally tampered with, John Roselli is named as the guardian of the estate. Our district of Alaska's law concerning women owning land are not completely straightforward. Thus, Chuck entered into the initial contract with John last year, as you know.

"As the guardian," Mr. Davis cleared his throat, "John owns nothing other than what he owns along with his wife, Havyn. But no other man can lay claim without the guardian's permission. Chuck put this in place to protect you until each sister is married."

Whitney swallowed hard. Heat filled her cheeks. Why were women made to feel inadequate if they weren't married?

Of course, she'd always *wanted* to be married when she

was younger. It's not that it was a bad thing. But men hadn't exactly proven themselves trustworthy.

Oh, there were John and Daniel, and she trusted them, but even though they were great husbands to her sisters, they weren't perfect. Her father hadn't been trustworthy. Even Granddad had lied to them on multiple occasions. Sure, it was to protect them, but a lie was a lie.

Mr. Davis droned on about her sisters' rights with their husbands. She shifted in her seat and squashed the desire to simply leave. This would be over soon, and she could go home and take her dogs out for a long run.

The lawyer picked up some papers. "Now, I'll continue with the reading of the will."

Just like he'd explained, everything was divided between the three of them. Blah, blah, blah. And more of the same legal verbiage. More blah, blah, blah. None of it mattered. Not really. It couldn't bring Granddad back. Or Mama.

Everyone went silent. Whitney glanced at her sisters, who both touched hankies to their eyes.

Mr. Davis coughed and picked up another envelope. "Then there's the letter Chuck asked me to read." The man picked up a glass of water and drank for several seconds. He caught Whitney's eye and looked back down at the paper and tugged a bit at his collar. "'My dear girls . . .'" Mr. Davis cleared his throat again.

"'My dear girls, I hoped the good Lord would heal my physical body enough to stay a few more years on this earth, but He healed me in another way. The better way. I'm so sorry to leave you all behind, especially after the loss of your sweet mother, but please do not mourn for me. I am forever with my Savior. Rejoice in that fact.

"'Sweet, fiery, merciful Maddy: I love you. Ever since the

day you were born and placed in my arms, a precious tiny bundle, you grabbed onto my heart and I knew you'd never let go. I know that Daniel will take amazing care of you. Keep loving those sheep, standing up for those less fortunate, and playing the cello. You make that giant violin sing.'"

Maddy laughed through her tears as Daniel wrapped her in his arms.

"'Havyn: Our secret keeper and violin virtuoso, who for some crazy reason loves to name every one of her chickens. As the middle child, you've been referee and more often the glue that held you and your sisters—and all of us—together. You have blessed me immeasurably. John is your perfect match, and I'm so thankful God brought him here. Name a rooster or two after me—especially the ornery ones—just promise me you won't fry them up.'"

"Oh, Granddad." Havyn put her face in her hands and cried.

The lawyer glanced at her again. Then went back to the paper. "'And last, to my eldest grandchild, the ever-unshakable Whitney. I've never in my life seen anyone work with dogs the way you do. It's a special gift—but even more of a gift is your talent at the piano. Your mother and I often sat in awe, tears streaming down our faces, as we listened to you play when you thought no one was around. Keep playing for God's glory. He will help you find your way. You are strong and beloved.'"

Mr. Davis turned the page.

Granddad's words were sweet, but instead of letting them in to soothe the raw places, she put them away in her mind. It was easier. Maybe one day . . .

The lawyer read the rest. Challenging and encouraging words. To stay strong and supportive of one another, to keep playing beautiful music for God, to take care of the farm. All things she expected to hear from Granddad.

Whitney's heart stung at the poignant words, but none of them explained how to make it through. How to go on after so much loss.

She swallowed and sat taller.

Mr. Davis handed a sealed envelope to Whitney. What was this?

"This envelope contains a letter from your grandfather with the information you will need to find his gold and everything else of value." Mr. Davis held up both of his hands. "Please, don't ask me questions about it, because Mr. Bundrant kept it a secret. The information is privileged and I have never seen it. Your grandfather informed me it was in some sort of coded note, for which I do not have any clues or collection of knowledge. He wanted to ensure that you would be the sole ones able to access anything."

Havyn let out a slight chuckle. "Granddad. He always did distrust banks and everyone else."

Madysen laughed a bit as well. "He'll probably send us on some sort of wild goose chase to find it."

Listening to her sisters made her smile. "Remember that time he created a scavenger hunt for us on Mama's birthday?"

Laughter filled the room, and Whitney tucked the letter into her reticule. They could read it at home. Each of them knew about Granddad's code. Granted, it had been many years since they'd used it, but when they were little, he'd given each of them a piece of the key. One of them couldn't decipher it on her own. They had to come together to do it.

"There's one more part of your grandfather's will that I need to read." Mr. Davis walked back behind his desk and put his spectacles on his nose. He sat in his chair and lifted another envelope. "Chuck had me write this out for him a couple weeks ago."

Whitney looked at her sisters. Hadn't everything been covered in the will? But Granddad was nothing if not thorough.

Mr. Davis held the note and read: "'It is my desire that Christopher Powell, his two children currently in Alaska, and his sister-in-law, Ruth, move into the family farm while Chris is searching for Stan. There's no need for the family to be separated, and since it was my hand that did the separating many years ago, I want to rectify that now. I know it is costing a good deal of money for them to stay in a hotel in town, and it must be quite cramped. So, girls, I'm asking you to invite your father into your home and back into your lives. This is my last wish. Maybe then you can see how the Lord creates beauty from ashes, and from old men's mistakes.'"

Mr. Davis laid the letter down.

Whitney stood to her feet. "I think that's a bit much to ask of us right now." Fidgeting with her bag, she pleaded with her sisters. "Maybe after we've had time to grieve, but not now." She shook her head. "Not now." Her heart pounded in her chest and that horrible feeling of being out of control overwhelmed her. More people at home meant more eyes to potentially witness her struggle. She had a hard enough time keeping her emotions in check as it was. No. This couldn't happen. How could Granddad ask such a thing of them?

Of her?

Madysen stood and took slow steps toward her. "I know this is a lot to take in, but we need to honor Granddad's last wishes. This was his farm. He built it. He paid for it. He made it what it is. And he's right. Dad has been separated from us for too long. We need the chance to be a family again."

Whitney sent pleading eyes to Havyn. Could she at least see how difficult this would be for her? But the compassion in Havyn's gaze showed her that she was outnumbered.

"Maddy's got a good point, Whit. We need to do what Granddad asked."

The protective wall she'd worked so hard to erect began to crumble. "Very well." She mustn't let them see how this shook her. Or how alone it made her feel. "I need a bit of fresh air. Is there anything else you need from me, Mr. Davis?"

"No. Not a thing." The man tapped the will. "I will take care of everything else."

"Thank you." With a glance to her family, she went to the door. "I'll meet you at the sleigh."

When she pulled the door closed behind her, she heard the muffled voices. All probably expressing their concern for her. She could just imagine it.

Poor Whitney, she hasn't recovered from the attack.

Poor Whitney, she was the only one unmarried.

Poor Whitney, she'll probably be a spinster forever.

If only things could go back to how they had been before. . . .

When she was strong. Sure of herself. Hadn't been hurt by that awful man. Hadn't lost the two most important people in her life.

But that was the past. *That* Whitney was gone. Who was she now?

As she climbed up into the sleigh, she took several long, deep breaths. It wouldn't do any good for her to fight her sisters on this. Best to make them think she was fine. That it was simply grief making her react this way. The way forward now was to keep herself busy. She could keep up the façade. She could. No one needed to know anything different.

Which wouldn't be a problem because the farm had plenty for her to do. She'd wanted to breed more dogs and train them. Goodness, there was enough demand for her trained teams that she could focus on that alone and keep herself plenty occupied.

She leaned back in the seat, a plan forming in her mind.

Voices sounded behind her. They would head home now, and she'd have to deal with figuring out where to put her dad, Eli, Bethany, and Ruth. Steeling herself for company, she slapped what she hoped was a congenial look on her face and waited.

John helped Havyn up into the front of the sleigh and then climbed in beside her and took the reins. He looked over his shoulder to Whitney. "Do you need anything while we are in town?"

"No, I'm fine. But thank you." It wasn't a lie. In front of her family, she would be fine. In private could be a different story. No need to worry any of them. She gripped her handbag a bit tighter and gave a sad smile.

Daniel and Madysen joined her on the back seat. Once they were underway, Maddy leaned forward and tapped Havyn's arm. "I had an idea and want to run it past both of you." She shot a smile to Whitney.

Oh boy. Here it comes. "Go ahead."

Maddy touched Whitney's knee. "Since the house has five bedrooms—not including the room where John stayed when he first came here—"

"Well, that wasn't technically *in* the house. . . ." Whitney didn't set out *intending* to stall things, but here she was, doing her best to keep them from talking about what she knew was coming.

"Good point. I guess there are lots of other rooms on the farm." Madysen tilted her head back and forth as she chatted. "Anyway, my thoughts were this—and bear with me, I know it isn't easy to think of moving things around so soon, but I think I have the solution. What if John and Havyn moved into Mama's room, while Daniel and I move into Granddad's room. Whitney can stay where she is. Dad and Eli can take Havyn's old room, while Ruth and Bethany take mine. What do you think?"

And there it was . . . everything would change. It was a relief to not have to move *her* things or shift into a different room, but that didn't negate the facts.

Havyn looked to her husband. "What do *you* think?"

"I will leave that to you ladies."

Havyn turned to face them. "Why don't we take some time to think and pray about it? We don't have to do anything right away. Is that all right with you, Whit?"

"Of course." Might as well go along with their plan. Speaking up in the lawyer's office had done no good, and frankly, she was too tired to care. If she pressed too hard now, it wouldn't end well. Besides, her head was aching, and all she wanted was a hot bath and to go to bed. Even if it was the middle of the day.

Whitney didn't miss the looks exchanged between her sisters. No doubt they were shocked by her agreeable response. But it ended the discussion, which was exactly what she wanted. She watched the town fade from view as they turned toward their farm. The two couples chatted in low tones, and she closed her eyes for a moment, willing her thoughts to still so she could relax.

A nudge to her shoulder made her open her eyes.

"Whit?" Maddy's voice.

"Um hm?" She sat up from leaning on her little sister's shoulder and blinked several times. "I didn't realize I'd fallen asleep. Sorry. Hope I didn't squish you."

"It's okay. But look. Isn't that Dr. Cameron?" Maddy pointed.

Huh. It did look like Peter. He was pacing by her dogs. She leaned forward and looked at John, "Could you drive out to where he is before you go to the house? It looks like the good doctor needs something."

As they drove closer, Amka appeared next to Peter. She waved frantically.

"I think something must be urgent." Havyn bit her bottom lip.

The sleigh swished to a stop, and Whitney hopped down. "Is everything all right?"

Peter approached, his face grim. "I need your help." He looked at Amka and then back to Whitney. "Amka's village has many sick children. As you know, there's only one way out there in the winter—dog sled. And I don't have one yet. I'm in need of transportation."

Everyone else had exited the sleigh, and Havyn and Maddy had their arms around Amka and were asking how she was doing.

"Of course. I can take you. How bad is it?" One of her strengths was keeping a calm demeanor, but her heart flip-flopped inside of her. *Not the precious children, please God.*

Peter shook his head. "From what Amka has told me, I'm afraid if I don't go immediately, we may lose several of them."

Gasps flowed from her sisters.

Whitney nodded and straightened her shoulders. "Let me go change and gather what I need. How long do you think we will be gone?"

"A day or two? I'm not sure. But you are welcome to leave me there and come back if you are needed here."

She looked to her sisters. "I'm sure they can manage without me for a bit. Just promise me you won't make any big decisions without me, okay?"

Havyn and Madysen nodded.

She turned back to Peter. "I'll do whatever I can to help." But the thought of driving a man alone out to the village brought her heart rate to a much faster pace. Memories of another man—an awful man—threatened to overtake her.

No. Stop it.

John piped up. "Do you need me or Daniel to accompany you? It is a good distance away and the dead of winter."

Amka stepped forward and put her hand on Whitney's arm. "I will go. I *need* to go. These are my people. I can handle one of your teams, that way we can bring additional supplies."

The tension released from her shoulders, although she hoped her fear hadn't shown. Peter was a good man—the best of men—but she wasn't ready to trust *any* man at this point. "That would be helpful, Amka. Thank you."

Peter nodded. "I would appreciate your assistance as well. They know you, and you can help them feel comfortable with me."

"Yes. I will help." Amka nodded at him.

"Good. Then I will head back to my office and gather everything I need. Now that I know there are two sleds, that will help me know how to pack."

"Amka and I will come to your office and pick you up in about thirty minutes." Whitney didn't even bother to look at anyone else. She just headed to the house.

This was what she needed. A mission. The headache would have to be ignored. There were lives on the line, and they needed her.

It felt good.

Havyn rushed after her older sister. Whitney was more than capable, but with everything that had happened, they needed to look out for each other in ways none of them ever imagined before. "Hey, Whit?"

Whitney looked at Amka. "Go pack whatever you need. I'll be right there."

Amka nodded and headed toward the quarters Chuck had built for her family by the milking shed.

"Do you have some things you want me to bring out to the village?" Whitney was always in her element when it came to her dogs and taking care of people.

"No, well, actually, I hadn't thought of that, but I was wanting to check on you. Are you sure you're going to be all right by yourself out there?"

Her sister frowned and crossed her arms over her chest. "Of course. I do this all the time."

"No . . . I mean . . . well, you'll be out there with a *man*." She didn't want to imply that Peter would ever do anything to her, but the question still had to be asked.

"Amka will be with me—"

"And I'd like to be too."

Havyn and Whitney turned.

"Dad!" Havyn rushed to him with outstretched arms. "Are Eli and Bethany with you?"

"No. Not this time. John told me where you're headed. I have a lead on Stan and could use a ride out there to the gold camp just past Amka's village."

"This is a bit of an emergency." Whitney's clipped words conveyed her lack of love for the man who was their father.

Dad held up his hands. "I understand that. And I will help too. But I don't want to miss the opportunity to find Stan for Ruth."

Havyn watched for her sister's answer. Ultimately, it was up to her. Her dogs. Her sleds. Her domain.

"Fine. As long as you help Dr. Cameron too, I'm fine with it. But you better pack light. As in, whatever you can carry on your back."

"I can do that." Dad squeezed Havyn's shoulder and sent her a smile. "I appreciate you giving me a ride. I've got a small bag with me." He looked between the two of them. "I'll go help John and Daniel."

The awkward silence that followed made Havyn's chest tighten. She wanted to talk to her sister like they always had, but she couldn't. And she wasn't sure why. "Are you sure you'll be all right?"

Whitney gave her an emotionless smile and patted her arm. "I'll have my guns and my dogs. I'll be fine."

Fine. Her sister's usual response nowadays. But Whit *wasn't* fine. Havyn's heart broke a little. There wasn't time to talk about it now. Would she get the chance soon? Before her sister was crushed by the weight of it all? She swallowed and pasted on an encouraging smile. "Well, we will all be praying for you. For the journey, for the village, for Peter to help them. And for your safe return home. You have God with you, Whit."

Her older sister turned. "I better go pack." As she walked away, she mumbled, "God is with me. For all the good that does. . . ."

Havyn froze. It was worse than she imagined. When had Whit become so bitter? And to talk about God that way? For a moment she couldn't breathe.

Maybe she didn't know her sister as well as she thought.

FIVE

Peter looked around his office one more time, then checked his list. He prayed the supplies they were bringing would be enough. But if the sickness was what he dreaded—measles—eradicating it could be a lot more complicated and take more time and medicine than he had on hand.

He'd done his best to prepare for epidemics. In remote locations such as Nome, it was crucial to think ahead. Supplies didn't come in regular shipments. Especially in the winter. And the number of people living in close proximity to each other made the spread of contagious diseases that much more rampant.

But even with his planning and foresight, it might not be enough.

The reports he'd gotten from Amka weren't good.

Father God, give me wisdom. Please help Amka's people accept my help. And Lord, please staunch the spread. Keep us safe as we travel, protect Whitney, Amka, and the dogs. And thank You that Whitney is willing to take me and the supplies there.

It would be wise for him to have his own team, but he'd

have to learn a lot before he was ready for that. He should watch Whitney's work closely on this trip, learn as much as he could, and then broach the subject with her.

He checked the clock. The ladies would be here in a few minutes. Once he made sure he had everything, he started hauling the crates outside his office. Within moments, the yapping and yipping of dogs brought his attention up.

Two sleds headed his way.

"Whoa." Whitney's calm voice had her dogs slowing to a stop. They ended up with the basket straight in front of him.

The dogs were a beautiful breed. He wasn't sure what kind, but he'd have to learn. Their fur was about two inches long, thick. Some black with white around their faces, some brown. A few with gray mixed in. The most striking feature was their eyes. Most of them had blue eyes. He hadn't ever seen that in a dog.

Whitney hopped off the basket, praising individual dogs by name and giving them a slight rub. Then she headed toward him. It had been a while since he'd seen such a bright look in her eyes. This was what she loved to do. That much was obvious.

"Is this everything you need loaded?" She motioned toward Amka, who steered her sled to a stop as well.

"It is. I hope it's not too much?" He buttoned up his coat.

"Not at all. The dogs can carry a good load, but since both sleds are carrying two people, that is extra weight. Still, we should be fine." She went to grab a crate.

Peter stopped her. "Two people? Who's the fourth?"

She sighed. "My apologies. It's my father. He's got a lead on Ruth's husband at one of the mining camps."

"Oh. It will be good to have him along." Another man would be great help, but Whitney had problems with her dad.

Hopefully that wouldn't make things more difficult for her. "I need you to teach me how to load a sled properly. Where to put the weight, how to secure it, et cetera."

"Of course. Why don't we start with the heaviest and go from there?"

"Sounds smart. Just show me what to do."

Judas peered out his office window. What were two teams of dogs doing outside Dr. Cameron's office? Wait a minute. He'd recognize that red hair anywhere. Whitney.

Mustn't miss an opportunity to speak with her.

Making his way out to the street, he put a hand to his hair to make sure it was all in place. Appearances were everything. "Good afternoon, Dr. Cameron, Miss Powell." He dipped his head.

"Mr. Reynolds." The doctor narrowed his eyes and stacked another crate. Now what had he done to receive such censure? Just because the man didn't want to peddle any of Judas's medications?

"Mr. Reynolds, nice to see you." Whitney's words held the slightest bit of warmth. That was enough for him.

"Are you headed out on a trip?" He pointed the question to her and turned his back on the *good* doctor.

"Yes, Amka's village has many sick children, so we are bringing supplies and medicine, and Dr. Cameron will do what he can to help them." She strapped down another crate.

Judas stepped closer and lowered his voice. "Well, might I speak with you in my office before you leave? I'd like to help if I can."

She looked around at the sleds. "As long as it won't take too long. It's a good thirty-mile trek to the Inupiat village."

"Of course, of course." He held out his arm toward his office. "Please."

Whitney glanced at Amka. "I'll be back in a few minutes. Just make sure everything is ready to go. My father should be here any minute. He needed to pick up something." She shrugged.

They walked in silence the short distance back to his office, and he ushered her in and shut the door. "Please have a seat. Might I offer you coffee or other refreshment?"

She took off her gloves and sat in the offered chair. "No, but thank you. I really am pressed for time. You said you wanted to help? Do you have any medicine or supplies you wanted to send with us?"

"Yes. Let me send my secretary for some extra blankets and lanterns. I'm sure you will need them." He held up a finger and went back out the door, gave his secretary instructions on what to pack up and fast. Back in his office, he went behind his desk. "There will be plenty of oil for the lanterns as well."

"Thank you." She stood.

He stood with her. "It's the least I could do. But that's not all I wished to speak to you about."

"Oh?" She waited for a moment and then took her seat again.

He followed suit. "Yes, and as much as I wish to be delicate about this, I know we don't have time, so let me be brief." He used the most concerned tone he could conjure. "It won't be long before the town is abuzz with the news of the inheritance you and your sisters received. The rumors will fly and grow, and I wanted you to be aware—and give you warning—that there are many men in this town who would seek to steal that away from you. As you probably know, I care for your family a great deal and I have long appreciated your strength of character."

"Thank you, Judas. But I—"

"I'm sorry to interrupt, truly I am, but I must admit that I am nervous and need to speak my mind." He swiped a hand down his face and shifted his weight. Would she buy his charade?

Her eyes widened and her lips shut.

"I have all the money a man could want and am making more every day, so you can rest assured that I am not after your money. I consider *you* a friend, but I would like to deepen that friendship. My dear, would you consider allowing me to court you?"

Whitney blinked several times and her jaw dropped open half an inch. Caught her by surprise.

Good.

He pressed on. "I know, and greatly respect, the fact that for the years I've known you, you've felt it your job to take care of your family. You've always been wise and knowledgeable. Mature and capable. But with the loss you've faced and with your sisters married, you are finally free to think of what you need and want for yourself. I'd like you to consider how I might be a part of that answer."

Several moments went by in a bit of awkward silence. He kept his expression eager . . . hopeful. His acting skills were great—even if he said so himself.

Then she stood to her feet and replaced her heavy mittens on her hands. "I admit your question has taken me aback. I need to ask you to give me some time to think on it. You have always been a dear friend of our family, and I appreciate your care and concern. I need to get on the trail, though. Maybe we could continue this discussion sometime next week?" She offered a slight smile.

"That would be lovely. I will anxiously await the time." He went to the door and opened it for her. It wouldn't take long for her to agree. Of that he was certain. "Do you have room on one of the sleds for the mail for the gold camps out that way?"

"If it's not too much, I'm sure we could manage."

"That would be wonderful. It's been over two weeks since we have delivered any mail to them." He reached for her hand.

As soon as they touched, she jerked her hand back and her eyes went wide. "I'm sorry."

"Oh gracious, please accept *my* apologies, Miss Powell. It was thoughtless of me to touch you without permission."

Her expression softened. "Thank you for your understanding. I find myself reacting most harshly at times. I do apologize." She lifted the hood of her coat back up and turned for the street. "I'll speak with you next week."

"I'm looking forward to it." Judas watched as she left and grinned. His plan would work.

Martin Beaufort ran up to him. "Judas, I'm glad I caught you. I need to speak with you."

Well. What was this about? "Of course, Martin. Please come into my office." Judas ushered the man inside. "Now, what can I do to help you?" He glanced out the window to watch Whitney, her steps confident and swift as she headed back to her sleds. Then she halted for a moment and looked back over her shoulder. Toward him. Her lips lifted slightly.

There. Perfect.

The mercantile owner sighed, and it brought Judas's attention back to the man in front of him. "Martin? Is everything all right?"

Beaufort's head drooped a bit. "I don't know what I'm

doing wrong, but sales have been down. There's not enough to make my payment this month."

Putting on his concerned façade, Judas gave a slow nod. "I hear you. Many businesses are struggling this time of year." He watched the man for several moments and then pulled out his ledger. "I'll tell you what, let's not worry about your payments until the first ship comes in."

Martin gasped. "But that's months away. Not until May. I can't ask you to do that."

"Oh, you're not asking. I'm offering. Like I said, times are difficult, and I want to help you. Your business means a great deal to this town." He knew because he'd been maneuvering sales away from the mercantile for several months now. Oh, he'd done it quietly—and with customers who knew how to keep their mouths shut if they knew what was good for them.

"I don't understand why sales are down. There are more people than ever. Our prices are good, and I haven't done anything different."

Judas put a hand on the man's shoulder. "Don't worry about it. Maybe once spring arrives things will pick up. We'll put a hold on the payment until then. That way, you can focus on the business."

The man let out a long sigh. Relief covered his face. "Thank you. I'm so grateful for your kindness. May the Lord bless you for it." He put his hat back on his head and walked out of the office.

Judas went back to his desk and sat in his chair. Beaufort would fail, and then he'd have to sign over the entire store. The once-thriving business would boom again with Judas at the helm.

Yet another piece of Nome he would own.

Picking up his pen, another thought hit him square between

his eyes. Martin was Daniel Beaufort's father. Daniel was married to Madysen, Whitney's sister. Judas would have to time the acquisition of the mercantile with the deftness of an experienced hunter. In a way that ensured Whitney and her sisters believed that *he* was in the right.

Then again, if he played it smart, he could show compassion over and over again—in a public manner, where the Powell women would see—and then Martin would have no other choice but to *give* his mercantile to Judas. His gracious extensions and loans had kept the man afloat the past year.

Hmmm. There were several avenues he could take to get what he wanted. Which one was in his best interests, now that Whitney was in the picture?

Tapping the pen on the desk, he grinned.

With Peter in the sled basket in front of her, Whitney urged the dogs into full speed. They were through town and out in the wide-open spaces of Alaska. Amka drove the sled behind her with Dad as passenger.

The expression on his face when she told him he wouldn't be riding with *her* was one she hadn't expected: disappointment. She seldom considered that he would get his feelings hurt concerning her. But then again, she hadn't given him a chance to be a part of her life, had she?

Not that there had been a lot of time for that. Her priorities and attention had been elsewhere. Surely he understood.

She shook her head of the thoughts. Relax. This was where she belonged. Out on the trail. With her dogs. With the peace and quiet of nature around her.

People were simply too much trouble.

She cringed at such a thought, but she couldn't help it.

People hurt her. Took advantage of her. Crushed her when they left.

At least Peter seemed content to be quiet. For the first mile, he'd attempted to read in a medical book. But it must have been too hard to focus with the swaying and shifting because he'd tucked the book back into his satchel.

He'd seemed antsy to get to the village. And quite serious. What the village was facing must be worse than any of them realized.

She appreciated his dedication to his work and the fact that he didn't need to break up the silence with conversation. As long as she'd known him, he'd been that way. Several times, he came to check on her after her head injury, and he'd often sit there, content to watch and listen. That was the kind of man she imagined as the perfect husband. Someone she could talk to when there were problems, of course, but also someone she could sit in silence with and feel perfectly content. She could imagine it being that way with Peter. He was different from most men she knew. That was probably why she thought of him as a friend. Trusted him.

Friend. She didn't have many of those. Then the earlier conversation with Judas came flooding back to her mind. Her skin warmed. Judas and Peter were around the same age, weren't they? Late thirties?

There was an age difference between her and Judas—at least ten years—but that wasn't bad. The look in his eyes as he spoke to her had sent a little shiver up her spine. She and her sisters had often remarked about the striking color of his eyes, but only because it was fascinating. Not because any of them had ever thought of him as a potential suitor.

Could *she* think of him that way?

It would be easier than being courted by a man she hardly knew. She'd known Judas for close to thirteen years now. A lot had happened in that time. And they'd spent a lot of time together at functions. Done business together on more occasions than she could count. Granddad had trusted him too. That said something.

The shock of him wanting to court her still hadn't worn off. The idea was worth thinking through. After all, she wasn't getting any younger. A fact that never bothered her until both of her younger sisters married *before* her. Then the comments started from well-meaning people at church and at the mercantile. Comments that they should have kept to themselves.

Maybe she *should* give Judas a chance. She'd never have to worry about anything ever again. The man practically ran Nome. He was kind, generous, wealthy, powerful, and if she laid down her ground rules from the beginning, he would most likely let her do whatever she wanted. Which meant she could keep raising and training her dogs. Run them whenever she wanted. And she'd never have to feel alone.

Ever again.

That thought was the one that resonated the most. Not that she needed a man, but without Mama and Granddad . . . she was alone. Oh, she loved her independence, but she had to admit that her heart ached to be loved and cherished. Her family had always done that. Her sisters and brothers-in-law did that still. But love from family was different.

Maybe she should make a list of all the pros and cons to courting Judas Reynolds. That way, she could analyze it and make a good decision before she returned home.

Judas was wealthy and kind. Pro.

He cared for her family. Pro.

Quite a bit older than her. A chance that she could be a widow at a younger age. Con.

Because she'd be alone again.

Her stomach turned. Maybe the list wasn't such a great idea. She reached into her pocket and let her fingers grip the bottle there.

Peter turned and looked over his shoulder at her.

Heat filled her cheeks.

Did he know what was in her pocket?

Six

The trip out to the village racked Peter's nerves. When he'd traveled with other dog mushers out to the remote villages, he'd sworn every time to never ride with that specific driver again.

Reckless and scary. That's what those journeys were. Every single one of them. So climbing into the sled with Whitney had been an act of courage, but he'd held on to the hope that she *had* to be better than the others. Besides, he knew her pretty well. Knew her stellar reputation.

Two hours had passed as the sleds shushed over the snow. For the first little bit, he'd tried to act nonchalant and do some research along the way, but that proved impossible. While the ride was smooth for the most part, he discovered in short order that he needed to pay attention to the curves of the trail. Then there was the fact that the dogs kicked up quite a bit of snow. He didn't want his books to be sopping by the time they reached the village, so he'd tucked them away.

The rest of the time, he'd worked to relax his muscles. His beautiful driver knew what she was doing and where she was going. Besides, he should rest as much as he could on the journey. Once they arrived at the village he would be needed every moment.

But instead of closing his eyes, he let them roam the sparse landscape around them. Deep snow covered everything as far as the eye could see, and if not for the snow glasses Amka had given them, he might very well be snow-blind. The narrow slits in the bands of wood strapped to his head muted the brilliance of the light on the snow and made it easier to see, and he wanted to see it all.

What a fascinating land! And while the terrain wasn't flat, it didn't boast the mountains that soared to the heavens like many other areas of Alaska he'd seen. He had come to appreciate and even love the wide-open spaces of Nome and the surrounding region. Even though they were cut off from most of the world.

That last fact was one of the reasons he'd come here.

Grief was a beast. One that liked to hang around and drag a person down. But as much as he'd fought the battle against it, he'd had to make a complete life change to feel like he could move forward. His passion was just as fierce as it had always been, but there was more driving him than ever before.

The need to offer his skills to those who didn't have access to medical care was the most prominent in his mind and heart. Maybe he could change the outcomes, the would-have-beens, so others didn't have to suffer or endure the pain that so many had.

Himself included.

"Haw!" Whitney's command to the dogs had them shift along the trail to the left, and the village came into view. She really was an expert with these animals. Not once had he feared for his life like he had with other mushers. Mutual trust ran between Whitney and her dogs.

Impressive. That's what it was. What *she* was . . . if only she could see that herself.

Several people came to the edge of the village to greet them as they approached. The task in front of him was daunting. But he had help. These were Amka's people, so she would help him gain the villagers' trust.

Lord, here we go. We need Your help.

Whitney slowed the team, and Peter prepared to hop off the sled and get to work.

And Father, don't let anyone die on my watch.

Never again.

Chris got off the sled and helped to unload the crates of supplies. Amka was a quiet woman, but she had raved several times about his daughters and their talents. Especially Whitney with the dogs.

He couldn't help but agree. Watching her in action on the trail had been a sight to behold.

If only he could reach her.

Not that he blamed her for keeping him distant. As a child, she'd seen—and understood—too much of his drunken behavior and the pain it caused. That she'd actually dragged him home . . . his throat clogged. How could he have done that to her?

For years, he'd fought the demons of the past, but God gave him a clean slate. Over the past few months, Havyn and Madysen had warmed and come around. But Whitney . . . his sweet Whitney. Well, the wounds he'd inflicted on her might be too much for either of them to overcome.

The best he could do was show her he was a new man. Maybe he could at least earn favor from her for his other children. If Matthew, Eli, and Bethany could be welcomed by his girls, he would be content. He didn't deserve forgiveness from his family. But by God's grace, he had it from the Father. That was what mattered most.

In short order, the sleds were empty and Whitney had the second team of dogs headed to a shelter. Chris watched the busyness around him and adjusted the rucksack he'd slung over his shoulder.

Whitney walked back toward him with quick strides. "I need to get you and the mail out to the gold camp before it gets too late."

Even though it was still early in the afternoon, the sun would dip below the horizon all too soon. "You don't need my help here first?"

She shook her head. "No."

Well, that was that. At least for now. With a slight nod, he followed her to her sled.

He climbed in, and she handed him the pack of mail. "Please hold on to it. That way I don't have to strap it down." Her tone was clipped. Hurried.

He watched over his shoulder as she lifted the hook from the snow, stepped on the runners, and called out, "Let's go!"

Without hesitation, the dogs took off. The motion jerked him back, and he had no choice but to face forward. The hum and warmth of the small community swished by, and Chris gathered every ounce of courage he had. He was alone with his daughter. For the first time in a long time.

Once they were out of the village, he shifted in his seat so he could see her over his shoulder. "I appreciate you bringing me along. I know Ruth is grateful as well."

Her eyes never leaving the trail in front of them, she nodded, but her lips stayed in a thin line.

"I was hoping we'd have a chance to talk."

Whitney's eyes hardened. With one hand she reached for her scarf and lifted it to her face. "I'm afraid that won't be possible right now. The temperature is dropping, and the light is fading. You better protect your face and bundle up." With that she wrapped her scarf up over her nose and mouth.

Point made. No talking.

Not now.

Maybe not ever.

Judas,

It has been a mere six hours since I posted the first letter to you. I cannot begin to tell you the relief that I have felt in writing to you. But the urgency remains. I will spend every cent I have to correspond with you—it is that important.

As I have been poring over the Scriptures, I find myself coming back to the first epistle of John each time I think of you. "If we confess our sins, he is faithful and just to forgive us our sins, and to cleanse us from all unrighteousness."

My dear Judas, please. I am begging you to turn back to God. To confess. Stop wasting your life on things of this world. He will cleanse you. He will welcome you with open arms and so will I.

In Christ's love,
Cain

Judas leaned back in his chair and peered out the window at the twilight sky. What a persistent fool.

He folded the letter and shoved it back into the envelope. Let the man waste his precious few pennies on letters.

It didn't make a lick of difference to Judas.

With a shrug he straightened and stashed the letter into his top left drawer with the other. He went back to the dwindling stack of mail. No time to think about Cain or his words. He had business to do. And money to make.

By the time they drove up to the gold camp, it was after three in the afternoon. The sun had already slipped into bed for the night, and twilight lingered. Whitney swallowed, her stomach plummeting. She hadn't thought about having to make her way back in the dark. Not because she never drove in the dark, but because she was at a gold camp. Full of miners, a lot of them unsavory at best. And a place where Garrett Sinclair himself had worked.

A shiver shook her shoulders.

No. Her thoughts wouldn't go there. She wouldn't allow it. Setting the hook in the snow, she jumped off and went to her father. "Deliver the mail. I've got to get back."

"But—"

"There are sick children back there, Dad. They need me." She went to the line of dogs and checked their paws, harnesses, and eyes. All of them dipped their tongues into the snow for hydration, which was good. It wasn't that far to the village. She could make sure they had plenty of food and water once she got back there.

She ran around to the driving position and lifted the hook.

Dad stepped in front of the team. "Thank you!" He waved a hand at her.

"Let's go!" She didn't even acknowledge him. With her boots firmly planted on the foot boards, she urged the dogs faster.

The hairs on her neck prickled, and she put her scarf back in place and scanned the horizon. No one appeared to be out there. But it felt like eyes were on her. And little fingers raced up her back.

With a quick glance to the rear, she put the fear to rest. No one was behind her. No one was beside her. No one in front of her.

So why was her heart still racing?

She looked every direction around her trying to rid herself of the anxiety. It wouldn't settle. "Go, Pepper, *go!*"

Her lead dog barked.

Thankfully, the dogs weren't worn out and loved to run, so the sled gained even more momentum. It wasn't the safest thing to go full speed after dark, but she had no choice. Not really. Not if she wanted to retain her presence of mind.

Her breaths came in short intervals, and no matter what she tried, she couldn't get rid of the creeping terror that she was being followed. That someone was watching.

That she would be attacked.

Again.

Panic took over, and she fought to stay focused on the task at hand. The village wasn't far. She could get there. Everything would be fine.

But her hands began to tremble on the handlebar. She needed help.

She reached for the bottle deep in her coat pocket. The

first sip warmed her throat but did nothing to steady her hands. So she took another sip. Then another.

Her mind drifted back to the horrible events of the past year. In the dark, it was too easy to do.

Another sip.

Stop it. Positive thoughts should be her focus. Not these. Another sip.

Then her mind went to the picture of her dad. The look in his eyes when she put him in Amka's sled rather than her own. The expression on his face when she left him at the gold camp. She shook her head. She wasn't responsible for his feelings.

The image that overwhelmed her in that moment was her dad lying in a heap in the street.

Then him wobbling back and forth when he was drunk.

Then his funeral, when they thought he'd died.

Another sip.

But this time it burned. Up through her nose. And she choked and sputtered.

She shoved the bottle back in her pocket as her eyes watered and overflowed. The tears froze on her cheeks, and she lifted her scarf back up over her nose and mouth.

She deserved the pain. The sting.

Havyn's words came rushing back: *You have God with you.*

As much as she wanted that to be true, she'd pushed Him away. Why would He welcome her with open arms after that? She lifted her face to the sky.

"Why?"

Several of her dogs took a quick glance back at her. It wasn't a command they were used to, but in the silence, they understood she was struggling with something. Of course they did. That's what she loved about them. They couldn't speak, but they sure could sense her emotions. Her turmoil.

"Go." The word was strained, but it was enough.

The dogs kept running.

She lowered her voice to a whisper. "Why? Don't You love me anymore? Am I not good enough?"

A flash of green started on the western horizon and shot across the sky.

"Whoa."

Her team came to a stop.

Waves of green and yellow filled the star-studded black dome of the sky. A faint crackling broke the silence of the night and then disappeared. She'd always loved seeing the auroras. But tonight, the sight lifted a bit of the weight from her heart. Made things seem normal. Comfortable.

As if God had sent it just for her.

She watched the sky's light show for several minutes, then felt the heaviness in her chest. What was she doing? Why had she turned to the tonic—and now whiskey—to rid herself of pain, anxiety, and worry?

Why hadn't she turned to God?

Even as the logical part of her brain struggled to sort it out, things became fuzzy, and then the headache started. But it wasn't a dull ache this time. It was sharp. Deep. She buckled to her knees.

What was wrong with her? Was she permanently injured? What if she died out here? Alone.

Covering her eyes with her hands, she heard several of her dogs whimper . . . bark . . . moan.

She *had* to keep going. They weren't far from the village. She could lie down there.

But the stabbing sensation in her temples grew.

You know what will help.

Yes, she did. Her trembling fingers pulled the bottle free. She took another sip. Then a long swig. She had to make it back. For her dogs. For Amka.

"Let's go!" She cried the command out against the pain that threatened to split her head in two.

Her vision blurred, so she relied on the dogs to follow the trail.

Help us make it back. Please, God.

She hadn't prayed in a long while. Would He hear her? Dipping her head, she leaned over the handlebar, willing the pain away.

The dogs slowed.

How much time had gone by? She risked lifting her head and saw Amka waiting outside the village for her.

Her heart lifted a touch. Amka would take care of her team.

She urged the team to Amka's side, but when the sled stopped, something wasn't right. Why were her legs so weighed down? And her arms as stiff as tree trunks. She stepped off the footboards and everything spun. The northern lights danced overhead and she was drawn into the swirling motion.

Then everything darkened as she floated down, down, down.

SEVEN

It was as he feared.

Measles. At least it was presenting that way.

Since so many were sick, that tracked it back to exposure up to two weeks ago. How many others had been exposed? Peter would have to trace all contact with other villages, with people in Nome, with the gold camps. If he wasn't careful, it could escalate out of control.

Exactly what he'd been trying to avoid. To prepare against.

Peter swiped a hand down his face. He scrubbed his hands in a fresh bowl of water, slathered them with soap, and scrubbed again. After rinsing them, he pulled a clean towel out of his bag and dried them before replacing the towel. If he was going to get ahead of this, he'd have to help everyone understand the severity of contagion. And how to reduce the spread with cleanliness.

At least he had come when he did. He could put Amka in charge of asking people if they had traveled and whom they'd been around.

He walked outside the tiny home he'd been in, where three little girls' fevers were quite high. He breathed deep, needing the fresh air, and looked at the sky.

One thing he'd never tire of seeing was the auroras. They were fascinating. They had a soothing, calming quality about them. But the frigid chill in the air bit at him. He should have put on his coat.

"Dr. Peter, Dr. Peter . . . come quick!" Amka ran toward him.

"What is it?" The woman was always so calm—something must be serious. *Not one of the children, please, God.*

"It's Whitney. She collapsed!"

His stomach plummeted.

Peter rushed to follow Amka to where Whitney lay in the snow on the outskirts of the village. "What happened?"

Amka shrugged. "I do not know. She was driving the sled, I heard the dogs coming and came out here to help, but as soon as they stopped, she fell down. Right there."

Kneeling beside Whitney, he pulled back her scarf and put a couple fingers to her neck to feel her pulse. Steady and strong, though it was slower than he liked.

Her cinnamon hair surrounded her face in a mass of curls. But her skin was paler than usual. Had she pushed herself too hard? Gotten enough rest? When was the last time she'd eaten?

All questions he needed to ask her . . .

Wait. Did this have anything to do with the tonic she'd been drinking? He leaned in a few inches and closed his eyes when he caught the smell.

He patted her face. "Whitney. Can you hear me? Wake up."

She didn't respond. So he patted her face with a bit more force.

She moaned, and her eyelids fluttered.

He glanced at Amka. "Quick. I need to get her somewhere warm. Can you take care of the dogs?" He lifted Whitney into his arms.

"Yes." Amka nodded and spoke to the team in soothing tones. They were certainly on edge about their mistress.

Peter carried her to the small hut he was staying in. As soon as he set her down, she came to.

She gasped, then wiggled as fast as she could to get away from him. She leaned up against the wall and glanced around the hut. "Where are we?"

Peter sat on the floor several feet away from her. "At Amka's village. This belongs to her family. You passed out."

Her cheeks flamed red, and she pushed hair away from her face. "I thought it looked familiar." As much as she tried to sound normal, Peter could see right through her. He'd spent enough time with her now to know her quirks.

"Have you been overly nervous of late, Whitney?"

She tilted her head as her brow furrowed. "What?"

"Anxious. Worried. Have you been eating and sleeping?"

"Of course I have. Now how are the villagers? The children?" She sat a little straighter and put a hand to the side of her head.

Peter stared at her. She couldn't avoid the questions forever. "Is your head still bothering you?"

Her eyes closed for a long moment. "Yes. It was much worse as I was driving in, but it's fading now."

"You didn't answer me about feeling anxious. Could that be why you fainted?" More than anything, he wanted her to feel comfortable and know that he wasn't accusing her.

The look in her eyes reminded him of a deer's eyes when it was caught without cover. "Well . . . uh . . . there's been a lot going on lately. We lost our grandfather. But I'm fine. Really." She stood and straightened her coat over her sealskin pants.

The tonic bottle fell out of her pocket onto the animal skins that covered the floor.

With a glance down, she snatched it up and stuffed it back into her pocket.

Peter kept his voice calm. Without judgment. "We're going to have to discuss that sooner or later." He pointed his gaze to where she'd stashed the bottle.

Her shoulders slumped. "I am fine. I admit there's been a lot of added stress lately. Yes, it's made me anxious. The headaches get worse with that. But I'm managing. I promise." With both hands, she wound her hair back into a knot and tied it with a leather strip. "How are the villagers? Have you been able to figure out what it is?"

Well, he had two choices. Continue his questioning and potentially push her away and lose her trust. Or give her some space and allow her to win this round. Since they'd buried Chuck two days ago, he would give her some leeway. "It appears to be measles. Which is what I suspected. But it worries me."

Whitney nodded, her eyes clear. "I've had the measles, so allow me to lend my help and support in any way that I can. It also helps that most of the children know me well. The adults too."

"I appreciate that, but I think you need to rest first. You can assist me first thing in the morning."

She put her hands on her hips. "I'm not an invalid, Peter Cameron. I'm fine. Let me help."

He held her gaze for several seconds. "On one condition."

"What's that?"

"You eat. A hearty meal. Right now." He raised his eyebrows and waited.

"You want me to cook something? Now?"

"No need. Amka's mother told me she would bring over some stew. Since the night will most likely be long as we take care of the patients, we should eat to keep our energy up. But don't hesitate to let me know if you need to sleep at any point. We can't have any more fainting spells."

Whitney rolled her eyes at him. "Yes, *Doctor*. Good grief, it's—"

The door swooshed open, and Amka entered with her mother. They carried trays of food.

Perfect timing. He smiled. "We can eat in here and then get back to the children."

Amka brushed her hands on her tunic after setting the tray on the floor. "Whitney, you will stay with me and Mother. Father and my brothers will move in here with Dr. Peter."

Amka's mother left without a word. Was it their culture that women not spend time with men they didn't know, or was the woman wary of him still? Many of the natives looked upon white men—especially doctors—as untrustworthy. With good reason. Too many supposed doctors had come through over the years, peddling their fake medicines and stealing from the villagers.

"How are my teams?" Whitney's voice turned tender.

"Good, good. Fed. Watered. And Yutu is playing with them now." Amka put a hand over Whitney's. "No need to worry. They are in excellent hands. Now eat."

"My thoughts exactly." Peter sat back down on the floor. "You will join us, won't you, Amka?"

The beautiful native woman looked between them, waiting for Whitney's nod. When it came, she smiled.

"I would enjoy that. Thank you."

Madysen shivered under all her layers of clothing as she left the cheese kitchen. Maybe it was her imagination, but it felt like the temperature had dropped a good fifty degrees since she came out here. That couldn't be right. She checked the sheep pens and milking shed while she was at it. At least the sheep were locked up tight and in shelter.

Heading to the house, the more steps she took, the more the chill reached her bones and the faster she went.

"There's my beautiful wife." Daniel's voice came from behind her.

She shot him a smile, but kept walking. "Your wife is exceptionally cold at the moment."

"But she's still beautiful." He caught up with her and put an arm around her shoulders. "John has everyone on the farm rounding up the animals. Inuksuk and Yutu went back to their village when they heard the weather would turn worse. With the sickness there, the villagers will need help keeping their animals sheltered."

"I locked the sheep up, but will they be warm enough in there?" She studied her husband's face.

He didn't reply right away. "I pray so. Since they are all together, the warmth from their bodies should keep the barns a decent temperature. The hardest part is gathering them all up. Thank you for doing that. They listen to your voice, that's for certain." He tapped her nose. "Havyn went to double-check on the chickens, I took care of Whitney's dogs, while John and the rest are out looking for the cows. They have the most grueling job."

"I don't envy them. Not out in this cold." She shivered again and raced for the door. "I can't wait to sit in front of the fireplace and get rid of this chill."

The sound of an approaching sleigh stopped her in her tracks.

Daniel stepped out into the lane. "Who could that be?" Then he waved to Madysen. "It's Granny."

Madysen joined her husband and waited for the sleigh to come to a stop. Not only was it Granny Beaufort, but she had quite the cargo with her. Ruth, Eli, and Bethany were huddled in the back seat.

Granny set the brake. "The Grand Nome Hotel caught fire about an hour ago."

Madysen put both hands up to her face. A fire in town could spread and devastate in no time. There were thousands upon thousands of people living in close quarters and not a lot of sturdy shelters, and Madysen's mind raced with the horror. "Oh no! Was anyone injured?"

Daniel's grandmother shook her head. "We don't know yet. I went over as soon as I heard the bell and saw Ruth and Bethany throwing their things out the window. The streets became chaos and the fire grew. So I grabbed your family and figured I would drop them off here and then go see what else I can do to help."

Black smudges covered the trio's faces. Daniel helped the ladies down and then put a hand on Eli's shoulder. "You holding up?"

Her younger half brother looked as if he might burst into tears at any moment, but he stiffened his shoulders. "I tried to help put out the flames, but then Bethany and Aunt Ruth needed my help."

Madysen stepped closer to him. "How very brave of you. We're glad you are safe. Let's get everyone inside."

Daniel helped grab their meager belongings out of the sleigh, and Granny stepped over to Madysen. In hushed tones, she spoke into her ear. "I know this hasn't been a peaceful week for you all, but I couldn't bear the sight of them standing out in the middle of the street with nowhere to go."

"It's not a problem. You did the right thing." She bit her lip as her mind shifted to Whitney. But no matter how difficult this might be for their older sister, it was what they needed to do. Whit would understand that.

"Well, I'm glad you agree. I didn't want to be presumptuous, but they need you. I better get back into town." She wrapped her scarf up around her face.

"Oh no you don't." Madysen gripped the older woman's shoulders with numb fingers and steered her toward the house. "You are *not* driving home alone in this weather. It's already dark, and the temperature will continue to plummet, I'm sure. We've got plenty of room. You can stay with us."

"Martin doesn't know that I've gone, though. He'll surely worry." Granny pulled back against Madysen's arms.

"*Now* who's the stubborn one?" She laughed. "It's not fit for man nor beast. Get inside, young lady. Martin is probably still helping with the fire. He knows you have good sense. He'll also see that the sleigh is gone. I'm sure he can put two and two together."

Here she was, the youngest of the adults, telling her elder what to do. Madysen attempted to keep a straight face, but it didn't work. She'd hear about her bossiness later.

As they entered the house, Daniel rushed toward them. "Oh good. You convinced her to stay." He was out of breath. "I was about to chase her down."

"See?" Madysen quirked an eyebrow at Granny.

"Oh hush. I'll stay." She removed her mittens and another pair beneath them. "Which is a good thing, because I don't believe I can feel my hands."

With a glance down at the aged hands, Maddy rubbed them with her own. "Let's get you over to the fireplace. That should help."

Daniel nodded and took his grandmother's elbow. "Everyone else is huddled there. Except for the men still rounding up the cattle."

The door slammed and stomping ensued. John's voice echoed from the entry. "All the cattle are accounted for, praise God. Now if we can keep it that way, we will do well."

Her brother-in-law shivered as he came into the parlor.

Havyn reached up and brushed ice from his eyebrows. "Are the workers safe? Do they have enough food and water?"

"They do. At least for a few days. I told everyone to check on the animals, but otherwise stay in their quarters. The other chores can wait until this cold snap passes. The most important thing is for everyone to stay safe."

Granny sat next to Bethany and held the young girl close. "How cold is it?"

"Our thermometer outside is registering nineteen below zero right now." John pinched the bridge of his nose as his shoulders slumped. "It could drop another twenty degrees tonight. According to Inuksuk, this will last for several days. And possibly get a lot colder."

January was always the fiercest month in Alaska. Every January, Granddad put extra measures in place. Madysen bit her lower lip. Had they prepared enough this year?

Then there were Whitney and Dr. Cameron. And her dad. They'd ventured out in this weather. Did they know what was coming? *Lord, please keep them safe and warm. Give them wisdom to stay put.*

John stood by the fire rubbing his hands together. "I wish Chuck was still here." He let out a long breath. "With the staggered breeding he set up, I'm worried about the new calves that should arrive in March. I would hate to lose any of them."

"You're doing a wonderful job taking care of the farm, John." Havyn went to her husband's side. "Granddad believed in you. And we've got a lot of help." She looked to Daniel and Madysen.

"She's right. It will work out." Daniel placed an arm around Madysen's shoulders and squeezed.

That little bit of reassurance helped to assuage her worry.

Ruth stood and clasped her hands in front of her. "I don't mean to interrupt, but you have a good deal to discuss, I'm sure, and we have added to the workload. So if it's all right with you, I'll take Eli and Bethany into the kitchen and we can work on a meal for everyone."

Havyn rubbed a hand on her stomach. "I appreciate that, Ruth. That would be a tremendous help. There's bread rising on the stove, and I fully intended to make a vegetable soup for dinner. But I've been chasing chickens down for a while."

All eyes turned back to John. Funny, they'd always looked to Granddad for direction until this last year. Now they'd come to trust and rely on John. He'd never set out to take over and fill their grandfather's shoes, but how amazing was it that God had provided the right man for her sister and a man who loved their farm just as much as they did.

"I guess now is as good a time as ever to discuss the challenges we are facing." John looked down. "I'm afraid this cold snap might result in loss of animals. Not just cows, but also sheep and chickens. The few pigs we have seem to be faring the best in this cold weather."

Havyn put a hand on her husband's knee. "I made sure

that the chickens were in the three different huts. And I closed the outer doors that give them access to the yard. It will be quite a mess in there, I'm sure, but at least they will stay warm. They're a hardy bunch, so I'm trusting that God will keep them safe."

Daniel leaned his elbows on his knees and clasped his hands together. He gave her a quick smile and then looked at the others. "The sheep too. Their wool coats are at their thickest right now, and we've blocked off access to the out-side. As long as we can keep them inside the barn, they should be fine. Noisy and stinky, but fine."

Madysen giggled. "The fun will be maneuvering around in there to milk. Since we've put the breeding of the sheep on a staggered schedule as well, it's a good thing we don't have any due for another couple of months."

Granny tapped her finger on the arm of the settee. "Sounds to me like the focus then should be on the cattle. That's the most likely place of loss."

John nodded. "Yes. You're correct. We stopped milking the cows that are due soon, so we've lost a good deal of income on the milk, butter, and cream side of things. But once the new round of calves are born, things will pick back up. We also have plenty of orders for beef. Once the April butchering time is here, we will see how many orders we can fill—of course, assuming we keep the cattle from freezing during the next few days."

"Best to remember the words of Job: 'The Lord giveth and the Lord taketh away. Blessed be the name of the Lord.'"

Amens sounded after Granny's words.

She placed her hands in her lap. "We do our best with what the good Lord has given us. But ultimately, it's out of our hands. We need to be content in whatever circumstances we are in and praise God for the hard times as well as the good ones."

"Amen to that." Madysen grinned. She looked around at the others. "On a different topic, I know that Havyn and I promised Whitney that we wouldn't make any big decisions without her, but this fire has created a bit of an emergency, wouldn't you say?"

Havyn tilted her head to the side. "I agree . . . even though I'm not sure how Whitney will take it. But I know what you're going to say. We should get everyone moved around since Ruth and the kids are already here."

Granny stood. "That sounds like something I can help with. Are we rearranging rooms?"

Madysen stood with her. "Yes, we probably should go look at everything and decide what furniture to move." She waved at everyone to follow and headed out of the room and down the hall. "John and Havyn will move into Mama's room. Daniel and I will move into Granddad's. Dad and Eli can take Havyn's old room, Ruth and Bethany can take my old room, and Granny you can stay with us for now."

The men of the family came to her side.

Daniel wiggled his eyebrows at her. "Just tell us what to do."

She grinned. "With pleasure."

EIGHT

Waking up in the chilly hut, Whitney pulled the fur blanket up and around her ears. She blinked several times and tried to focus on the ceiling. For three days, she had helped Peter treat the sick in the village. It had been more exhausting than even the manual labor on the farm, and every time she ventured outside, the temperatures had dropped so low she wondered if she'd be able to breathe without freezing her lungs. But the urgency of the situation had kept her busier than ever.

Exactly what she needed.

Life had become foggy. Dim. Without color. In just a few days' time, her world had changed. Again. And she wasn't sure she could bounce back this time.

But here and now? People needed her. The world righted itself and she had a purpose. At least for this brief respite.

Why didn't she feel that purpose at home?

As sisters, they still needed each other. At least that's what the logical side of her brain reminded her.

Granddad and Mama would both echo that fact. So why was she struggling?

Perhaps it was easier to close herself off because of the headaches. The pain overwhelmed her.

Then there was her father.

Ever since their ride out to the mining camp, his face kept coming to mind. Like he actually cared.

It had been months since he'd returned to Nome. Maybe it was time she let go of her anger toward him. Eli and Bethany were sweet, and she longed to know them better, and yet, she held them at arm's length.

Why?

As the question tumbled around in her mind, one thing continued to make sense.

She was a mess.

Whether it was Mama's death, or Granddad's, Dad's surprise return, or Sinclair's attack—whatever it was, something wasn't right. That was why she felt so alone. Abandoned by God. Numb.

Broken.

Slipping out from under the blanket, she looked around the room. No one else was there. The women had tended to business and let her sleep. Just as well. She had no small talk left to give and certainly didn't want to involve herself in any discussion of importance.

What was wrong with her? Mama would scold her for such an attitude. Maybe if she took the dogs for a run, she could clear her head and get rid of these feelings.

As she pulled on her layers of clothing, she patted her pockets. Where did she leave the bottle? It wasn't in her coat pocket. Where had she put it? Scrambling, she searched through her bedding—and found it underneath the fur blanket. She put a hand over her heart and tried to calm the racing.

She'd found it.

Relief filled her as she looked at the tonic bottle, but the weight was too light. She swirled the precious liquid. Probably a sip or two left. She'd have to wait until she got home to refill it. Which meant she could only use it if it was absolutely necessary.

Never mind. She could keep the headaches and anxiety at bay by simply staying busy. Mind over matter. Granddad used to tell her that all the time. She could do it.

Amka slipped into the room. "Peter needs to speak with you."

"Is something wrong?" She tucked the bottle into her pocket. Did Amka see it? "I mean, are things worse?"

Her friend nodded. "It's very bad. Many are ill and more are coming down sick. Dr. Peter is so good to care for them. He has calmed their fears of a white doctor."

Whitney finished tying her boots. "Where is he now?"

"I left him in the main lodge. We put as many sick there as we could . . . like a hospital."

"That's a good idea. I'm sure it saves him time." She got to her feet. "I'll go find him and see what I can do to help."

Amka nodded. "I will rest for a while. Let me know when I am needed."

Whitney made her way to the largest of the village buildings and stepped inside. A large fire had been built up to warm the room. Dressed as she was, it wouldn't take long for her to overheat. Removing her heavy coat, she spied Peter across the room and then stopped in place. His gentle manner as he bent over an older man made her breath catch. Peter smiled down at the man and then laid a hand on his arm.

As she stood frozen in place, she watched him go from patient to patient. Always with a smile. A gentle touch.

He'd come to check on her many times after she'd hit her head. Each time, he'd treated her with that same care. What would it be like to have Peter caress her cheek not as a doctor, but as a man—?

Oh! Whitney turned on her heel and nearly knocked down one of the elders as she grabbed her coat and fled the room. Where had *that* thought come from?

The very idea of a man touching her had been repulsive since the attack. Besides, *Judas* was the one she should be thinking about in that way. After all, he'd proposed courtship.

She hurried to where the dogs were being kept. Yes, she should be helping the good doctor. But that wasn't wise at the moment. Not until she got her thoughts under control.

The chill of morning air took her breath away. The sun wouldn't be up for hours yet. But she doubted that would help. The wind was whipping its way through and stung every piece of exposed skin. Thoughts of Peter persisted, and she pressed them down as quickly as they came to mind.

She made it to the small wooden building where the villagers had laid straw and hay so that the few animals they had could stay warm and slipped inside. Several cows lowed in protest against the icy air.

Most animals raised in Alaska acclimated and did fine in the cold winters. That was, until a cold snap like this came through. Losing their animals, which were sources of food, could devastate a small village like this.

Thank heaven the dogs had an indoor shelter as well. It wasn't heated, but at least it was out of the wind.

Inside, Yutu was feeding the animals, including her dogs. "Thank you." She smiled at him and then knelt down by her pups.

"You are very welcome. They love the seal blubber. It will help them stay strong and give them plenty of fat for when they need to run again."

"That is a treat I don't give them often. I appreciate your sacrifice for them."

"You do much for our family and our people. We are grateful. Bringing the white doctor here was scary at first, but the children are getting better. We thank you for that." He hand-fed each one of the dogs, and they licked at his fingers with yips of appreciation.

"Thank Dr. Cameron. He has a gift with medicine and cares about people. He reminds me of Doc Gordon." Whitney petted two of her team and then moved on to another two. She'd come in here to stop thinking about Peter, yet there he was again, the hero of the hour.

"Too bad all white doctors cannot be like Dr. Gordon and Dr. Cameron." Yutu crouched beside Pepper.

Wasn't that the truth. When Judas told them about Dr. Kingston and how he'd sold fake medications, she'd wanted to blame the doctor for her mother's death. When another patient's father shot the doctor dead in the middle of the street one night, no one mourned the man. She'd actually been relieved he was gone.

Maddy expressed sympathy for the man and hoped he'd had a chance to know God. That made Whitney feel guilty for her horrible thoughts . . . but now she saw it was one more thing that proved she was broken. Unfeeling.

The door creaked open. "Whitney. Oh good, I'm glad I found you." Peter closed the door and jumped up and down a few times. "Gracious, it's cold."

"Do you need help with the patients?" She made it to the last two of her dogs and gave them belly rubs.

"I'm out of medicine and supplies, and we've had a few more cases come to our attention. Is there any way we can go back to Nome and pick up more supplies?"

Life and death were before her. She jumped to her feet. "Of course. If we leave soon, we can make it back by lunchtime."

Yutu came forward and waved his hands. "I think a storm might be coming."

"All the more reason we need those items." Peter nodded. "If we don't get them, the younger children may die. When do you think the storm might come through?"

"Today. Probably this afternoon."

Peter looked to her. "What do you think? Do we have enough time?"

The fact that he asked her meant a lot. After all, it was her dogs she'd be putting at risk. "Let me go look at the sky." She opened the door and studied the inky sky. Not a star shone through anywhere. Still . . . the wind *had* died down. That was a good sign.

And the sick children needed them.

She went back inside. "The wind has calmed, but we need to go right away. I don't want to risk getting caught in a storm in these temperatures." With a quick glance at the men, she clamped her jaw.

Yutu looked from her to Peter. "A storm is coming. If it is calm now, that may mean it won't be here until tonight, or it might mean that it will come much sooner." He dipped his chin and stared at her. Much more was conveyed in his eyes than he said out loud. They'd known each other for many years, and this man understood the weather of the north far better than anyone else. His expression sent a tremor down her spine.

"The children . . ."

He gripped her shoulder. "I will help you get the team harnessed and pack food for the dogs. They will need it in this cold."

"Thank you." She tried to shake off the foreboding. They

had to go. She turned to Peter. "You need to dress in as many layers as you can. I'll bring some emergency supplies, but we need to travel as light as possible. Can you be ready to leave in ten minutes?"

"Yes. Of course." He raced out the door, and she did the same.

Eight minutes later, they were on the sled. She reviewed the checklist in her mind . . . they were as ready as they could be. She lifted the hook. "Let's go!"

Yutu and Amka stood at the edge of the village and waved them off. The air was still as could be, so why didn't it make Whitney feel any better? Was this churning in her gut telling her they'd just made a horrible mistake?

The first few miles passed in relative quiet. The fresh snow was deep and concealed most of the trail, but the dogs knew the way. Peter kept a lantern in his lap to help give them light, but the sky pressed down on them. Lower and lower the clouds closed in until they filled the surrounding air. Thick and full of crystals.

Oh no. Ice fog.

It made watching the trail even more difficult, but she let the dogs use their instincts and senses. They'd been on this trail hundreds of times, and their sight was far better than any human's.

Several minutes passed, and Peter leaned forward with the lantern. But all that did was light the bubble of fog they were in.

Pepper barked four times. Her signal for needing direction from Whitney. The sled slowed.

She couldn't see a thing.

Then the wind picked up from the north with such force that it almost knocked Whitney off the sled. She looked up, and the fog was being pushed away by the wind, which should have brought relief, but instead increased her dread. Glancing back to the north, she braced herself for what she feared was there.

A wall of gray clouds headed toward them like a stampede.

"Whoa!" She shouted with every ounce of strength she had.

The dogs obeyed. Scanning the horizon, she searched for shelter. To the south there was a small bank of tall scrub brush. At this point, it was their only hope. She glanced back to the north and then called out, "Haw, *haw*!" Her team pulled to the left and went straight for the scrub.

Peter hadn't said a word, just sat in the sled and held the lantern high. His silence and understanding were much appreciated.

They were in trouble.

The storm had come much faster than even Yutu thought.

The brush was right in front of them. "Whoa!"

While the dogs were stopping, she jumped off the sled and grabbed the hook. "Good dogs." She set the hook. She'd have to position the sled on one side of them and the scrub brush on the other. Another look to the storm surging down on them and she ran to Peter.

"We don't have much time. We need to dig a trench for us." She ran the line of dogs. "Stay. Stay." Waiting for them to lie down, she saw the concern in their eyes, but they obeyed. She grabbed the two small buckets she carried for food and water and handed one to Peter. "Dig as deep into the snow as you can on the south side of the scrub. I'll position the sled on the other side. It's got to be big enough for us and the dogs. I've got a small tent we can put up, but I'm not sure it can withstand the wind, so the trench is our best bet."

He nodded.

They started digging. The buckets weren't large, but it was better than using their hands.

Thankfully, the snow moved with relative ease. Probably because of the protection of the scrub. Within a few minutes, they'd dug a couple of feet deep. Now if they could just get it wide enough and long enough. Before long, she was huffing and puffing. Sweat trickled down her forehead and froze, but there wasn't time to worry about that. They needed shelter and fast.

She stood and peeked at the sky. "We don't have much time." Snow pelted them.

"I'll keep digging. You go get the sled and the dogs." Peter didn't even look up, just kept slinging bucket after bucket of snow.

She raced to the sled. Unhooking the main harness from it, she kept the dogs tied together and walked them several paces away from the shelter so they could relieve themselves. Her dogs must have sensed her urgency, because they made short order of the task and sat at attention. She pulled Pepper next to her, and the other dogs followed. She took them to the far end of the trench and anchored their harnesses into the snow. "Down." She pointed.

In a neat line, they went into the trench. Dug themselves a little nest and lay down. They curled up next to each other as if they understood exactly what the storm meant. Whitney took a large piece of burlap and covered that end of the trench with it, anchoring each of the corners with sticks. Glancing up, she saw Peter watching her. "Helps to keep their heat in." As fast as she could, she positioned the sled on the south side.

With the brush on the north, and the sled on the south, if she could get the tent over them, they might have a fighting chance. It depended on how much snow the storm dumped on them and how long the blizzard lasted.

Peter yelled, his voice barely audible above the roar of the wind. "Is this enough over here?"

"It's going to have to be. I need your help to get the tent up." It might well blow away in a good blizzard, but she at least had to try.

He scrambled out of the trench. "Just tell me what to do."

She paced out the dimensions of the tent and moved the sled closer. Peter had managed to dig almost four feet deep. That would definitely help. The tent might have a chance. She gave him two long wooden stakes. "Drive those into the snow." She pointed. "There and there. I'll get the other side. Then we have to get the oilskin over the stakes, and then I'll place the center post."

They went to work, but the blizzard was already upon them. By the time the stakes were in the ground, they could barely see each other. Fighting against the wind and snow, they managed to get the oilskin in place on the north side. Then on the south. She shoved Peter into the trench and followed him, pulling down each of the flaps and securing the oilskin to the stakes.

With wide eyes, Peter looked around. "That was close."

In the glow of the lantern light, their temporary shelter looked even smaller. She swallowed against the lump in her throat and sat down in the trench by her dogs.

Peter set the lantern down between them. "Thank you. You saved our lives."

She shrugged. They were only feet apart! A tingling swept up the back of her neck and across her face, so she got up and reached into the sled for the meager supplies she'd brought.

"This has brought up bad memories, hasn't it?"

Peter's voice was soft. Gentle.

She handed him a blanket and kept the other for herself.

Yes, she felt guarded. Unsure. Since the attack, she'd been fearful around men. Even Judas, and she'd known him forever. But when she looked into Peter's eyes . . .

She wasn't afraid. Just a short time ago she'd been thinking of his gentleness and his caring touch with his patients. She breathed deep.

The space might be tight, but she had nothing to fear from Peter.

"Whitney?"

How long had she been staring? "I'm fine." She turned her gaze to a safe place—her dogs. Down in the trench, she had a good view under the burlap.

He wrapped the blanket around his shoulders and shifted so he was facing her. "Look . . . you use that phrase a lot. But you're not fooling me, Whitney Powell."

What she wouldn't give to take a sip from the bottle right now. "I'm not trying to fool you, Peter. Really. I'm fine."

"So why don't you tell me why your hand just went to the bottle in your right coat pocket."

She snapped her gaze back up to his and resisted the urge to yank her hand out.

"Would you like to tell me about it, or shall I keep pushing?"

"I don't know what you're talking about." How did he know her so well? And he wasn't afraid to say what he thought to her. Something that endeared him to her and aggravated her at the same time. She looked down at her dogs.

"About the fact that I've smelled whiskey on your breath more than once. I'm not judging you, but we need to discuss whatever it is that has pushed you to drinking."

She fisted her hands at her side. How *dare* he! "Peter Cameron! I don't *drink*." She narrowed her eyes at him. "I take a little medicinally. You should know that. You gave it to me."

"What I gave you was a tonic for your headaches and anxiety." The smoldering look in his eyes dared her to disagree. "There were herbs in my treatment. It was medicine."

She wasn't about to back down. "Which you said yourself was mostly whiskey." Her voice raised with the howl of the wind. The defense in her tone was whiney to her own ears. She hated that. But what could she do? He'd called her out, and there wasn't a response to give.

"That didn't give you permission to refill the bottle with *only* whiskey after it was gone. Why didn't you come to me?"

The calm, quiet timbre of his voice infuriated her.

How did he know? She crossed her arms over her chest and refused to respond. Just stared him down.

"Look. Again, I'm not judging you. I'm simply concerned. As your physician. After Sinclair confessed to the entire town, it was pretty clear what he tried to do. That you were able to get away with only the blow to the head is a miracle. But it's my job to help you through your recovery, and I can't do that very well if you won't open up to me."

"Please. Never mention that man or what he did again." She spat the words.

"I'm sorry, Whitney." He sighed.

"It's not exactly something a lady wishes to speak about." There. Maybe he'd leave her alone now.

"Fair enough."

"Good." Several moments of silence passed. She closed her eyes and leaned her head back.

"All right, then."

She snuck a glance at him through her lashes.

"Why don't we discuss how many times you've refilled that bottle?"

NINE

Three more letters. Three! Was Cain writing every day? Judas tossed the unopened envelopes onto a corner of his desk and sifted through the rest of his correspondence.

He didn't have time for this nonsense. He needed to focus on his plans. On Miss Whitney Powell. Not on a pathetic little preacher from Portland.

But the more mail he opened, the more his gaze was drawn to the three letters.

With a huff, he slit each one open with his silver letter opener, then set it back down in its velvet holder. He had an obligation to at least read the sender's words. It didn't mean he would do anything about them, or even reply. But he would read them.

He lifted the heavy crystal decanter off his desk and refilled his glass. He'd need it to get through the garbage that was certainly inside these missives.

Perhaps the letters would give him the laughter he needed today. Nothing had gone as planned with the blizzard upon them. And he was stuck inside.

Judas,

One day you will stand to face your judge. You will face the consequences of your actions over all these years. If not on earth, then you will most definitely face your eternal Judge.

You have put the love of money above all things. You might think of yourself as a success, but we both know the truth. You should be storing up treasures in heaven. Not here where they are worthless.

We know you were hurt by Olivia years ago, but that was no reason to turn your back on God. It's been too long. My chest is heavy with the weight of this—the outcome of your soul. It's not too late. But I'm afraid that soon it will be. Please don't wait any longer.

Repent, Judas. Turn from the life of sin you are living and grab hold of God. You know the truth. You know it.

In Christ's love,
Cain

The next letter held more of the same, with plenty of Scripture and declarations that it was all born out of love. By the time Judas read the third letter, he wanted to set a match to every single one of them.

He shook his head and laughed. Who did Cain think he was? He barely had enough to feed his family. The man was a preacher—and not a very good one. He lived in poverty, surrounded himself with the poor and needy, to do what? Make himself *feel* better?

A man of Judas's position didn't need to worry about someone like Cain, no matter what history they shared. He lifted his brows and glanced at the letter again. The man was destitute. Let him waste his money writing. It wouldn't do any good. Because Judas didn't need God.

Not now.

Not ever.

———

He'd crossed the line now. Whitney wouldn't speak to him ever again.

But after a long silence, she opened her eyes and stared at the sled. "It's my own fault. I should have never taken him out to demonstrate the dogs without an escort. I barely knew the man."

As much as Peter prided himself on holding his temper, he was mad. "Don't you *dare* blame yourself, Whitney."

She held up a hand. "Here I am doing it again, too. I took *you* out with no one to accompany us. But I figured you knew better than to make trouble with me. I always have more than one gun on me. And my dogs will attack on command."

The sad little smile she sent him made his heart ache. "This is no laughing matter."

"Oh, come on, Peter. Can't you take a joke?"

"Whitney, you are not to blame for what Garrett Sinclair did to you."

She looked away again. "Yes, I am. At least in part. I've never had much luck with relationships with men. Look at my father, and even my grandfather. They lied to us and fooled us. No wonder I trusted Garrett at his word. I simply don't want to give any other man a chance to make a fool out of me again."

"Is that why you refilled the bottle?" He hated to push, but he had to. Sitting here in the middle of this blizzard, watching her, he realized his care for her was strong. More than he wanted to admit.

"No. Of course not. I refilled the bottle because it's the one thing that helps with the pain."

"If you're still having pain, you should have come to see me."

"Why? So you could question me about it?" The fire was back in her eyes as she shifted her glare to him. "Whiskey doesn't demand answers from me. It helps me to forget." She winced and looked away.

"What? Are you in pain now?"

"No."

"Then what made you react like that?"

She shook her head. "Nothing."

But when he watched her face, he knew. He'd pushed her far enough for now.

Whitney closed her eyes. Shutting him out.

Their makeshift shelter shuddered in the wind, and Peter leaned back against the wall of snow. His thoughts all over the place. Whitney was at the forefront.

More than anything, she hated that her father had been a drunk. That much he knew. But she had loved Chuck deeply. Respected him. So why would she lump him in with her dad? That didn't make sense. Or was it all about men in general? Ah, that might be it. Trust. She'd said she didn't want to let another man make a fool out of her again. Even those she cared about.

This was more difficult than he thought it would be. He should be honest. Straightforward. "Is this about your dad's drinking, or about all men?"

"I'm *not* like my dad." The words were flung at him.

"I didn't say you were."

Her eyes had become tiny slits. "But I saw the look on your face. It's what you were thinking, wasn't it?"

He let his shoulders slump and shook his head. He couldn't in good conscience let this go on. He was her physician and her friend. He had to confront her. In love. *God, I need help. What do I say? How can I help her?*

"I'm sorry." She appeared to deflate in front of him. "As you can tell, there are two topics that will get my temper up pretty fast. My dad being a drunk, and men pulling the wool over my eyes. You just happened to touch on both." Wrapping the blanket tighter around her, she pinched her lips together and pulled her knees up to her chest. "I don't know what's wrong with me, but losing Granddad has made me feel . . . broken. I don't mean to take it out on you." She closed her eyes. "Like I said, I'm fine. I need some rest. I recommend you try to sleep too. We'll need to be ready to move as soon as the storm is past."

And just like that, she closed the door on any more conversation. At least for right now. But she'd opened up to him more than he'd anticipated. Admitted to things as well. That was an enormous step.

Watching her from his perch a mere three feet away, he took note of her breathing. It was steady. The muscles in her face even began to relax. She must be exhausted to fall asleep with such speed.

The roar of the storm outside made him shift. He squirmed. The only thing separating them from a fierce blizzard was a thin piece of oiled leather. Maybe he should take Whitney's advice and get some rest himself.

But when he closed his eyes the sounds of the storm were more prominent.

So he studied Whitney again. At least asleep she seemed peaceful.

How often had he seen the ravages of alcohol in his

patients? He would have *never* given her that tonic if he'd thought her becoming dependent was even a remote possibility. Her abhorrence of alcohol had been in her favor.

Or so he'd thought.

But grief and pain could do horrible things to people's minds. Especially strong, independent people. When men tried to do things on their own, without the help of the good Lord above, it resulted in disaster.

He should know. He'd tried to do so many things on his own. Still did. It was a lesson that he had to keep learning. Maybe that's why he wanted to help Whitney so much.

Or maybe it was because he found her fascinating.

He shook his head. Everyone he'd ever cared about he'd lost.

Another strong burst of wind pushed against their tiny shelter. Growing up in Kansas, he'd been terrified of tornadoes. The devastation was always so great. No matter how many times they'd taken cover in their root cellar, he'd never gotten used to the sound of the wind. Or seeing the terror on his mother's and sisters' faces.

Life on the farm had been beautiful. Until he lost his dad to a farm accident. A storm had come upon them in the blink of an eye, and the cattle had stampeded right over him. At thirteen years old, Peter had found his dad, crumpled and broken in the field but still alive. He didn't know any way to help him. Grandmother had been a midwife and healer, but she couldn't save his dad either.

So began his dream of being a doctor.

Mom fell ill right after he finished medical school. When he couldn't save her either he'd wondered what good it was to be medically trained, and even have a certificate, if it didn't help him save the people he loved.

It wasn't until his grandmother fell ill that he understood and could put his head knowledge together with his heart. As she'd struggled to breathe and function the last few weeks, she helped him understand that he was simply a caretaker. God was the one who decided what was to be, but the outcome shouldn't stop him from using his gifts and trying to help. It was his job to do his best and leave the results up to God.

For several years, he'd been able to keep that outlook. Until Charlotte—

No. He didn't want to think about her . . . couldn't allow himself to go there. It had taken six years to get this far.

He clenched his jaw against the memories.

He'd started fresh. He was helping people. He'd do his best and leave the results up to God. He would.

He recited the phrase in his mind several times. Then he closed his eyes and tried to block out everything around him.

There were children who needed his help.

Movement under her arm made Whitney flinch awake. Where was she?

She sat up and blinked away the remnants of sleep. Pepper wriggled her muzzle closer. Whitney patted the top of the lead dog's head. Oh, that was right. They'd had to seek shelter before the blizzard hit them full on.

She could always rely on her pups.

She took a deep breath, and her gaze landed on Peter. He was asleep, the center of his brow creased into a deep *V*.

Was that her fault? Was he worried about her? Or simply their predicament?

Even with the time she'd spent with him over the past few months, there was little she knew about him. Or his past.

Why had he come to Nome in the first place?

What manner of man was he? Truly? He'd been good to her. Good to her family. They trusted him. But he'd started to push her. A little too much.

She was comfortable with him. Maybe because he didn't let anyone tell him what to do. Or how to run his practice. As much as she adored Judas, it had made her giggle when she found out that the new doctor had told him no. Something, she was quite certain, Judas didn't hear often.

Granddad had all-out approved of Peter. Said they needed more doctors who took the natural approach.

Tipping her head, she studied him. His dark hair had a bit of a wave to it. And while he always dressed nicely, he wasn't afraid to get his hands dirty. Clothes weren't of utmost importance to him. Neither was appearance. But he conveyed a strong moral code. Trustworthiness. At least to her.

No. That wasn't true. She'd seen how well he treated the natives. Gave them the same attention and courtesy that he gave to white people. Now *that* was something she wished she could see in everyone.

Mama used to tell them that when someone was trustworthy, it was part of their nature. They didn't go out of their way to prove it because it was simply who they were. And they showed it in how they lived their everyday lives. She also said that you could tell a lot about a person by how they treated older people, the native people, or people of different classes. Not that they had the crazy society rules there in Nome, but Whitney had grown up learning exactly what Mama meant.

How many people—men and women alike—had she witnessed say horrible things to the Inupiat people? Or even treat others they deemed beneath them with contempt or derision? It had infuriated her on more than one occasion.

But then, she'd also seen people who weren't out to impress anyone. They never avoided difficult things for fear of failure or looking foolish. They helped the downtrodden.

Peter hadn't been afraid to ask her those intense questions. He didn't seem bothered by what other people thought about him. He did his best and helped as many people as he could.

He stood behind his convictions.

Mama had been that way. Even though she'd been full of grace and compassion, she'd stood firm. She never wavered on her expectations of her girls. Never allowed them to veer off the narrow path without major consequences. And when they made a mess out of things, she reminded them she loved them and helped them through the horrible effort it took to clean up things, but she never took the punishment away.

Memories cascaded in and made Whitney miss her mother even more. So she pushed them away. The less she thought about Mama, the better it would be. Might even make it easier to let go.

Havyn's and Madysen's faces were then at the front of her mind. With Mama gone, Whitney had wanted to be there for them. Fill the void. But she'd failed at that. And look at her now.

What a mess. *She* needed more tending to than they did. A fact she didn't like to admit.

They were happy. She was not.

They were married. She was not.

With a shake of her head, she tried to banish the thoughts.

Maybe Judas's offer *was* her best option.

139

TEN

Whitney opened her coat and reached inside for the watch pinned to her chemise. It took quite an effort since she'd put on every piece of clothing she'd brought with her. But she was grateful for the five layers she had. Wouldn't even have minded another layer or two.

Four hours had passed since the storm had barreled in on top of them. Prayerfully, it wouldn't take another four for it to pass. As quickly as the storm had come upon them, and with such intensity, she hoped it would run out of steam soon.

The thought of children suffering—even dying—all because of her made her stomach turn.

Oh, it wasn't her fault they were sick. But it *was* her job to get them the supplies they needed. Storm or no storm.

The storm howled and railed against their shelter. She braced herself and counted to ten. She expected her oilskin tent to go flying away on a gust at any moment, but it held fast. *Thank You, God.*

She didn't *feel* particularly close to God at the moment, but the prayer came easily and she found comfort in it. Was it familiarity? Habit?

It didn't matter. God might be shuffling her off to the side right now, but He was still God. And He cared about those children. Everything she'd believed about God her whole life told her that was true. Nothing that had happened to her, not even the most terrible thing, could justify negating her mother's teaching. Maybe God was close to *her*, no matter how she felt.

The wind blasted again, and her heart picked up its pace. How she longed to break out of the tiny shelter and breathe some fresh air! But that wasn't wise. Blast, she hated this anxiety. She'd never dealt with any of this ever before. Why now? Wasn't it enough that she'd had to lose dear family members? Why torture her by yanking her confidence from underneath her? It wasn't fair. *God, are You listening?*

Stop it. Stop thinking about it. It wasn't doing any good. Whitney took a deep breath. Then another.

Her stomach growled. She should go through the supplies and see what they had. It may not be wise to eat any of it yet, but at least she could make a list.

With a glance at Peter, whose light snoring a couple feet away soothed the frantic beating of her heart, she moved as stealthily as she could to the sled positioned above her. Outside the trench. Leaving the warmth of her spot made the dogs shift and look up at her. But then they put their heads down again.

They knew how to survive and how to retain their warmth. Amazing how God had given them those instincts. If only she had as much.

They'd had to pack light for speed. Why hadn't she prepared better? Yutu knew a storm was coming. Why hadn't she listened?

She clamped her eyes shut. Given the same circumstances,

she wouldn't have packed any differently. Sometimes storms were hours away. Sometimes they moved faster than anticipated. It was the way of nature. They'd taken the risk because lives were at stake.

They were fine. That's what mattered. They had shelter. None of them was injured. And other than being a little cold, they were *fine*.

She emphasized the word over and over in her mind. Sooner or later she'd convince the fearful side of her brain to settle down.

Reaching into the leather bag Yutu had packed, she found several packets. Oiled cloths covered each one. The first and the largest held a good deal of seal blubber. Good. That would keep the dogs for another day. The fat would help them keep their bodies warm. Underneath the blubber for the dogs, she found two packets of smoked salmon and eight flat pieces of Amka's fried bread.

Relief made her smile as she looked up. What would she do without these precious people in her life?

Peter shifted beside her, and the movement drew her gaze. He must feel safe to sleep so soundly. He had such confidence in her. Otherwise, he wouldn't have asked her to take him to the village.

She trusted him too or she wouldn't be here. Right? Peter always seemed to take away that edge of frantic upheaval in her heart. His gentle and calm nature reassured her even when she didn't realize it.

She studied him.

He was a nice-looking man. A hard-working man who sacrificed on a daily basis for his patients. Why wasn't he married? Was it because he gave everything for his patients?

She weighed the options. Many women would have a problem sharing their husband with a long list of patients.

But Whitney wouldn't.

Whoa. Where did *that* come from? She raised her brows and stared at him. Did she care for Peter that way? She hadn't thought she was capable of it after the attack. Though the way this man cared for the native people touched her deeply.

No, her heart wasn't ready. If she wasn't ready, then what would she tell Judas? Especially since she hadn't even thought of him in recent days. And not the way she'd just thought of Peter.

A shiver ran up her spine, and she tucked away thoughts of caring for Peter. He was her friend. A wonderful doctor. She . . . trusted him.

That was all. So why did she feel differently toward him?

His eyes cracked open and he smiled. "I'm being watched over by an angel with red hair."

Caught.

Whitney's face grew warm, and she looked away, pretending to be busy with petting Pepper.

He shifted to a more upright position and ran a hand down his face. "How long was I asleep?"

"I'm not sure. But it's been a little more than four hours since we set up the shelter."

He shook his head. "Sounds like it's still snowing and blowing out there."

"Yes, it is." She pulled out two of the pieces of fried bread and one of the packets of salmon. "Are you hungry?"

He put a hand to his midsection. "I am. How are we on supplies?"

"We have enough for several meals if we are cautious. But I'm optimistic that this will pass soon. And if I'm correct, we need to have our strength up to dig ourselves out and get back on the trail."

"How tough will it be to get back to Nome?"

"The dogs will have to work extra hard. The blizzard has dumped several inches, if not a foot more, of snow. We'll have to watch out for the drifts, because they could be well over the dogs' heads at any given point. If they end up in one, we'll have to dig them out, so prepare for slow going." She handed him some smoked fish. "I may even have to teach you how to break the trail."

"Thank you." He took the food. "I'll do whatever you need me to do."

They ate in relative silence, and then Whitney divvied up some blubber among the dogs.

As the wind died down, the surrounding quiet seemed more pronounced. Should she start a conversation? But what did she want to talk about? Nothing about God at this point. Definitely not answering his question about how many times she'd refilled the tonic bottle.

After finishing his piece of bread, Peter leaned back and stretched. "I hear you and your sisters are taking a break from performing at the Roadhouse."

She hadn't expected that, but at least it was a safe topic. "We felt it was right since we are mourning Granddad." She wouldn't tell him she'd often had thoughts of quitting lately. Not that she could quit music . . . but things hadn't been right for a while. She couldn't put her finger on what it was that made her feel detached from her sisters and their performances. Hesitant. Something had affected her spirit. Her heart. And God hadn't stepped in and fixed it.

Maybe that was the problem.

"You're not thinking of quitting, are you?"

How could that man read her mind like that? She turned away and pretended to check the dogs' harnesses. "I'd rather not speak about it right now." So much for a safe topic.

Peter let out a long sigh behind her. "You know, Whitney, for someone who doesn't want to feel alone, you sure do enjoy pushing people away."

Her sharp intake of breath made her lungs hurt. "*What?*"

"I'm not trying to hurt you, I promise." His eyes pleaded with her. "I'm sorry. Forget I said anything."

If only she could. Her anger burned because she had no defense against his statement. He was correct. But she couldn't admit it. She didn't even know what to do about it herself.

"Sometimes I should think before I speak." He wrinkled his nose.

One of the things she liked most about Peter was that he spoke his mind. At least . . . *most* of the time she liked it. But how mature was she to tell him he could only speak his mind when it suited her? That wasn't fair.

Without a suitable response, she kept silent and tended to the dogs. The awkward moment stretched into several minutes.

Once the dogs all had a bit of the blubber, and she'd petted each one, she stilled. "Listen."

Peter sat up straighter. "It sounds like the worst of it has passed."

"It does. We should check the skies and wait to be sure, but I don't want to waste any more daylight if we can avoid it."

"Just let me know how I can help."

She nodded and put her attention back on the dogs. Gracious, Peter didn't seem bothered by her awkward moments, her cool indifference. It wasn't like she was doing it on purpose. But how could she fix it?

He cleared his throat and clapped his mitten-covered hands together. "You know, I've been wanting to talk to you about getting my own team and sled. Would you be willing to teach me more than breaking the trail?" He raised his eyebrows.

She could hug him for changing the subject. "It's a great idea to get your own team. I can even raise a team specifically for you and train them with you."

"I was hoping you'd say that. I hear your dogs are the very best."

She sent him a smile. "They are, but they will take a great deal of care and work on your part as well. You've got to be invested in them."

"It's clear you love working with them. How much time is involved in the training?"

"At least a couple hours each day. Are you up for that?"

He leaned forward. "Of course. I want to be available to help the outlying villages. The other doctors have informed me they don't have time. The truth is, I don't think they care much about the native people."

Was that a hint of disgust in his words? "Sadly, that's an attitude many whites take toward the Alaskan natives. It doesn't matter which tribe they are from, they are looked down upon. The color of a person's skin or where they are from or how they speak shouldn't matter. We are all children of God."

"I agree. That is why I want to be able to drive a sled out there myself." He lifted one corner of his mouth. "It's not like I can take up your precious time every time I need to check on the villagers."

The man could cut to her heart one moment, then smooth it over in the next breath. She returned his smile and looked him in the eyes. "There will be more to it than learning to drive the sled. You have to develop bonds with the dogs, learn

147

how to command them, earn their trust, and become their leader. You'll also need to relocate. There won't be room for the dogs in town. At least not where you're currently living."

His brow creased. "I have been thinking on that. I could keep my office where it is in town. Maybe you could help me find a place to build a home that would accommodate the dogs and their needs?"

Warmth filled her cheeks again. Why? Just because she'd be spending more time with him? No matter. She didn't have time to examine her feelings or what they meant. "Sure. I'll help."

"I doubt there's much land available that I can afford, so that should narrow our choices. You can show me what you think would be best."

"Of course." She hadn't thought about the financial strain this would put on him. The sacrifice this man was making to take care of others reminded her of her mother. Mama would have loved Peter. And Granddad would have offered to build something on their farm for the good doctor.

Why hadn't she thought of that before? She frowned. They were already adding more on the farm with Dad and his other family. Even so, perhaps she could bring it up with her sisters in a few weeks. It was the least they could do to help the doctor. Besides, it would take a good deal of time to teach him, so having him right there on the farm would help her too.

"Thank you. I really appreciate it."

"You are welcome." The intensity in his gaze made her turn away. She repacked the leather satchel and crawled over to the flap of the tent to take a peek. The sky was indeed clearing, with no ominous line on the horizon.

"Looks like it has stopped snowing. Stay here with the

dogs. I'm going to check the skies and see if anything else appears to be on the way."

Chris glanced around the room one more time.

The blizzard raged outside the thin walls of the gold camp's one lopsided building. Most of the men had made their way from their flimsy tents into the meeting room to share warmth and to pool their resources for food. The others were probably digging away inside the caves and tunnels, oblivious to the storm outside. That or they were lost to the blizzard. Not a pleasant thought.

Was that what had happened to Stan? There'd been no sign of him. No one had a clue where his brother-in-law had gone, and it had been months since anyone had seen him.

As much as Chris hated the thought, if something didn't happen soon, he'd have to tell Ruth the news she didn't want. He didn't want it either—didn't wish that kind of loss on anyone. But the reality of the situation was all too clear.

Life often dealt horrible blows.

He swiped a hand down his face. Only by the grace of God was he still standing. Alive. With six beautiful children, whom he didn't deserve. They were the reason he kept going.

He'd lost his second love—the woman who'd led him back to God and away from the bottle—long before he should have. But in her short life, she'd taught him much. Then he'd lost his first love before he could make things right. He hadn't even gotten a chance to tell her he was still alive. To apologize for everything he'd done wrong.

How many times had he cried out to God that it should have been him? *He* should have been the one to die. Not Esther. Not Melissa.

But then he thought of his children. The good Lord still had him here for a reason. And most likely, it was to make things right with his children.

Bethany and Eli were still young enough that they had forgiven him easily. But Melly's girls—Whitney in particular—had a tough time coming to forgiveness. And Matthew, his eldest with Esther, had treated him differently ever since finding out the truth that he'd been married to Melissa when he began his relationship with Esther.

Was his connection with his son salvageable? He wasn't sure.

Some days it seemed it would be easier to go back to the bottle and disappear. His children would be better off without him. The pain and grief he had to endure would be gone. At least momentarily.

But then he was reminded of what Jesus did for him on the cross. How incredible to be forgiven and made a new man! He wanted to share with the world that if God could change *him*, He could change anyone. That they *all* had the opportunity to be redeemed.

Redemption. What a beautiful word. The one word that motivated him each and every day.

Thank You, Father for Your redemption. For loving a sinner such as me.

As he poured out his heart to the Lord, a strong sense came over him to pray for Whitney. Hard.

I don't know what she's going through, God, but You do. Show me how to help her. Even if she never speaks to me again, Father, I don't care. But my heart is awful burdened for her right now. Keep her from danger. Protect her. Show her how much You love her. Thank You.

The sense of urgency didn't leave him, but peace settled

around his shoulders. Opening his eyes, he looked around the room. Every man here needed to know about Christ's sacrifice and the love of the Father. No better time than the present to tell them.

At the moment, he had a captive audience.

The driver had quite a time keeping the sleigh from getting buried in the drifts. Judas glanced at his watch for the fourth time.

"My apologies, Mr. Reynolds. But I had a feeling it would be a longer trip than usual."

"Just get me there, and everything will be fine." He peered over his shoulder. The storm had brought a lot more snow than any of them expected. But this was Nome in the dead of winter. He tugged his gloves on a little tighter. He should have instructed the man to put more heated bricks in the sleigh. The one at his feet was already cold.

But it would be worth it when he made it out to the Bundrant farm and saw Whitney.

Thirty minutes later, they finally pulled up to the familiar home. Judas made quick work of climbing down. "I shouldn't be too long."

"Yes, sir."

Havyn and Madysen came out to greet him. "Mr. Reynolds, how good to see you! What made you come out after such a storm?"

Their warm greetings always made him smile. These ladies adored him. Pretty soon their older sister would as well. "I'm simply checking on all of you, of course."

"That's very kind." Havyn waved him in. "Won't you come in for a cup of tea? It's awfully chilly out here."

He nodded and removed his hat. "I would love that. Thank you." Once inside, they led him to the parlor. "Where's Whitney?"

Madysen took a seat across from him. "Dr. Cameron needed her help to get out to one of the villages."

So she was still gone. With the doctor.

"I saw them on their way out. I thought they'd be back by now."

Curse that Cameron! Ever since he'd arrived, he'd all but thumbed his nose at Judas. He'd refused help—and medications—from Judas. Even went so far as to purchase his little storefront outright so he wouldn't have to rent. The man was a thorn in his side.

"We heard there were many sick, and you know Dr. Cameron. He'll stay and make sure that everyone is on the mend. It's only accessible by dog sled this time of year, as I'm sure you are aware." Madysen placed a napkin on her lap.

"Yes, and it's a treacherous journey to be sure. Whitney is an expert with those dogs, though, isn't she?" Judas accepted a cup of tea from Havyn. "Thank you, my dear." He blew on it and put it up to his lips, shaking his head. Cameron was getting in the way. Again. "I'm shocked your sister would be foolish enough to travel alone with a stranger after everything that happened to her reputation last fall."

Madysen dismissed his comment with a wave of her hand. "You've always been so protective of us, but there's no reason to worry. We know Peter quite well. Besides, Dad and Amka went with them—they took two teams—so she was hardly alone."

Havyn passed a plate of cookies around. "And you know Whit. She would never deny children a doctor. If there's anything she can do about it, she'll do it."

As much as he was miffed at the idea that Whitney was still gone and in the presence of that doctor, he gave the girls a smile. "Just one of your sister's admirable qualities, yes." He took another sip of tea. So he'd wasted all this time getting out here.

"It was thoughtful of you to come out and check up on us." Madysen was so tiny, it would be easy to mistake her for a young girl.

"You know how much your family means to me, and with your grandfather gone, I felt it my duty to make sure all is well." His disappointment would have to stay hidden. It wasn't a complete waste of time and effort. Especially if the ladies shared with Whitney about his sacrifice to check on them.

"Would you like us to play some music for you?" Havyn's face beamed with the offer.

"No. That's quite all right. I'm satisfied that you are far-ing well. Besides, the road is quite difficult with all that fresh snow, so I better get back before dark." He set his teacup down and stood.

Madysen stood as well and reached for his hand. "Oh, please stay. At least for a little bit longer. You need to catch us up on the news."

Two hours later, he walked back into his office. Keeping tabs on Miss Whitney Powell shouldn't be this hard. He dropped into his chair and stared at the ceiling. Was competition building from the good doctor?

Judas laughed. No. Peter Cameron wouldn't stand in his way. Ever.

A knock at the door made him sit up straight. "Come in."

The door opened, and in walked Charles Beck.

Judas waved him to a seat. "My favorite judge. What can I do for you this evening, Judge Beck?"

"I have an idea."

Good grief, Beck was always bringing him ludicrous ideas. That's how he owed Judas so much money. All his unwise and underhanded dealings had done nothing but pad Judas's pockets even more. Oh, the man had made plenty himself with his schemes and gambling, but where the judge got his harebrained ideas was a mystery. Granted, they made money, but the judge couldn't stick with one thing for the life of him. It was always something new. Exhausting.

Beck blathered on for twenty minutes. "What do you think?"

But this time, Judas really didn't want to waste time or money on it. No matter how much it made him off the poor fool. "I think I will have to pass on this one, Charlie."

The man cocked his head. "That's the first time you've turned down one of my ideas."

"And?"

"I'm not sure what I think of it." The judge sat a little straighter.

"What you need to think is what I *tell* you to think. You would do well to remember that."

The man's head dipped in a slow nod, but his eyes narrowed. What was he thinking?

"It occurs to me you have no heir, Judas. You really should get your business affairs in order. Especially with this sickness going around. There's talk of an epidemic."

So that was his play. The man thought he could get into his good graces—and his will? "I fully intend to marry soon."

"Do tell. Who is this lucky woman?" Beck leaned forward a bit too eagerly.

"If you must know, it's Miss Powell. She's upstanding, of high moral character, and I believe she holds me in high regard."

"A good deal younger too." The judge stroked his beard. "That will aid in producing an heir."

"Exactly." Judas leaned back.

"Good. Sounds like you have found a perfect match, my good man. Let me be the first to congratulate you. And please, don't hesitate to come by my office. As soon as you are wed, I can draw up the necessary paperwork for your will so you can take care of your wife and family."

The judge was too smooth. Well, two could play at this game.

"Of course, I appreciate your generosity and willingness to help with such a crucial matter."

"Well then . . ." Judge Beck stood. "I shall be on my way. I look forward to seeing you soon."

As the greasy man left, Judas tapped a finger on his desk. While it was good to have the judge in his pocket, the man was becoming more and more of a nuisance. Perhaps he needed to bring up a new judge. Someone he could control a bit better. Who didn't have his own agenda.

Yes. Judge Beck had worn out his usefulness.

The only problem now was how to get rid of him.

No matter. It wasn't like he hadn't gotten rid of plenty of other obstacles over the years. What was one more?

ELEVEN

The sun began its slow descent on the horizon. "I'm headed out to check on my girls!" Havyn called to Madysen.

"Need any help?" Her younger sister's voice echoed from the kitchen, where she was working on preparations for dinner.

"No, but thank you. I won't be long." She wrapped her scarf around her neck and tugged on her gloves and boots. Pretty soon it would be much more difficult to bend over. She was already feeling quite a pull from the baby. Her skirts still fit, but for how much longer? The waists were feeling much too tight. And she couldn't wear the sealskin pants anymore.

As she straightened up, she put a hand to her ever-growing belly and headed out the door. "All right, little one, you stay warm in there and grow big and strong. Let's go talk to the chickens."

A wonderful sensation crossed her abdomen. Like a little fluttering of wings moving from left to right.

She held her breath and waited for it to happen again. This time, it started on the right and moved to directly under her hand. Tears sprang to her eyes. "Do that again, sweet one!" She placed both hands on her abdomen, wanting to embrace her little one.

For several moments she stood there outside the house and relished the beauty of a life growing within her.

Her husband walked over from the milking shed. "Everything all right, my dear?"

"I felt the baby move! Come here, you've got to feel this." She waved him over with frantic movements and then placed his hand on her stomach. "Go ahead, little one. Your daddy wants to feel you too."

She stood still as John looked at her with adoration. This time, the movement was like tiny little bubbles being tossed around. "Did you feel that?"

He shook his head but kept staring at her. "But I love watching your face light up."

Her shoulders slumped. "I can feel it on the inside, but maybe it is too light for you to feel with your hand yet. But just wait! Our baby is growing every day."

John leaned down and captured her lips with his own. "I adore you, Havyn Roselli."

"And I you." Her cheeks grew warm. "Now, let me get back to the chickens. You distract me, my handsome husband."

He wiggled his eyebrows at her. "You distracted me first." He laughed. "But I need to finish chores too. I'll see you at dinner."

Havyn walked out to the chicken yard and looked at the piles of snow. It would be some time before the men could get out here and shovel pathways. There were other priorities after the blizzard. Her poor girls. They hated being cooped up. But the snow was too deep. How was Whit faring in this?

She missed her sister. Not just her presence right now, but *Whitney*. The Whitney who started a slow disappearance after Mama died. Then after Sinclair—Havyn didn't even want to think the man's name—nothing was the same. Granted, Whit was in a lot of pain lately from the headaches, but there seemed to be so much more going on.

God . . . help. My heart tells me something is wrong, but I don't know how to fix it.

She brought a fresh bucket of water out to the first hen house and tapped on the door. "Good afternoon, my beauties. How is everyone doing today?"

Chatter erupted from inside the structure. Laughing, Havyn opened the door and went inside. Her girls all chattered at once and pranced around her feet for her attention.

By the time she made it to the third hen house, her arms were aching from hauling the water and feed. But at least she was almost done.

Opening the door, she wasn't prepared for the onslaught. Out came Angry Bird, squawking and pecking and flapping her wings, followed by Buttercup and Sophie.

Before Havyn could get the door closed, the three hens had escaped the enclosed yard and scrambled through the gate to the larger yard, where they spent a good deal of the summer. "Get back here, you silly birds." Havyn went after them.

But now, *all* the chickens were riled up, and the noise from each one of the hen houses was deafening.

"Oh, *hush* now!"

Of course, they didn't listen.

When she made it through the outer gate, she searched the yard for the three rebels. Dumb chickens. They were probably buried in the snow, waiting for rescue.

She finally caught sight of them and couldn't help but

laugh. Angry Bird was leading the others in some sort of crazy game of chase as they zigzagged their way over the top of the snow. Apparently, they weren't heavy enough to sink into it. The problem was, the snow was as high as the fence, which meant the chickens could go wherever they wanted.

Oh brother.

As soon as she gave chase, she realized it was futile. The chickens were headed down toward the pond.

Now what was she supposed to do?

———

Whitney and Peter made it back to Nome a couple hours after dark. Every muscle in her body ached, and exhaustion threatened to take over. Even with her nap earlier in the day. Breaking the trail had been much harder than she'd expected, especially for a storm that had only lasted a few hours.

When she dropped Peter off, he objected to her traveling the rest of the way home alone, but she pulled out the pistol to assure him she could take care of herself. She promised to take him back to the village first thing the next morning with fresh supplies, then headed home.

The lights of the farm greeted her at a little past six. The dogs barked their excitement to be home and pulled the sled straight to their yard. As she unharnessed them, Daniel and John made their way to her.

"Glad you're back!" John rubbed the heads of each of her dogs.

"Did you get stuck in the storm?" Daniel carried a bucket of water.

"We did." She let out a long sigh. "I'm just glad it didn't last for days."

"What did the storm front look like? Was there a lot

of wind before it?" Daniel was always fascinated with the weather.

"Just a big wall, to be honest. We were caught in ice fog before that, and it was calm as day. Then the wind picked up and blew out the fog, and we saw it. Peter and I were coming back for supplies when it barreled its way through."

"I bet the trail was a beast after that." John grabbed fresh straw for the dogs to bed down while Daniel filled the feed bowls.

She leaned back and stretched out her shoulders. "Yeah. And we need to go back tomorrow. Probably should head back tonight, but we're both too tired. More people are sick, and Peter ran out of supplies."

John put a hand on her shoulder. "Let us finish with the dogs, then. You go on in and we'll be right there."

With a nod she headed to the house. A few months ago, she wouldn't have allowed John or Daniel to touch her dogs. But now, they were family. It was good to have help.

She walked into the house and glanced around. The bottle in her pocket was empty. She needed to refill it before she headed out tomorrow—

Havyn and Madysen came to greet her at the door with hugs and smiles. "We're so glad you're back!" Maddy bounced on her toes. "I made your favorite for dinner. Just in case."

Havyn helped her out of her coat. "Why don't you go get cleaned up, and we'll get everything on the table."

"Sounds good. Thanks." That would give her the perfect opportunity to sneak into Granddad's office.

Listening to her sisters move around in the kitchen, she padded her way to the office and lifted the key from where she kept it on a chain around her neck. Maybe she *should* move the bottle into her room. That would be easier.

She took the bottle of whiskey and went to her room. She set it down and changed her clothes. The dogs had been cuddled up next to her, so the smell of wet pup clung to her.

But it wasn't nice for her to delay everyone's dinner, so she made her way back to the dining room.

To her surprise, Ruth, Bethany, Eli, and Granny were also there.

"It's good to see you, Whitney." Granny placed her napkin in her lap.

"You too, Granny." While she *wanted* to like the fact that the dear woman was with them, she was too exhausted to care.

Bethany gave her a sweet smile. Eli came over, grabbed her hand, and pointed to a chair. "Will you sit next to me?"

Her stepbrother was growing into a young man. The fact that he wanted to sit next to her melted her heart. "Sure." It was good to feel something other than numb.

"Do you think I'm big enough to help with the dogs now?" His voice squeaked on the end.

"Of course. I can always use the help, and they love the interaction. In fact, Dr. Cameron has asked for a team, so there will be extra work training them and him."

"I'll do whatever you tell me to do. I want to learn all of it. I've been watching real good. I promise." The eager look on Eli's face couldn't be denied.

Whitney gave her younger brother a soft smile. "As soon as I get back from this next trip, we'll start, okay? Until then, you can help John and Daniel feed and take care of the dogs that are here."

After John prayed and thanked God for the meal, all the dishes were passed. Fried chicken with roasted potatoes. Her favorite. Something they had made once in a blue moon until

Havyn finally agreed they could raise a flock of chickens for fryers. She'd have to hug her sister later.

What was Peter having for supper? Poor man. She'd deposited him at his office and just taken off. How thoughtless of her—she should have asked him to have dinner with them.

No. Such thoughts were ridiculous. Peter could take care of himself. He didn't need her worrying over him like a mother hen.

John passed the large bowl of potatoes to her. "You know, I've been wondering how we could help the good doctor. Won't he need to build a new place to live if he's going to have a team of dogs?"

Whitney could hug her brother-in-law. Now she wouldn't have to bring up the subject herself. "We spoke about that on our journey." Would the rest of her family come to the same thought she had? She spooned potatoes onto her plate and let the conversation sink in.

"He's done so much to help us and our town—not to mention the villages—we should do something to help him." Havyn squinted and wiped her mouth with her napkin. Then she lifted a finger. "Why don't we offer to build Peter a small home here? We've got plenty of room, and he wouldn't have to build another shelter for the dogs since we already have more than enough space."

"That's a great idea." Daniel lifted a piece of chicken to his mouth.

"I agree too." Maddy shrugged her shoulders. "Are you okay with that, Whit?"

"Yes, I think it's perfect. I just hope it won't be too far for him to go in and out of town for his patients there."

John waved a hand. "I doubt that will be a problem."

"I take it Amka is still out at the village?" Granny passed a steaming bowl of cinnamon apples.

Whitney nodded. "Yes, Peter and I had planned to get the supplies he needed and go straight back, so Amka stayed with the other team and sled. Dad was still out at the gold camp. Of course, the blizzard changed our plans, but we'll have to head back in the morning. Peter is quite concerned about some of the children. But I believe he's gotten the sickness under control."

"Good. That's a relief." Daniel poured himself another glass of water. "Peter is a wonderful doctor. The town sure did win a prize when he came."

Whitney took a bite of potatoes and savored them. "I still miss Doc Gordon, but I'm praying he'll return this summer. A couple of the other new doctors are too young . . . and they won't go visit the villages. Peter and Doc Gordon would get along well and be great for Nome. Wouldn't it be wonderful to turn our town into a respectable place rather than the crazy, gold-digging, mining town that it is?"

"I wouldn't get my hopes up." John pointed his fork at her and then dug back into the food on his plate. "Once the gold is gone, don't you think they'll head out for the next great strike?"

"Probably a good thing." Daniel nodded and then looked at Granny. "Although that would hurt the mercantile's business, I'm sure."

"We'd do fine. There are plenty of good people who have made Nome their home." Granny dabbed her napkin at her mouth.

"Speaking of good people . . . Judas Reynolds came out here this afternoon." Havyn sent a little smirk her way.

What did that mean?

And why did Granny look none too happy?

"Oh?" Whitney put on her best nonchalant face.

"Yes, he was asking about you. Wanted to make sure we were all right after the storm." Madysen put another helping of chicken onto her plate.

"That was very kind of him." How was she supposed to answer? Sooner or later, she'd have to tell her sisters that he had asked to court her, but she hadn't made a decision about her answer yet. Though she was leaning heavily in the direction of a yes. Whether her heart was ready or not. Something had to change in her life.

She dug into her food and allowed the conversation to shift to the farm. As words drifted around the table—from the cows, to the sheep, to Havyn's adventure chasing three of her chickens down the lane—comfort spread its wings over her. This was normal. She belonged. Perhaps her grief had clouded everything for too long. Maybe she was on the road to healing.

"I'm thinking we should let Mr. Norris know we can play this weekend at the Roadhouse again. What do you think?" Maddy's question brought Whitney's good spirits to a crashing halt.

"Must we so soon?" Did that sound like a whine? She worked to keep her breathing slow and steady but couldn't stop the rapid beat of her heart.

All eyes shifted to her. Why had she even bothered to open her mouth? Why did Maddy have to bring up the subject in the first place?

"Is something wrong?"

"Are you not feeling well?"

"We all miss Granddad . . ."

Everyone spoke at once.

Whitney dabbed her napkin to her lips. She was too tired to deal with this right now. Laying the cloth down, she took a steadying breath. "I don't mind if you and Havyn play without me." She looked at Maddy's shocked face. "But I don't want to. I'm not sure if I'll want to do that anymore. I'm sorry."

Shock seemed to be the expression of the moment. Then Havyn started crying.

Which made Maddy wrap her arms around their sister and cry too.

Which made Daniel and John comfort their wives.

Which made Whitney feel like a heel.

She stood. "Excuse me, I'm going to head to bed. I'm really tired."

But as she left the room, her feet took her to the piano instead. The music to *Fantaisie-Impromptu* lay open. Right where she left off.

Her fingers itched to play.

It wouldn't do any good. She didn't learn the piece when Mama asked. Didn't play it for Granddad.

She'd missed her chance. And now . . .

Well, Maddy and Havyn had Daniel and John. They didn't need her. Their music would be beautiful without her.

She closed the music and tucked it back onto the shelf and then shut the lid to the piano. There. For now, it was best.

As soon as she walked away from the piano, she regretted it. What was *wrong* with her? She loved music. Loved her family.

When she made it to her room, Ruth was there, waiting. "Punishing yourself isn't going to do any good."

Whitney frowned. Pushed past Ruth into the room. "I'm not punishing myself."

"I saw how you looked at the piano just now. You can't fool me."

She shot a glare at Ruth. "You don't know me. I know you think you do, but you don't. You don't understand what I've been through. Everything that I've lost. Everything that has changed."

"Whitney!" Havyn's voice, full of shock and shame, came from the hallway.

"Keep at it, sis. You've almost got that motherly scolding voice down." Where was this snippy tone coming from? She put a hand to her forehead. Here came the pain. Good grief. She needed a drink. But she needed all of them to leave so she could have one.

Havyn put a hand to her belly and took a long, deep breath. A sure sign she was tempering her words. "Look. I came back here to tell you what happened. We didn't discuss it at dinner. I know we promised not to do anything without you, but the hotel caught fire and we had to move Ruth and the kids here. We went ahead and moved everyone's rooms around. Just like we talked about."

"All except yours." Maddy tossed in from behind their sister.

"I see." Whitney darted her gaze to Ruth.

"I think we need to get some rest. Tensions have been high lately, so why don't we talk in the morning?"

Since when did Havyn boss them all around? Boss *her* around?

The shooting pain in her temples chose that moment to start up again, so she just closed her eyes and nodded.

Everyone left in an awkward silence. She'd hurt them, but she couldn't seem to figure out her own feelings—much less her outburst. Headaches and bitterness toward Dad and God tormented her. *Nothing* was right anymore. It was almost as if she didn't know her own family anymore. Didn't know who she had become.

Dressing for bed, she couldn't take her eyes off where she'd hidden the whiskey. A little before bed should take the edge off the pain. Then tomorrow, she'd talk to Peter about it. Surely he had another remedy for her headaches and anxiety.

Yes. She would do that. Then she wouldn't need the strong drink anymore.

But . . .

What if Peter couldn't do anything else? What if she became an invalid and a burden on her family?

The pain overwhelmed her, and she closed her eyes and counted to ten. No. She was fine. She had a handle on things.

Climbing into bed, she pulled the whiskey with her. Too tired to refill the small tonic bottle, she just drank out of the larger one. Just until the headache settled down. She took a small sip and tucked the bottle next to her. Just in case.

Relaxing against the pillows, she reached for it again and this time took a long drag on the mouth of the bottle.

The liquid warmed her.

In the morning, she could apologize.

The room smelled of antiseptic. A smell Peter was used to, but at the moment, it turned his stomach.

Then he saw her.

Charlotte.

Her hair drenched from sweat, her face bright red. No matter what he did, he couldn't stop the flow of blood. And his wife was suffering because of it.

"I can't, Peter . . . I can't." She fell back against the pillows and breathed heavily.

"Yes, you can. I'm here with you. It shouldn't be that much longer. Hold on, Charlotte. Stay with me. Please."

What good was his medical training? He had no idea what to do. And Dr. Willis—his mentor and teacher—was out on another call. A young man had been gored by a bull. Peter sent word, but so far, the good doctor hadn't come.

His wife and child were dying, and he couldn't stop it!

The scenery changed, and he was outside. The humid summer of Kansas threatened rain. The scent of damp, freshly turned earth filled his nose.

He stood beside the grave. A simple pine box held his wife. And his son.

"There was nothing any of us could have done, my boy. Not a thing. Your wife simply couldn't carry a child." Dr. Willis had a hand on his shoulder.

The man reassured him over and over again that nothing could have prevented the disaster that took his whole world. They hadn't known that his wife had a malformed uterus, or that the baby hadn't developed correctly. Then the placenta had ruptured.

All Peter knew was that he hadn't been able to save them. Neither one of them.

He'd failed. Plain and simple.

The scenery changed again. Whitney was there, walking a narrow ledge, a bottle in her hand. Her expression was so sad.

"Whitney!" He rushed toward her. "Don't move. You'll fall!"

And then she was gone over the side.

Crouching at the edge, he watched her fall until she disappeared into the blackness—

"No!"

Peter jerked up in bed and took stock of the room around him. He wasn't back in Kansas. Struggling to breathe, he thrust his hands into his hair and gripped the sides of his head.

Another nightmare. This time laced with a new element. Whitney.

TWELVE

Tuesday, January 17

The room was dark as Whitney blinked and pushed herself up to sit. If only she could sleep longer, but the need for the privy pushed her.

With a groan, she stretched and worked to free her mind of the cobwebs. Why was her brain so muddled?

"Good morning, sleepyhead." Madysen's usually sing-song voice was anything but. It held a tinge of anger.

Whitney turned toward the sound. "What are you doing in my room?"

A lantern lit. Havyn's face wasn't any happier than Maddy's voice.

The warm glow helped her to see her sisters standing at the foot of her bed. Grim. Serious.

In Havyn's right hand . . .

The whiskey bottle.

No! Whitney surged to her feet.

Havyn held out the bottle. "We're trying *not* to jump to any conclusions here, but we heard a thud as we were heading to the kitchen. It was this. And you were dead asleep."

171

"What's going on, Whit?" Madysen put her hands on her hips.

Whitney's stomach roiled. She understood their accusatory tones, they'd grown up with the same father she had. But still . . . she didn't want to explain. "Peter gave me a bottle of tonic to help with the headaches and uneasiness after the attack."

Both sisters softened a bit. Good. At least they were listening.

"Since the tonic was mostly whiskey, I refill the small flask with that." She nodded toward the bottle still in the white-knuckled grip of her pregnant sister.

"You refill it? Often?" Maddy's voice softened. As if she couldn't believe it.

"No." What could she say? "Only as needed."

"Might I remind you that this home has never had alcohol in it because of the demons it produced in our father?" Havyn's brows knit together.

"*You* are the one who reminds us time and again of the pain Dad caused with his drinking. How *could* you?" Maddy looked about ready to cry.

Whitney's body tensed, and it was her turn to place her hands on her hips. "You know very well that Granddad had that locked up in his cabinet for medicinal purposes. That's what this is. Peter knows about it. You have no idea what I've had to endure and the pain these headaches cause me."

"Aren't you afraid of ending up like Dad?" Havyn's voice had lost some of its edge.

How could she get them to see? She wasn't like their dad. Not. One. Bit. "I'm not drinking for the sake of drinking, I promise. I can't even stand the taste of the stuff. It's only for the pain."

Havyn shook her head. "I don't know, Whit. This scares me. You wouldn't wake up."

Guilt pricked at her conscience, but she wouldn't give it entrance. "I'm fine. You both have enough to worry about without having to fret over me."

"You're our *sister*! Of course we're going to worry. You haven't been acting like yourself." Maddy stepped forward and tried to put a hand on Whitney's arm.

She jerked back. "Have you thought about the fact that everything has changed? Did you consider how both of you running off to get married could impact me? It's not enough that I have to grieve my mother and my grandfather, but a man tried to ruin my reputation! He hurt me. Worse than I want to admit. You two have your husbands to run and cry to . . . I don't have anyone. So mind your own business and stay out of mine. I think I have a right to not act like myself."

The shocked looks on her sisters' faces made the silence deafening.

Oh, curse her temper! She slumped. "I'm sorry. My head still hurts."

Maddy sniffed.

Havyn set the bottle down on the bed. "We were concerned, that's it. I better go fix breakfast." She turned on her heel.

Maddy followed. Without a word.

Whitney collapsed onto the bed. Why couldn't she get past the pain and grief like her sisters had? Why was God allowing this to happen to her?

Tears sprang to her eyes. She tried to keep them at bay, but it was no use. Now the headache would rage again, but she didn't care. Nothing was right or normal.

She'd never talked that way to her sisters. Never! What had she done?

The red of Whitney's curly locks caught Judas's attention out the window.

Of course, she was back in front of that doctor's office. What now? She'd just returned, or so he'd heard.

This was not going according to Judas's plan. Well, he was about to change that. Right now.

He went to the hat stand and grabbed his coat and then headed out his office door. Within moments, he was a few strides away. Pasting a smile on his face, he slowed his pace and stepped close to her.

"Good morning, Mr. Reynolds." There was a wariness in her eyes.

"Please, call me Judas."

Her lips tipped up. Barely. "All right. Judas." This time, she held eye contact.

"Have you had a chance to think about my request?" He kept his voice low. His tone sweet.

She dipped her head a bit. "Yes, I have."

"And?"

"If I agree to court you, I need to be clear that I am not promising to marry you."

"I would never expect that you were, my dear." If he were a betting man, he'd say the odds were in his favor, though.

"I appreciate that you are a God-fearing man of good character. Those are important things that I would like in a husband. But things are difficult right now. You must understand that." She gazed off in the direction of her farm. "You were there for me when Mr. Sinclair lied. In fact, you came to my rescue and salvaged my reputation. I will be forever grateful for that. But I don't want you to think that my decision is made lightly or out of any response to that."

"It is apparent you've put a great deal of thought into this." She was coming around. Excellent.

"I have." She turned back to face him. "The truth is, I'm not sure I'm good wife material. There are many things I need to figure out for myself before I enter into a relationship like marriage."

The lady was thinking about marriage. It couldn't be going better if he'd orchestrated the whole thing himself. "You have my deepest respect for your honesty, Miss Powell."

"Please. We've known each other long enough. Call me Whitney."

"Whitney it is." Judas lifted his shoulders a bit. Time to pour on the charm. "You are the most level-headed and practical woman I've ever met. That's exactly what I've been searching for in a wife. That's why you haven't seen me about town courting anyone else. No one has met my standards. But you . . . well, you don't have your head in the clouds with unrealistic dreams about marriage like most young women. You're not a gold digger either. I need someone who is sensible, honest, loyal . . . and frankly, I see all of those plus so much more in you, Whitney."

Her cheeks tinged pink. "Your words are very kind—"

He put a hand over his heart. "They are from my heart. God's honest truth."

She shook her head. "I've never seen this side of you, Judas. It's refreshing. Forthright. I appreciate that."

Oh, if she only knew. "Does that mean you'll allow me to court you?"

She tilted her head to the side and studied him. "Yes, I believe it does."

"How about this evening?" No time like the present. The sooner he could secure the lovely lady in marriage, the sooner he could work his way into the family business and add it to his empire.

"I don't think I can tonight. I'm about to take Peter—Dr. Cameron—back out to the village with more supplies. I'm not sure how long I will be gone."

He reached forward and took one of her hands. This time, she didn't pull away. "I will eagerly watch for your return then and ask again."

"Thank you, Judas."

She released his hand and pulled her hood up over her head. Judas turned—and found Cameron frowning at him. Perfect.

The dogs were having a heyday out on the trail, but even with their eagerness and chipper barks, Peter couldn't dispel the dark cloud of his mood.

All he could think about was hearing Whitney agree to court to Judas Reynolds. Didn't she see what kind of man he was? Good grief, she'd known the man more than a decade. Had he really pulled the wool over all of their eyes?

His hands fisted in his lap. He should tell her to pull the sled over so he could give her a piece of his mind on the subject.

But he wouldn't do that.

One, because that was simply his temper talking.

Two, because he didn't understand what to do with the feelings he was having at the moment.

Yes, he cared for Whitney. She was his patient. He cared

for her whole family. But somehow . . . those feelings had deepened into something more with her. The how and when were beyond him.

Plain as the nose on his face, though, he had to admit they were there. No getting around it after he'd watched her with Judas.

He was jealous.

The thought was ridiculous. Yet true.

And he wanted to hit something. Which he couldn't deal with at the moment. Why was he angry? Because he didn't think he'd care for anyone after Charlotte? Was he betraying her in some way?

Or was it because he despised Judas so much?

Or maybe . . . because he'd hoped Whitney would turn the despicable man down?

The lead dog stumbled through a drift, which caused the rest of the team to come to a halt as the sled slid sideways. Thankfully, they hadn't been going full speed.

Whitney appeared at his side. "The snow has been blown over the trail we broke yesterday. Sorry about that."

He hopped out of his seat in the sled. "Can I help with anything?" Maybe physical work would help his attitude.

"Sure." She shrugged. "It's like the other day. We've got to break trail. But first we have to dig them out."

They worked together in silence, and Peter found that petting the dogs as he dug them out was good for his foul mood. It didn't make him feel better about Whitney, though. These new emotions were dangerous. If he had feelings for her, why didn't he open his mouth and tell her?

Probably because he hadn't realized it until this moment. Or didn't want to admit it.

If it was the latter, he had some serious soul searching

to do. Keeping his feelings locked up in a little box wasn't healthy, no matter how much he tried to convince himself it was best.

If it was the former . . . well, the same could be true. Had he been tamping down his emotions all this time? He let out a sigh.

Exactly what Dr. Willis had warned him against. He'd scolded Peter on multiple occasions because Peter said it was easier to compartmentalize everything when he was working with patients. Dr. Willis insisted that the best doctor was the one who was personally invested. One who cared about each and every patient. Prayed for them. Took time with them.

"Peter?"

Whitney's voice jolted him back. "Hmm?" He blinked away the memories.

"Are you all right?" One eyebrow quirked up. "You've been petting Ginger for several moments now. Not that she minds, but I need your help digging us out." She sent him a prodding smile as she pointed over her shoulder with her thumbs.

"Sorry. My mind was elsewhere."

"I figured as much." With a shake of her head, she giggled.

No more shoving his feelings down. "I was actually thinking about you and Judas."

Her expression shifted to serious. "Oh. You heard us talking?"

"I did."

"I take it you don't approve?" The edge to her voice told him he was on thin ice.

It was his own fault. He'd opened this can of worms. "I know your family has been close to Reynolds for a long time. . . ." The words hung in the air. Should he finish?

"Sounded like there was a *but* coming?"

He'd expected her to get defensive and angry. But instead, her tone had changed. The look she sent him was vulnerable. Almost as if she was seeking his approval.

He high-stepped through the drift toward her. "But . . . I don't believe he's the right man for you." There. He'd said it.

"How am I supposed to know who the right man is?" She threw out her arms and huffed. Exasperated. That's how he would describe her.

Well, he'd backed himself into a corner. He couldn't exactly say, "I'm here!" He shrugged. "I don't know."

"Well, then how on earth am I supposed to know that Judas is wrong for me unless I allow him to court me?" Whitney leaned down and tugged another pup out of the snow. It took her a few swift maneuvers to untangle the dogs' lines.

"That's a good question. I'm not trying to tell you what to do, Whitney. I'm simply telling you as a friend what I see."

She mumbled something under her breath.

"Sorry, I didn't catch that."

"Probably because I didn't want you to." She put a hand to her forehead, then went back to the dogs. "Everything has changed in the past year. *Everything*."

As much as he wanted to, he couldn't do anything to fix that. "I'm sorry."

"Don't apologize. It's not your fault." With a side-glance at him, she let her hood fall back. Her curly hair spread out over her shoulders. "I appreciate you speaking your mind with me, Peter, but there are some things I'm going to have to figure out on my own. Without Mama or Granddad to talk to . . . I feel lost."

"I wasn't trying to make you feel worse or to confuse you." There didn't seem to be any way out of the mess he'd created. "I'm sorry. Maybe you should ignore the fact that

I said anything." He swiped a hand down his face and blew his breath out. "Just know that I care and I'm here if you need someone to talk to. All right?" He turned away.

"All right. I appreciate that. I always wanted a big brother."

Good thing she couldn't see the scowl crossing his face. The last thing he wanted was her thinking of him like a brother. "How about a good friend?"

"I suppose so, although I've never been certain men and women could be friends without issues of something more coming to interfere."

He glanced over his shoulder. "Interfere? In what way?"

"You know. Inevitably one or the other starts thinking about the other in a way that takes them beyond friendship. Without meaning to they might think of how nice the other person looks or how great they are at . . . well . . . at most anything."

"And that's a bad thing?"

She shrugged. "It is if you want to keep the relationship uncomplicated and free of—"

"Interferences?"

She snapped her mouth shut and studied him for a long moment. "Yes."

They went back to digging on the trail and maneuvered the team back into the shallower snow. It was backbreaking work, and there wasn't any need to fill the air with conversation. Even so, Peter enjoyed the time in her presence.

She didn't force a façade. Had been honest enough to admit that she was struggling. Felt lost. Her faith had been sorely tested. Was there anyone else she could truly be herself with? Maybe that was why she was allowing Judas to call on her.

Heavenly Father, please comfort Whitney during this time.

Help her to see that she's not alone. Help me to be the friend she needs.

Too many times of late, he'd tried to do things on his own. It never ended well.

His heart clenched. He wanted to be more than Whitney's friend. There. He admitted it.

But could he ever tell her?

Thirteen

Urging her dogs into a full run, Whitney took the trail back to Nome. As soon as she'd arrived with Peter and the supplies, Amka had asked her to fill a list for the villagers from the mercantile. The sickness had taken its toll, and many were without staples. Which, in the dead of winter, could be a dangerous thing. Deadly, even.

So she'd helped unload Peter's supplies and turned back around.

It gave her time to think. Too much time. Because after Peter gave his opinion about her courting Judas, she'd begun to doubt. About Judas. Her future. Everything.

For the past two hours, she'd replayed the conversation over and over in her mind.

Something in the way that Peter looked at her made her think there was more he wanted to say. Did he dislike Judas? Or was there something else?

The doctor was a good man. When she hadn't trusted any man other than John and Granddad, Peter had shown himself true. Safe.

If only she could talk to Mama about this.

The pain that hit her at the thought of her mother made her want to curl up into a ball and cry. The ache seemed as real as if something was stabbing her in the chest. With everything in her, she wanted to reach into her pocket and pull out the bottle.

No. She kept her hands firmly planted on the driving bow. She wouldn't give in to that. It was for headaches and anxiety. Havyn and Maddy were overreacting. She wasn't like their father. She didn't have a problem with drinking.

The town came into view, and she breathed a long sigh.

Thank heaven. There would be plenty there to keep her busy and her mind off of Peter and his words.

She drove the sled through the bustling town, toward the mercantile. Mr. Beaufort should have everything she needed to fill Amka's list. Whitney would not want anyone in the village to suffer because of lack of supplies.

"Whoa." Her command to the team was immediately obeyed. She set the hook and ran to the front of the sled, petting each of the dogs and checking to make sure they were in good shape.

Their tongues hung out, and the dogs' eyes were bright and eager. Even after the long haul back and forth, they seemed in good spirits. After making several circles in the snow, her dogs settled down in front of her sled.

"Good dogs." She sent them a smile and headed into the store. She tilted her fur-lined hood back and removed her gloves.

"Miss Powell!" Mr. Beaufort called from the register. "It's good to see you. How are Amka and her family?" The man's smile was genuine.

"They are doing well, although the sickness has spread a bit. That's why I'm here. They are in need of supplies." She reached into her pocket and pulled out the list from Amka. She slid it across the counter in front of Mr. Beaufort. "Do you have everything in stock?"

He perused the list. "Sure do. I'll get this filled in a jiffy."

"I'll be out with my team. Thank you, Mr. Beaufort."

He leaned closer and tapped the counter. "It's Martin. After all, we're family." The smile he sent her made her feel at home. "I'll bring it out as soon as I get it gathered up."

"Thank you, Martin." She slapped her gloves against her palm and lifted her hood back up over her hair. With a tug, she put her gloves back on. Her mouth watered as she passed the barrel of pickles, and the tangy scent overtook her senses.

The bell on the door jangled as she exited, and the chill in the air threatened to take her breath away.

"Miss Powell." Judas walked up to her. "Whitney." His voice turned soft and intimate. "How good to see you made it back."

She gave him a smile and studied his eyes. Peter's words rang in her mind, but she couldn't find any guile or deceit in Judas's face. He truly seemed to care for her. "Amka was in need of supplies, so I came back."

"How very kind of you. I'm glad that those people have you to help them." He held out his arm for her.

Even though her sled was mere steps away, she took it.

"When do you head back?" His tone was kind. Interested. His focus completely on her.

"Tomorrow morning. It will be best for the dogs since they've been on the trail so much today already and we still need to get home."

"Good." He stopped beside her sled and turned toward her. The space between them a mere foot. "Perhaps, then, I can persuade you to dine with me this evening?"

A little shiver went up her spine. Her first *real* invitation to be called upon by a man. There was no need to think it through. She'd already agreed he could court her. "That would be lovely."

"Wonderful. I think the Golden Palace Restaurant would be nice. I will bring out the sleigh to pick you up at, shall we say, five o'clock? That way, I can return you home in plenty of time to ensure you have adequate rest for tomorrow."

How considerate. "That sounds perfect." All the doubts she'd had earlier dissipated. Tonight, she would pay close attention, and if she needed to, she could speak to Peter and even Amka about it when she returned to the village. But at this point, she couldn't see any reason why Judas Reynolds wouldn't be an adequate partner for her.

"I'll see you later this evening." He tipped his hat to her and smiled. Then with a squeeze to her elbow, he turned and headed back to his office.

Whitney watched him walk for several moments. Even though it flattered her that such a distinguished man would show attention for her, she realized she didn't actually feel anything toward him other than their regular familial friendship. She turned to her dogs. "Well, it appears I have a dinner engagement this evening." She looked down at her sealskin pants and long parka. "I should probably trade in my mukluks and attire for a dress and boots, don't you think?"

Dressed in her favorite green dress, Whitney watched out the window for Judas's sleigh.

"You'll have to tell us all about dining at the Golden Palace. I hear it's really fancy." Havyn stepped around her, tucking curls of her hair here and there. "Your hair looks magnificent!"

"Thanks. Maddy did a beautiful job." Whitney had been nervous about telling her sisters that she'd agreed to court Judas Reynolds. And even though there had been a moment of shock for each of them, they had gathered around her with encouragement and praise and offered to help her get ready for the evening out. It had been a balm to her heart.

Even though her last words to her sisters hadn't been kind, they didn't say a word about it and no tension filled the air around them.

Forgiveness was a beautiful thing. So was family.

For the first time in months, things didn't feel like they were spinning out of control. Unease didn't press in on her chest. No awkward moments with her sisters. The ache of loneliness—missing Mama and Granddad—didn't haunt her at every turn.

Maybe this was exactly what she needed to move forward. Now if she could keep the headache at the back of her head from becoming a full-blown, throbbing monster chasing her down, she would be fine.

"I found some green velvet ribbon." Maddy waved the strands as she glided into the parlor. "Let me weave them into your hair, and it will be perfect."

Whitney sat in a chair so her sister could work her magic. "Thank you both." Emotion clogged her throat, and she swallowed it back. "I wouldn't have been able to do this without you."

Havyn stepped in front of her and grinned. "What are sisters for?" She put a hand on her belly. "Oh, the little one agrees."

It all felt so . . . normal.

Something they hadn't had in quite some time.

"You know, when you get back from bringing the supplies

out to Amka, we really should decode Granddad's letter. I know we're not in dire straits financially, but it would probably be a good idea for us to know what we have so at the next family meeting we can plan accordingly." Madysen tapped her chin as she spoke.

"Look at you, thinking ahead and talking about plans." It made Whitney release a light laugh. She turned to her other sister. "Havyn, I believe our little sister is all grown up."

Maddy shook her head and made a silly face. "Just remember that next time I forget it's my turn to cook dinner or I can't remember where I left my shawl."

As they giggled together, Whitney's heart felt lighter.

At precisely five o'clock, she heard the jingle of bells from Judas's sleigh. She stood up and smoothed her skirt. "Well, I better grab my coat."

"Have a wonderful time." Havyn wrapped an arm around Maddy's shoulders.

"Thank you."

The ride back into town was relaxed. Whitney had never ridden in a sleigh that was so comfortable. Not only were the seats covered in thick cushions, but the bumps in the road didn't seem near as rough as usual. She wanted to lean over the side and look at the runners but held her curiosity at bay. Whatever it was, it was the most pleasant ride she'd ever had.

Judas had ensconced her with heated bricks and several blankets, which made the trip almost as luxurious as sitting in front of the roaring fire at home.

"Thank you for agreeing to dine with me this evening." Judas seemed relaxed beside her.

So far the conversation had been sparse as Whitney had settled and taken it all in. "I appreciate your invitation."

"The weather continues to be frigid."

"Yes. It does." Should she say something else? How could a conversation with this man, whom she'd known forever, be awkward just because they were courting? That shouldn't change things, right?

"How are your animals faring?"

"Quite well, thank you." Was small talk the norm for an outing such as this? Thankfully, he seemed comfortable enough with the quiet.

Silence stretched for several minutes, and she turned to gaze out at the snow-covered landscape. It shimmered in the moonlight as the stars above twinkled. The air was fresh and clean. Not that she minded the scents of the farm, but she always appreciated the winter air. Almost as much as she appreciated a spring rain—how it washed everything clean.

Judas asked her questions here and there, but most of them required a simple word or two of response. Hopefully, things would improve, because she couldn't imagine a life of chitchat.

As they drove into town, the charred remains of the Grand Nome Hotel made her catch her breath. Thank goodness the fire hadn't spread. It could have burned down the whole town.

At the restaurant, Judas pulled up to the front door. It wasn't just a storefront—this was an actual solid building of brick, with large windows that let out the warm glow from inside.

Whitney smiled. Lovely. She hadn't been to this side of town since the restaurant had been built.

As he came around to assist her down from the sleigh, she looked up at the large staircase to the double-door entry.

"I hope you like it." He held up a hand to her. "I had it

built hoping it would be reminiscent of my favorite restaurants in San Francisco."

She'd forgotten that this was another of his businesses. How many did he own in Nome? Perhaps that was a question she could ask later in the evening. "It is very nice, Judas."

He snapped his fingers and a man from the porch came running. "Please park my sleigh in the barn and make sure the bricks are reheated for when we are ready to take our leave."

"Yes, sir." The man nodded.

Judas held out his arm and Whitney took it. They walked up the steps, and then he opened the door for her.

The lush red carpet was a luxury for Nome. Chandeliers hung from the ceiling with little dangling crystals that caught all the light.

It was amazing.

"Your table is ready, Mr. Reynolds." Another man in a fine suit bowed to them.

"Thank you, Reginald."

They followed the man through the dining room to the back corner, where there was a dining area enclosed on three sides.

Whitney glanced around. It appeared every corner of the restaurant held one of these more private dining areas. She allowed Reginald to take her coat while Judas held out the chair for her and tried to keep her discomfort at bay. At least the room didn't have a door that shut them off. That wouldn't be appropriate. She could see how people could want to dine without having others overhear their conversations. Perhaps it wasn't so bad.

"This is my personal table. I hope you like it." Judas took his seat across from her and laid his napkin in his lap.

"It's quite nice." Maybe this wasn't such a good idea. Why was she feeling so uneasy? Her stomach tumbled inside her, and her head twinged. Not another headache. Not now.

"Would you mind if I ordered a bottle of wine with our dinner?" He leaned back and looked down at his menu. Completely at ease with himself.

Was this how normal people dined out? She didn't see any harm in it. "That's fine." She pointed her gaze at her own menu.

"Let me know if you have questions about the menu. I worked with the chef personally to put it together." Judas's voice was smooth and calm.

It did nothing to soothe her jitters. "Thank you. It all sounds delicious."

When Reginald returned, she ordered a steak with mushroom gravy, mashed potatoes, and glazed carrots. Judas ordered something she couldn't even pronounce, and then took the bottle of wine the other man offered. After Reginald left, Judas poured himself a glass and held up the bottle. "Would you like me to pour you a glass as well?"

Heat filled her cheeks. How was she supposed to respond? She'd never done this before, so might as well be honest. "I've never had wine. I may not like it and wouldn't want to waste it."

He waved his other hand at her. "Don't worry your pretty little head about that." He poured a tiny amount into the glass in front of her. "Go ahead. If you don't like it, you don't have to drink it."

She gave him a tentative smile and lifted the glass to her lips. Taking a small sip, she let it swirl over her tongue. Funny, she was expecting something strong like the whiskey, but this had a much more pleasant taste.

Not that she would say that to him.

The deep fruity flavor warmed her as it went down.

"Would you like more?"

"Yes, please." It couldn't hurt, right?

He filled her glass, and she took another sip. This time, a mouthful. After several more sips, she finally relaxed and the throb in her head abated.

Judas smiled at her and asked about her dogs.

Their conversation fell into an easy rhythm. Then food arrived, and she found herself oohing and aahing over each bite.

Not only had the wine taken the edge off her headache, but she could relax. Be herself.

The evening passed in warm camaraderie. Perhaps she *could* handle this courtship thing. Judas was a nice enough man. Handsome. Kind. Wealthy.

So it wasn't all romance and lovey-dovey gifts and words. Not that she'd ever longed for that, but those were her expectations. Why?

Judas ordered dessert for them, and she excused herself to use the privy. But as soon as she stood, the room spun. "Oh . . ." She sat back down in her chair and waited for the tipsy feeling to pass. Everything seemed a bit . . . lopsided.

"Are you all right, my dear?" Judas held the bottle over her glass to refill it.

She put a hand over the goblet. "I've had enough, thank you." How many times had he refilled her glass? How much wine had she drunk?

"My apologies, Whitney." He snapped his fingers and Reginald appeared within seconds. "Would you please bring us some coffee? We'd like it with our dessert."

"Of course, sir." The man bowed and turned.

Judas leaned across the table. "Are you feeling all right?"

"A little unsteady, but I believe I'm fine. Maybe we shouldn't stay for dessert. Would you mind taking me home?"

He patted her hand and shook his head. "I can't very well bring you home in this state. What will they think? Let's get some coffee in you and you'll feel much better. I would never want anyone to think that I had taken advantage of such an upstanding woman. It's best to stay here to keep your reputation intact."

"I hadn't thought of that." Heat filled her face and neck. She definitely didn't want her sisters to see her like this. Then they'd really be on her case about drinking. What had she done?

Reginald returned with two cups, saucers, and a pot of coffee.

After he filled the two cups, Judas reached out. "Just leave the pot here, if you don't mind."

Whitney took a sip of the steaming liquid and went back over their dinner and conversation. Was there anything she couldn't remember? Had she said anything untoward or inappropriate? For several moments she kept the cup close to her lips and sipped on it as she reviewed the evening in her mind. Thankfully, nothing was a blur. And while she had definitely relaxed and talked a good deal, she couldn't think of anything that would be ascertained as unladylike.

Their dessert arrived, and she nibbled on the cake while drinking several cups of coffee. Keeping her mouth full gave Judas the opportunity to fill the silence with talk of his plans for Nome. Which was fine and dandy, but as her mind sobered, deep shame filled her middle.

After she'd finished her fourth cup of coffee, she looked up at Judas. "Forgive me for my behavior this evening."

"There's nothing to apologize for. I'm the one who offered you the wine."

She held up a hand. "Please. Allow me to finish."

"Of course."

"It was a lovely complement to the meal, but I think I've discovered that in the future, I should be careful about how much I drink. You were most gentlemanly by refilling my glass and taking care of my every whim at dinner, but perhaps next time I should limit it to one glass."

A smile stretched across his face. "Whatever you desire, my dear. I'm simply grateful you have agreed to a next time."

"Please don't speak of this to my family."

He put a hand over his heart. "I promise."

Setting the coffee cup down, she stood. Things still shifted, but at least she was a bit more clear-headed. "If you'll excuse me, I need to avail myself of the ladies' room."

"Would you like me to get your coat and bring the sleigh around?"

With a hand to her waist, she gave a slight dip of her chin. "I think that would be best."

"Of course. I will wait for you outside, then."

After using the facilities, Whitney walked around the outside of the building, hoping that a bit of fresh air would help to completely clear her mind. But as she came around the front of the building, she ran smack-dab into the last man she wanted to see.

Her father.

FOURTEEN

Madysen's bow screeched across the *A* string of her cello, and she cringed at the sound. "Sorry, Havyn."

"What's gotten into you today? That's the fourth sour note in the past few measures, and Baby Roselli doesn't like it too much." Her sister laughed and put the hand holding her own bow over her abdomen.

Madysen sighed and shook her head. "I have no idea." That wasn't true. She knew exactly what it was. "But let's try again."

"All right." Havyn lifted her violin. "One and two and three and four and . . ."

The cello rang out with the first note, and then Havyn's instrument joined in. But there was something missing. No matter what they tried to do, they couldn't cover it up.

Whitney.

This time, Havyn was the one to play a horrid note, and she moaned as she stopped and let her bow fall to her side. "You feel it too, don't you?"

She hadn't wanted to say anything, even thought it best to

keep it to herself, but then tears welled up in her eyes. "I've tried to be strong about this whole thing, but I can't do it anymore. I miss Whitney."

Havyn set down her violin and bow and walked over to her. She stood behind Madysen's chair and wrapped her arms around her. "I know what you mean. It's like even though she's here . . . she's not really *here*."

"Exactly." Madysen sniffed. With her cello cradled up against her chest and Havyn hugging her from behind, she felt a bit more complete. "I'm worried about her."

"Me too." Havyn released her and stepped over to the piano bench and sat down. Pulling a hankie out of her sleeve, she dipped her head and then dabbed at her eyes. "I was so angry when we found that bottle of whiskey. But if Dr. Cameron knows about it, what are we supposed to do? It must be okay . . . right?"

"It's not just that. She hasn't been herself for months now. I guess I expected Whitney to continue being the strong one for all of us, no matter what we went through. I mean . . . that's what she's always done. I never thought anything could shake her."

Havyn's lips pursed, and tears streamed down her face. "But we were wrong." She swiped at her face with the hankie. "Maddy . . . what if we made it worse by relying on her so much? I thought that was what she wanted, but what if she needed *us* to help fill the hole that Mama left in *her* life?"

No. She couldn't have caused more hurt to her sister. Maddy swallowed hard. Whitney loved being the one they relied on. She loved being the big sister, taking them under her wing. But what if Havyn was correct?

Tears sprang to her eyes as her stomach plummeted. She sat up a little straighter and inhaled slowly. "I think you've hit on it. She still wants to be strong for us, to fill the gap from Mama—because that's her job as the eldest. But she can't endure all of this alone. She needs us too."

"Let's make a pact." New light shone in Havyn's eyes. "No matter how much Whit tries to push us away, we won't let her. We won't leave her alone. We'll pray for her throughout the day and do what Mama always did. She loved us but wouldn't let us step off the narrow path. We've got to hold up our sister like Aaron and Hur helped keep Moses's arms up as Joshua fought Amalek and his people."

Her heart swelled with love for her family. "Agreed." Peace filled her along with a sense of hope. They could help their sister. They could.

Then everything would go back to normal.

Judas couldn't have planned it better if he had arranged the meeting himself.

Chris Powell stood directly in front of the sleigh. He looked at his daughter. "What are you doing in town?"

Whitney's eyes shifted to his. "I was having dinner. With Mr. Reynolds."

Powell turned and looked over his shoulder. "I see."

"I thought you were out at the gold camp." Whitney shifted her weight and stumbled a bit.

Her father reached out and steadied her.

Oh, to see the man's face! Tamping down the urge to smile, Judas listened to the exchange.

"One of the miners came back for supplies and brought me back. I thought you might need help bringing more supplies out to help with the sick."

"How did you know I was back in town?

"We stopped at the village and spoke with Dr. Cameron."

"Oh, that's very generous of you." Whitney looked to Judas . . . for help?

He didn't need to be asked. "I think it's time I brought your daughter home, Mr. Powell."

Powell watched his daughter walk to the side of the sleigh. He tilted his head and furrowed his brow when she stumbled again.

Judas scooted over from his perch in the sleigh and reached down to help her up.

"Thank you." Was that embarrassment he spied in her cheeks?

"Could I impose on you for a ride out to the farm?" Powell stepped close to the side.

Judas watched Whitney's face. She closed her eyes for a moment and then sighed. He looked past her to the man beside the sleigh. "It might be a bit tight, but I think we can manage."

"Thank you."

Whitney slid across the seat closer to him, which didn't bother him one bit. Judas tucked the warmed bricks around her and positioned the blankets over her. With Powell in the seat as well, they would stay quite cozy since it was built for two. But she tensed beside him. Was it because of his nearness, or because she didn't want to ride with her father?

Judas knew more than enough about Christopher Powell and his past. He made it his job to know about the people in his town. Powell had been a drunk and run around on his first wife. Even had children with the second woman. Little hussy. Now the man was back in his daughters' lives, which didn't seem to please Whitney at all.

In fact, she scooted even closer to Judas once her father was situated.

He smiled inwardly.

As they started off for the farm, Powell asked several questions of Whitney, which she didn't answer, stating that her head had begun to hurt. Naturally, Judas jumped in to save the day. That was what knights did, after all.

Even as he kept the conversation flowing with that good-for-nothing father of hers, his thoughts went back to the evening. How easy it had been to get Whitney talking once she'd had a little wine. And she hadn't even noticed that he'd refilled her glass whenever it got below half-filled.

She'd been quite a thirsty lady, too. She must have had five or six glasses. They'd gone through two bottles. A fact that surprised him, but that he could definitely use to his advantage. Perhaps next time, once the wine had loosened her tongue, he could ask about gold on their property.

It wouldn't be long before it would be his.

What was his daughter doing out with a man like Judas Reynolds? Chris couldn't wrap his mind around it. While he knew Reynolds was an old friend of the family, he also had heard of the man's business dealings, and more than one miner showed their fear of the man and his temper. While no one said a negative word about the wealthy man who practically ran the town of Nome, there was an undercurrent of something shady that Chris wanted to explore.

Especially if his daughter was going to be involved with the man.

When he'd first come to Nome, he wouldn't have had a problem with one of his girls making a match with the guy. What father wouldn't want his daughter taken care of, provided for, and married to a powerful man?

But the longer he stayed, the more he watched Reynolds's dealings. And the more he didn't like them.

When they reached the farm, Chris hopped down and thanked Judas for the ride. He then held up a hand for his daughter, praying she would accept help from him.

But Judas held her attention. He said something to her in a hushed tone and then lifted her gloved hand to his lips and kissed it.

Oh brother. It was worse than he'd imagined. What did the man want? Or was he in truth smitten?

Who wouldn't be? Whitney and her sisters were the most beautiful women in all of Alaska. They took after their mother. God rest her soul.

Whitney turned and took Chris's hand. As he helped her down, he studied her face.

A bit pale, but it was pretty cold out.

When she took a bit longer to steady herself, though, he held on to her hand.

Judas pulled away and turned the sleigh around to head back to Nome, and she lifted a hand in a wave.

"I think we need to talk." Chris was not about to let this moment pass.

"I'm tired, Dad. Can't this wait until morning?" Her voice was weaker than usual.

Maybe he should take compassion on her. "All right. How about after breakfast?"

"I forgot. I'll be taking the supplies back out to the village first thing in the morning." She wouldn't meet his eyes as she headed to the house.

"You're not going to feel like taking anything out anywhere in the morning."

She stopped in her tracks and looked over her shoulder at him. "What do you mean by that?"

"You know exactly what I mean, Whitney. And you forget that I know the signs of drinking all too well."

With a shake of her head, she stiffened. "You are mistaken, Dad. I have a headache. Nothing more."

"Are you sure?" He kept his voice calm. He wasn't angry. Simply wanted her to understand that he cared for her. No judgment. "There's no need to lie to me."

As he reached her side, her eyes shuttered. Closing him out. "I'll see you in the morning, Dad."

Dismissed, he managed a nod as she went toward the door. But he hadn't missed the droop of her shoulders. "I love you, Whitney. I hope you'll think about what I said."

His poor daughter. Hiding her drinking wouldn't do any good. But what would it take to get her attention?

God, please don't let her fall as far as I did before she comes to her senses.

The shame and almost-ruin he'd brought upon his two families caused him to cringe. He couldn't let that happen to his daughter.

No matter the cost.

FIFTEEN

Peter checked the temperature of another of the elders. As he wrote down the findings in his log, he saw many similarities to another epidemic that had killed too many of the Eskimo people from this region. He looked up at the walls of the small hut, and it seemed as if they were closing in on him, an inch at a time.

Lord, I need Your divine intervention here. What do I do? How do I help these people?

He tapped his pencil against his thigh and closed his eyes, pouring out his heart in prayer. When he ran out of words, he knew that God still understood him. The groanings of his heart.

An hour later, he was back in his own small shelter going over everything that he could find in the medical journals on the Great Sickness of 1900. The combination of infectious diseases—measles and influenza—that had never reached the native Alaskan populations before became deadly. The epidemic took a quarter upward to half of their population, while the non-native population saw little effect.

A knock at the door made him jump to his feet. Please, not another family coming down with it.

When he opened the door, Amka greeted him with a smile. "I brought you some soup."

"Thank you. That is much appreciated." When was the last time he'd eaten? He couldn't even remember. The savory and rich fragrance of thick broth, herbs, and smoked fish made his mouth water.

She set the tray down and turned to go.

"Wait, Amka, please. May I ask you a question?"

"Anything you need, Doctor, I am willing to answer what I can." She clasped her hands in front of her and dipped her head.

"Do you remember the sickness of 1900? Many called it the Great Sickness?"

Her chin tipped lower, and when she lifted her face, her eyes shone with unshed tears. "Yes. It killed thousands of our people."

"Did it hit your village here?"

"No." She put a hand to her chest. "Thankfully, it did not. But many of our brothers and sisters along the rivers—the Yukon, Kuskokwim, and Nushagak—told us of the devastation they faced."

"I see." He narrowed his eyes and glanced back over to the books. "That must be why it is hitting your village so hard this time."

"I do not think I understand?" Her brows came together in the center.

"Since this infection is new to your population, no one has immunity."

"*Immunity?* This word I do not know."

"Our bodies were designed by God to build up an *immu-*

204

nity to sickness, a way to resist it, fight it off. Once we have endured some sicknesses, we can't get them again. Or if we do, it's not as severe."

"Ah, yes. Like the chicken pox. My mother's generation got very sick when white men came through to trade. But then those who have had it do not get it again. Is that what you mean?"

"Yes, exactly." Peter went back to the books. It didn't help that there were probably several other villages that had no immunity to the measles or flu. "How many of the native people were not hit with the Great Sickness a few years ago?"

She squinted and pursed her lips. "Maybe twenty . . . twenty-five villages?"

His eyes widened. "That's a good deal more than I expected." If he took an average of one hundred people per village, that could mean between two and three *thousand* people could be leveled by this growing epidemic. And if it affected them the same way it had in 1900 . . .

They might lose over a thousand people. The thought sickened him.

"Are you not feeling well, Dr. Peter?" Amka stepped closer.

He blinked away the horrid thoughts and attempted to give her a reassuring smile. "I'm fine. But thank you for your concern and for helping me with my questions."

"I will go now and feed the others." She slipped out the door without another word.

Peter turned to the tray with the soup as his stomach growled. As much as he needed to get back to Nome and check on his many patients there, the pull to help train the people here on how to care for each other was stronger. He *had* to show them how to keep things clean. And how to keep from spreading the sickness to other villages.

Maybe Amka could deliver messages to the many villages. Or Whitney? The people trusted her.

As soon as he thought her name, a picture of her face came to mind. After his jealous realization the other day, he found himself thinking of her in a different way. His thoughts drifted to her more often than he'd realized, but now that his attention was on her, he couldn't deny his feelings.

Whitney Powell was an amazing woman.

But he couldn't allow his feelings to go too far. She was in a delicate place. Still grieving. She was also his patient.

Her headaches bothered him. And with the way she'd been reluctant to speak about how she was handling them, it didn't take much for him to imagine a scenario he didn't like. Especially since they seemed to be increasing in severity and frequency.

As he dipped his spoon into the soup, he flipped through the pages of *The American Year-Book of Medicine and Surgery*. Perhaps somewhere in this digest he could find some helpful information to treat her. He had to do something.

By the time he finished the soup, he'd gone through every medical book he'd brought with him. Nothing about head injury explained why Whitney was still having the headaches. The first few days—even weeks—after the injury, yes, but this long after that? The pain should have tapered off, not gotten worse. Once the stiffness in her neck was gone and there was no swelling on the back of her head . . .

No. It simply didn't add up.

He stood and paced the room. Medical challenges kept him sharp. Inspiration usually came after much prayer and research. He lifted his eyes to the ceiling. *Father God, I need Your divine inspiration here. If it is Your will, please show me what I can do to help Whitney.*

A knock at the door tore his attention away. "Come in."

Amka entered and retrieved the tray from his meal. "One of the children is crying out in pain."

Peter went to the basin and washed his hands. "I'll be right there."

An hour later, he held the toddler in his arms and rocked back and forth. Nothing had helped the poor child until he cried himself to sleep. Now the children were resting, and it was a beautiful thing to look around the room and see the many sleeping faces. Most of them were past the fever, but they would take several days to recover completely.

Normally one of the women was in the room watching over the children, but he'd sent them away for a time of rest. He was awake anyway. And he'd never had a problem sleeping in a chair if it came down to it. He had to keep the whole village as healthy as possible, which meant ensuring the caregivers were getting rest.

The little boy in his lap curled closer, and Peter felt the boy's pulse.

Then it hit him.

Thank You, Lord!

As soon as one of the women returned, he'd look it up in his medical books. But if he was correct, he might know how to help Whitney.

Whitney reached for the door and then stopped. No. She wasn't about to let her father have the last word. She whipped around. "I don't have to justify myself to you, but fine, if you have to be nosey . . ." She let out a breath. "I had my first glass of wine with dinner tonight. I didn't realize that it would make me tipsy. I thought it would be more like juice.

After all, they drank wine in biblical times, and the Good Book even says that it's good for the stomach."

Her father stared at her for several moments. "One glass isn't enough to make you tipsy."

Even though his words were soft, they struck their mark with force.

"You know where alcohol took me, and I don't want you suffering the same fate."

So he knew she'd had more than one glass. But did he know more than that? She wasn't like him. She took sips out of the tonic bottle for medicinal purposes. It helped with her headaches and anxiety. No matter how many times she repeated that last statement in her mind, it still made her cringe. But she wasn't about to tell him that.

"Look, it's far too cold for us to be standing out here chatting. Let me go along with you tomorrow when you go back to the village. That way you don't have to be alone."

"No. I'll be fine. I don't mind being alone." Why did he always get her ire up?

"Whitney, I insist. You're not going to feel very well in the morning." He stepped closer.

Enough! "You have no right to insist about *anything* in my life. I *hate* you. I hate you for what you did to our family. I hate you for perpetuating the lie that you were dead. You all but killed our mother because you broke her heart. And now that she and Granddad are both gone, I want nothing to do with you. Did you hear me? *Nothing!*"

Sadness filled his face, but he didn't lash back at her like she had hoped. Instead, his voice held compassion. "Your feelings are completely understandable. What I did was unforgivable. I know that. But God forgave me, and I'm asking for it from you all the same. Even though I know I don't deserve it."

His search for pity might work on someone else, but not on her. "I have no interest in forgiving you. Not now. Not ever." She whipped around and stormed through the door. Shedding her boots and coat, she mumbled under her breath every insult she'd wanted to fling at him. How *dare* he?

But when she walked toward her room, she stopped at the entry to the parlor. Everyone was gathered there. Their expressions let her know that they'd overheard. Of course they had. She'd been yelling and having an all-out tantrum.

No one said a word, and the uncomfortable silence stretched.

Whitney ran to her room, locked the door behind her, and leaned up against it. Tears flooded her eyes, and great sobs shook her shoulders.

What kind of person was she? No wonder God hated her—she deserved it. What had she become?

Feeling more lost than ever, she reached under the bed and grabbed the bottle of whiskey. Was it true? Would she turn out like her dad?

The sharp throbbing took up residence in her head again. She had no choice but to take a long swig and hope that sleep would overtake her.

Numbness in her shoulder woke her up. Where was she?

She pushed up and wiggled her arm to get the feeling back. Everything ached. Not just her head. But what could she expect? She'd slept on the floor in her clothes.

What a mess.

Getting to her feet, she put a hand to her head.

Just like Dad had said, she didn't feel like going anywhere or doing anything, but she had no choice. The villagers needed her. Peter needed her help too. She would have to ignore the throbbing in her head and make the best of it.

Whitney lit the lantern and turned the lamp down to a soft glow. It was a good thing the sun wouldn't come up for a while. Because light did *not* help her headaches. She reached for her watch and looked at it. Ten minutes after five in the morning. If she hurried, she could get out to the dogs without anyone seeing her.

Changing out of her nice dress as quick as she could, she made a list in her mind of what she needed to grab. If she was gone for another day or two, maybe things would settle down here and she could apologize to everyone.

But the more she moved, the worse her symptoms became.

"I hate that Dad was right." Her mumbling under her breath didn't help. Only proved that she had an awful lot of hate in her heart. Another way she was failing.

God, what is wrong with me?

When no answer came, she reached for her things and headed out of her bedroom as quietly as she could.

Her stocking feet on the wood floors didn't make a sound, and no light came from the kitchen or parlor. Relief washed over her as she put on her coat and thick boots and headed out to the barn.

All was quiet on the farm in the chill of the early morning. Whitney took several breaths and worked to calm the wild beating of her heart. Now was not the time to have anxiety. She was fine.

She reached into her pocket and gripped the tonic bottle. She pulled it out and—

What was she *doing*? Had it become that much of a habit that she reached for it without even thinking it through?

Shoving the bottle back into her pocket with more force

than was necessary, she shook her head. Dad might be weak when it came to alcohol, but she wouldn't be. She was stronger.

The dogs greeted her with their usual eagerness. Many of them jumped, barked, and wriggled to get as close to her as possible. She thought about taking one of the other teams for practice but decided against it. Her personal team was one she could count on, and the situation was such that it was important everything go smoothly. There would be time enough to work with the other dogs. After all, Peter wanted a team.

Peter.

His name sent a flurry of thoughts racing through her head. She compared him to Judas. Both men were quite nice to look at. Both were successful in what they did. But that was where the comparisons ended. Peter loved God, and his heart was one of service and kindness. Judas was a businessman through and through and knew how to make deals that would profit him. But did he care about people?

Well . . . didn't he take care of everyone in town?

Unlike Judas, Peter didn't care about profits. He wouldn't accept payment from the villagers most of the time. Only if they offered him goods to barter for his services. Probably because he knew they had so little.

She searched for answers as her mind volleyed back and forth between the two men. The fact that she cared about Peter warred with the courtship she'd agreed to with Judas. What did it all mean?

One of the dogs howled, and within two seconds, the rest of them were howling along. Whitney shook her finger at Aurora. "I know, you wanted my attention. But see what you've started? Now hush. We'll be on our way soon."

This was ridiculous. She needed to focus on the task at hand—not compare Judas and Peter.

It didn't take her long to get a sled loaded up and the dogs in their harnesses. She left a note for John that she might be gone a few days to help Dr. Cameron and to please take care of the dogs for her. It reminded her that Eli had wanted to learn more about the dogs. She'd promised her younger brother that he could help. Something else she'd have to tackle when she returned. Just because she was a mess didn't mean that the rest of her family had to suffer.

After double-checking everything, she headed out to the lane with the dogs.

And almost ran straight into her father and sisters.

"I packed light." Dad tossed his bag into the sled basket and shot her a smile. "Let me just shift a few things around here so I have a place to sit." Without getting her permission, he went to work. Still smiling, no less.

Havyn and Madysen stepped forward. "We packed you some food. Please give Amka our love." Havyn's hair was still braided from sleep, but she wiped at her eyes and came forward to hug her.

"Of course." Whitney attempted to swallow the lump in her throat. She couldn't exactly tell her father now that he couldn't come with her. Had they planned this?

Maddy petted the dogs. "I love you, Whitney. Promise to be safe." The cheeriness in her voice was a bit much, even for Madysen.

So that was how this was going to be. Everyone ignoring the fact that she'd yelled hateful words at their father last night.

Well, that was better than another confrontation. She wasn't sure her heart could take it at this point.

So she hugged her sisters and got Dad situated in the basket. Lifting the hook, she sent them a smile and then gave the command for the dogs to run.

Once they were away from the farm, she urged them into a steady speed and wrapped her scarf up over her nose and mouth.

Then Dad turned around in the basket in front of her and stared at her. "So . . . you want to tell me why you tried to leave without me this morning?"

———

Sleep eluded Judas for the third night in a row. He took the stairs down to his study, lit a fire in the fireplace, and poured himself a generous glass of bourbon. He downed the contents and poured another.

This wasn't like him. Normally, he slept like a baby. Never had a guilty conscience. Never worried about money. Never concerned himself with anyone else, really. With a shrug, he sat in a leather chair that had cost him a small fortune. As he ran a hand over the buttery leather, he smiled. Worth every penny.

His eyes darted over to the table beside him. Just as he'd suspected, it seemed Cain was writing every day. Judas had brought the letters home so he wouldn't have to deal with them at the office. But they called to him even more here. Haunted him. Distracted him.

He ran a hand down his face. Was that why he couldn't sleep? Those stupid letters? They were nothing but foolishness. The drivel of a cranky man who *had* nothing and would *die* with nothing. No one would remember him. No one would mourn him.

Sad, when he thought about it. But why should he care?

He lifted the page that lay on top. Scanned it. Huffed.

You need God, Judas. He's the only true need you have, and yet you've pushed Him away like an angry child throwing a tantrum.

The words rang in his mind. How *dare* he presume to tell Judas what he did or didn't need? The man was judging him as if he had any say whatsoever. Cain was powerless. He held nothing over Judas. Nothing. Judas was wealthy—wealthier than anyone could imagine—and he was influential, strong, formidable. A man without equal. That's who *he* was.

He'd proven Cain wrong countless times. He was in control of his own life. Not some invisible deity in the sky.

Heat flushed through his body as his pulse sped up. If someone were standing in front of him right now, he'd pound him with his fists.

No one told Judas Reynolds what to do. No one scolded him.

He was in charge.

He was the master of his own destiny.

He didn't *need* anyone or anything.

With a final swallow, the contents of the glass were gone. He threw the glass into the fire as hard as he could, relishing the explosive shattering and the surge in the flames.

Cain's words held no power over him.

Sixteen

Peter stepped out of a hut and breathed in the crisp air. The villagers were finally beginning to improve. Three of the families this morning showed no signs of fever. While there were more reports of the sickness's spread elsewhere, he could leave this place knowing that Amka's village was at least equipped to deal with the sickness a bit better. They understood now how to keep things clean, how to prevent spreading. And most important, they knew he would come if they asked him to.

That was a giant leap in the correct direction.

The yapping of dogs in the distance made him turn toward the sound. It wasn't even light yet, and Whitney was returning with supplies for the village.

His heart swelled with an emotion he refused to name. But one thing was certain, he was anxious to see her again. As the sled approached, he shortened the distance between them and went to greet her.

It appeared her father had come with her. Good. She hadn't come alone. Maybe things were better between the two.

"Whoa." Whitney's calm voice echoed through the early

morning quiet. She steered the sled up to him, her fur hood framing her face. "How is everyone doing, Doctor?"

"Better." He sent her a smile. "Much improved, actually."

"Good." She started unloading supplies.

"Good to see you, Mr. Powell." Peter stuck out a hand in greeting. "Did you have any luck finding your brother-in-law?"

The man shook his head. "No, not yet. It's getting difficult to hold out hope." Whitney's father lifted a box out of the sled. "I wanted to help you with the sick. I hear it's hit the gold camps too."

Peter frowned. Not good news. "I hadn't checked in with any of the gold camps outside of Nome. Is it bad? How long have people been sick?"

Powell ran a hand over his beard. "That I don't know. That was the news as we left camp yesterday."

"Well, be sure to let me know if you get any specifics or find out where the sick are. This spreads fast, and the sooner we can get a handle on things, the better."

The sound of voices behind him made him turn.

Amka rushed Whitney and hugged her. "It is so good to see you. Thank you for fetching the supplies that were needed!"

Within seconds, two of the younger boys had food and water for each of the dogs. Peter watched the animals. He needed a team sooner rather than later. It didn't hurt that this would give him more time with Whitney.

He looked up at her and watched her lively conversation with Amka and her family. The weariness had eased from her face as she talked with her friends. She reached down and lifted one of the littlest ones. How natural she seemed with the child. She laughed and covered the toddler's face with kisses. He could imagine her doing the same with her own child—a little redheaded girl with curls like her own.

She glanced at him, a question in her eyes. Had she noticed him watching her? Peter forced his gaze away and fiddled with the crates.

The people went to work distributing the supplies, and Whitney walked over to him. "I'm glad to hear things are better. Are the children past the worst?"

"I believe so. Last night, the rest of the fevers broke, which is a good sign." He shoved his hands into the pockets of his coat.

"Good." She lifted her arms and then let them fall at her side. "I was hoping to be able to help you with your patients, but if things are better, do you need me to take you back to Nome soon?"

"Your father was telling me that there was sickness among the miners."

The news made her frown. "That can't be good. Especially with the conditions at the camps and so many people within close proximity."

He nodded. "Exactly. But as of right now, I don't know which camp to check first."

"And there are quite a few of them out here." She toed the snow with her boot. Her brown eyes shadowed.

Was she not feeling well? "Do you have another headache?"

She rubbed the back of her neck. "It's a twinge really. Not as bad as they have been."

Now was the perfect time. He took a tentative step forward. "I had an idea last night about your headaches."

"Oh?"

He took the opportunity to step even closer. Gold flecks in her brown eyes caught his attention. How had he never seen that before? A few curls had escaped her long braid and moved with the wind. Her attire, which matched that of the natives, was very fetching. The deep caramel color of her sealskin pants and tunic was quite a contrast to her fair skin.

"Peter?" She leaned forward and tapped his arm. "Peter?"

"I'm sorry." He coughed into his hand and tried to cover his embarrassment. "I'm wondering if you might actually suffer from what we call hypertension."

Her brow wrinkled. "Hypertension? What is that?"

"It's when the blood pressure within your body gets too high."

She put a hand to her throat. "My blood pressure? Is that serious?"

Peter touched her elbow and used his most calm tone. "It can be if it gets too high and stays that way, but I don't believe that is the case with you. At least, not right now. You see, when your blood pressure elevates—probably caused by anxiety and stress in your life—it can be the cause of horrendous headaches." He held his hand out. "Would you accompany me back to my hut? I have some medicine I want you to try."

She nodded.

The deep furrow of her brow told him he should do a better job explaining. With a hand to the small of her back, he steered her beside him. "There's no need to worry. I really believe that if this is the cause, then your headaches could diminish over time. You see, I think the incident you endured caused your body to react. It wasn't simply the trauma to your head, which has healed beautifully, but all of the injuries you sustained—both physically and emotionally. It caused your blood pressure to rise. Anxiety—uneasiness, nervousness—within you because of the attack also causes it to rise. Stress, loss, grief, all of these can also cause it to rise, and you've been dealt all of the above. And when your blood pressure is too high, it can make you feel even more anxious and overwhelmed. Possibly depressed or even panicked. Causing an unending cycle of one making the other worse and so on."

She let out a sigh and stopped walking. "So you're saying the headaches could go away? And the anxiety as well?" A glimmer of hope shone in her eyes.

"I'm optimistic, yes."

With a hand to her forehead, she shook her head and began walking again. "All this time, I've been worried that something horrible was wrong with me."

Her words struck him in the heart. Had he done that to her? "I'm so sorry. Was it something I said that made you believe that?"

"No. Just the pain. And how often it comes. I was so afraid I'd become a burden to my family."

The fact that she shared that with him told him more than her words. No wonder her anxiety had continued to grow. They reached his tiny hut, and he opened the door. "Wait here."

He grabbed his bag and found the Indian snakeroot and sphygmomanometer and went back outside. "Here."

"What is it?"

"Indian snakeroot. I cut the root into sections for doses. You grind up the root and pour hot water over it—once in the morning and once in the evening—and after a week we will check and see how you are doing."

"And you think that will get rid of the headaches and anxiety?"

"I'm hopeful. But you also need to learn how to relax and let go of your worry." He paused and pulled out his sphygmomanometer. "I need to take a reading today so we know where you're starting from and can assess whether the medicine is working."

"All right."

"I just need your arm." He hoped his smile was reassuring, because her eyes were full of questions. "My wife used to say worry robs us of the joy God's Holy Spirit puts in us, so it can't be good."

She looked away while he placed the cuff. "She sounds like she was very wise."

"She was. She was also smart . . . like you." He leaned over and moved his head to catch her gaze. "There's no needle or anything."

Her shoulders lifted with her breath. "Oh. Good." But then she pinned him with her stare.

Was she afraid of the device? Maybe he should just keep her talking. "Charlotte knew a great deal and wasn't afraid of hard work. I always admired that about her. I admire it about you as well."

"Hard work was always a way of life. At least until Granddad found his fortune." She seemed to relax. "Even then he pushed us to always be busy at something. He and Mama used to say that if we were busy doing chores, we couldn't very well be busy doing evil."

"Sounds like something Charlotte would have said too." He started pumping the bulb. "Deep breaths. Nice and steady." Her nearness made him want to get even closer.

Several seconds passed. Her breathing steadied. When he looked back at her, her gaze drew him in. His heart was in his throat, so he looked back down at the glass dial. He tilted his head. "Just what I suspected. Your numbers are high. Now let's see if we can bring them down." He removed the cuff.

"How did she die?"

The question caught him off guard and brought his eyes

to meet hers abruptly. The intense appeal there couldn't be denied. Best to just tell her the truth. "I failed her." He shook his head as the memory poured over him. "She was in labor, and I failed them both. There were problems that I didn't know about. Problems with her body and the pregnancy."

"And how was that your failing?" Whitney's tone was very matter-of-fact.

"I should have known. Somehow . . . I should have known."

"I can't see how that was a failing on your part. Only God knows if a person will live or die." She clamped her mouth shut and studied him.

Peter was glad for her silence. He hated remembering those horrible moments. To his surprise, however, Whitney picked the conversation back up.

"Were you very much in love?"

He swallowed the lump in his throat. "We were."

"Then she lived and died knowing she was loved. That's so important." Her brow furrowed. "You talk about failures. Some people don't even have that."

"You surely aren't talking about yourself."

"Why not?" She shrugged. "The people who loved me are either dead or have someone else to focus on."

"And that means they can't love you?"

Whitney gave another shrug. "I know my sisters love me, but it's not the same. They are caught up in the love they have for their husbands—just as they should be. I'm not unhappy they've found true love, if that's what you think."

"Then what?" Feeling brave, he stepped forward and helped her get her arm back into her coat.

She didn't pull away. Her voice came soft, vulnerable. "I can't really say. I suppose a part of me is sorry not to have found it for myself. But it's more than that. The loss of

Granddad and Mama and my sisters' marrying so quickly—it changed everything for me. I'm alone."

"Only if you want to be." He didn't want to break their connection.

Inches from him, she lifted her eyes back to his.

Peter hoped she understood his implication but needed to get the conversation back to safer ground. It was for the best. For both of them. "Trust God, Whitney. He loves you for sure."

She blinked and shifted her weight. "Easier said than done, Doctor."

"That it is. But our God is faithful to provide."

She winced. "And to take away."

He reached for her other arm, but she wriggled out of his grasp and buttoned up her coat. "Whitney . . . no. That's not how God works. . . ." A hundred platitudes raced to his mind, but he couldn't voice any of them.

Fast-paced footsteps approached. He turned and saw Chris running toward them.

"Yutu brought one of the other miners to see me because he heard I had been looking for Stan." He bent over and caught his breath. "He said he knew where my brother-in-law was." Chris turned to his daughter. "Would you mind taking me out to another of the gold camps? I don't want to lose this lead. Especially if it helps me to find Stan for Ruth." His voice pleaded.

Whitney looked back and forth between her dad and Peter. "Um . . ."

"May I go along as well? That way we could make the rounds at the gold camps and see if the rumors of sickness are true. I would hate for an epidemic to start because I didn't check on the miners."

She nodded. "Of course. But we'll have to take both of the sleds to carry all of us and your things. That means once we drop off Dad, you'll have to drive one of the sleds back. Are you ready for that?"

Nothing like jumping in with both feet. "Will the dogs be all right with it?"

A slight smile lifted her lips. The intimate moment was gone, but her confidence was back. "Since I'll be in front with the other sled, I don't think you'll have a problem. We can go slow if you would feel more comfortable."

He'd wanted to learn. He guessed the best time was now. "Let me pack up my things and speak to Amka about what needs to be done for those recovering."

"Let's try to leave in half an hour." Whitney held up the bag of snakeroot. "I'm going to fix myself some tea."

Boosted by the thought of spending more time in Whitney's presence, Peter went in search of Amka. His hard work had paid off, and the people weren't suffering any longer. God was good. If only he could prove that to Whitney.

The thought brought rebuke to mind. That was hardly his job. God was fully capable of proving Himself.

Sorry, Lord. I wasn't trying to overstep my bounds. It's . . . that I care for her. Maybe I even . . . love her.

"Angry Bird, you get back here right now." Havyn pointed to the ground in front of her and placed her other hand on her hip. Seriously. This chicken would cost her what little sanity she had left.

Once the hen had initiated the escape from the hen house after the latest blizzard, she'd tried the same thing every time Havyn came out to check on her girls.

It had ceased being comical several days ago. And she was tired of chasing chickens around.

Thankfully, she'd gotten the door closed before any of the others tried to follow, but when the chicken didn't listen to her scolding, she refused to run after it. *Again*.

Angry Bird ran across the top of the deep snow, over the fence, and into the next pasture. The dark-feathered chicken looked over her shoulder at Havyn and kept on running.

"Fine. Go ahead and run away. I'll have to deal with a lot less trouble without you around." Havyn threw her words at the feisty hen. It wasn't like the girl wouldn't come back for food.

The baby chose that moment to move again, and Havyn looked down at her stomach and laughed. "You like it when I scold the chickens, huh? Well, just wait—one day that will be your job too."

With a rub to her belly, she let out an easy breath and carried the empty feed pail back to the barn. As much as she loved her chickens, she realized as soon as she found out she had a baby growing within her how much she would love this child. She'd wanted to be a mother—just like her own—since she was about sixteen years old.

If only her baby could have met Mama. Her heart twinged. Her eyes stung. Blast . . . more tears. Pregnancy had made the waterworks nonstop.

No. She wouldn't allow the grief to tamp down her joy of carrying a life.

At least she could share all the stories so her mother wouldn't be forgotten. That brought a smile back to her face. Millions of memories and things her mother taught her could be shared with this next generation.

As she entered the house and took off her boots, a sense of urgency washed over her, and she shivered. "Maddy?" She headed to the parlor.

"I'm here." Madysen sat with her cello in front of her.

Havyn put a hand to her cheek and sat on the piano bench. "Do you know where John and Daniel are?"

"They were in the milking pen with the sheep a little bit ago." Her sister's brow furrowed. "Why? What is it?"

Clutching both of her hands to her chest, Havyn closed her eyes. Her heart pounded. "It's Whitney. For some reason, I feel like we need to stop and pray for her. Right now."

Maddy put her instrument down and rushed to Havyn's side. "I had the same sense a moment ago, but I didn't realize what it was and was going to keep on practicing."

Havyn put her arm around Maddy's shoulder. "I don't know what Whitney is facing right now, but we know she's been struggling with pain and grief lately."

"Then there's the whiskey." Her sister's words were whispered.

"I know. I've been asking God how we can help her . . . and now . . . well, I feel the pressing need to pray for her like never before."

"May we join you?" John's voice came from the doorway.

She looked up, and her husband walked toward her with Daniel right behind him. "Yes. Please do."

As the men settled in next to them, they joined hands.

Madysen started the prayer with Scripture, claiming God's promise to guide them and give them a way out of temptation. As each one of them prayed for Whitney, they poured out their hearts. Asking for God's will to be done, for her pain to be taken away, and for healing.

Little by little the pressure on Havyn's chest lifted, and she lifted her tear-stained face toward the heavens. "Thank You, God, for giving us Whitney. We love her so much, but know that You love her even more than we could ever imagine. We're asking for You to intervene right now. Whatever it is that she is going through. Give her Your strength and Your peace to make it through."

It took twenty minutes to reach the gold camp that Yutu's friend had told them about. But as soon as they arrived, they knew something was very wrong.

Most of the men were sick.

Peter went to work immediately. Whitney followed him and helped however she could, but the stench was quite unbearable so she kept her scarf wrapped up around her nose and mouth.

They left one of the tents and breathed in the fresh air. Peter's head shook back and forth in slow motion.

"It's bad . . . isn't it?" She hated to voice the question, but she had to. What were they going to do?

"Much worse than anything at the village, but the symptoms seem to be along the same lines. Some of the men seem to have measles, while others appear to have influenza or dysentery."

"Tell me what to do, and I'll do it." She squared her shoulders. She'd do whatever she could to help this man who cared for people unlike anyone she'd ever known.

His eyes connected with hers. A darker blue than Judas's, there was something else different about them. Something . . . deeper.

She and Peter stared at one another for several moments.

He reached forward and gripped her hand. "Thank you. Not only for bringing us out here, but for jumping in and helping. But I also want to protect you. You'll need to keep your hands clean. Keep that scarf over your face too. I wouldn't want you to get sick." He squeezed her hand and let go.

As soon as his touch was gone, she missed it. Wished he would hold her hand again. She shoved the thoughts away. These men needed medical attention. "I can do that. What else?"

"You'll have to run back and forth to the sleds to fetch supplies. Since these tents are so crowded, there's not a lot of room for anything but the sick. Which also proves *how* the sickness has spread. But we can't do anything about that now. Can you stay for a day or two, or do you need to get home?"

"I'll stay with you. I've got a shelter I can set up for me and the dogs."

"Thank you. I should see if they have a tent I can set up next to yours. I don't want you to be by yourself here."

She hadn't thought about that. While most of the men were sick, those who weren't could hear her voice. Know there was a woman among them. "I would appreciate that."

He nodded at her and headed toward the next tent.

This group of men appeared to be more feverish. Lots of coughing filled the air.

"Dr. Cameron?" Dad's voice came from behind them. "Can I help?"

"Did you not find Stan?" Whitney hoped for Ruth's sake that the man was still alive.

"No. But the man I was told to ask is asleep. Seems to be pretty sick. He's in the next tent." He thumbed at the exit.

All four of the main tents at this camp were filled with sick men.

"Whitney, come quick!" Peter was holding a man upright as he coughed.

She scurried over, working her way between cots. "What can I do?"

"Give me your whiskey." Peter held out his free hand while the man convulsed with hacking.

What? What if *she* needed it? Her heart began to race as heat rushed to her face.

"What are you doing with whiskey?" Dad's accusatory tone filled the tent.

"Keep your voice down." Whitney spat the words at him.

"You do have it with you, don't you?" Peter's words were low and compassionate.

She gave a slight nod and reached into her pocket, but as she gripped the bottle, she couldn't bring herself to lift it out of her pocket. What would she do without it?

Her mouth went dry.

"Whitney . . . please." The look in Peter's eyes did her in. He knew what a sacrifice it was for her. Understood her pain. No one else did. "I promise you it will be all right."

She pulled the bottle out and handed it to him.

He didn't say anything, but as he took it, their fingers touched. And he left them there for a moment. Then with a nod, he turned back to the patient.

"Whitney?" Dad put a hand on her shoulder.

She jerked away and ran out of the tent.

Her legs took her to the outskirts, past her dogs, past the signs of other people. When she was out of air, she collapsed on her knees in the snow and let the tears fall. She hadn't asked for this revelation that now stared her down. Handing over that bottle had made it real. She couldn't deny it any longer.

She'd become dependent upon alcohol.

She hated herself for being so weak. Hated what she had become. Hated that she couldn't give it up.

Just like her father.

SEVENTEEN

I know that wasn't easy."

The snow crunched around Whitney as Dad approached.

She swiped at her eyes, then realized it didn't matter. No wonder she was broken. Best to sit here in her mess.

The man she'd abhorred for so long walked right up to her and sat in the snow too. "How long have you been drinking?"

All the anger she wanted to fling at him fell flat. She was no better than he. "I never considered it drinking. Not until today."

"Because at first, you had a sip or two when you needed it?"

Maybe Peter wasn't the only one who understood her. She couldn't look him in the eye, but she nodded. Might as well be honest. What did she have to lose? "Yes." Deep breath. She couldn't hide any longer. Not even from . . . *him*. "It was a spoonful or two from the tonic bottle after that man attacked me. Peter—Dr. Cameron—gave it to me to help with my headaches and anxiety."

"Did it help?"

"It did. But then over time it took more to alleviate the pain . . . and the pain and anxiety happened more frequently." She should smack herself for ever allowing it to get to this point.

She knew better. "I should have known the first time I refilled that bottle that something was seriously wrong."

"I understand."

But she didn't want him to understand. This was his fault. She jerked her head to face him. "*Do* you? Granddad told me the reason people drank was to forget, but for the life of me, I couldn't figure out what it was that you would want to forget. Me? Our family? What?"

"No. I'd never want to forget you or our family." There was so much depth to his eyes that she'd never seen before. Even though she'd lashed out at him, he remained calm.

Which only infuriated her more.

He crossed his arms over his chest. "What is it that *you* want to forget?"

The question made her sit up straighter and lift her shoulders. "*Everything*. Granddad's death, the attack, Mama's death, *you* showing up, your new family . . . the ways I've failed. I want to forget it all."

"You don't mean that." Were those tears in his eyes? Hurt? No. He was supposed to be the same ol' drunk that abandoned them. The man who was hollow and good for nothing.

It was easier for her that way.

"Maybe I do." But her bravado left in a great whoosh. Pictures of Eli and Bethany danced through her mind. She wouldn't want to forget them. No matter how they came to be part of her family.

"No. You don't. I can see it on your face. But as to the failing part . . . I get that. I drank for the same reason—to forget the ways I'd failed your mama and you girls. I was unworthy to even live. I wasn't any good to any of you, so when Chuck told me to leave . . . I did." He blinked several times and pursed his lips, but a single tear escaped.

"If you really loved us, you would have fought for us." It sounded so childish once the words were out.

Dad looked down and pushed snow around with his gloves. "That's not true and you know it. Because if it was, then I would say that you must not love your sisters because you're not fighting hard to be there for *them* right now. I heard you quit playing at the Roadhouse."

Ouch. Of course he would bring that up. "They don't need me the same way. They have husbands. And they can play *just* fine without me."

He turned his head and made a face. "That's not true either. The three of you together are amazing. It's like a three-stranded cord. Take away one strand and it's not as strong. No matter how talented your sisters are."

No great argument came to mind, and she felt deflated. Why was she so insistent on remaining angry at him? A little nudge to her heart made her look at him. Really look at him. Maddy and Havyn had forgiven him. A little too readily for her liking, but they had done it anyway. *God, what is wrong with me?*

"Ya know, Esther made me memorize some Scripture verses when I first had to conquer my demon of drinking. 'Cause it sure did have a hold on me. From Ephesians chapter six: 'For we wrestle not against flesh and blood, but against principalities, against powers, against the rulers of the darkness of this world, against spiritual wickedness in high places. Wherefore take unto you the whole armour of God, that ye may be able to withstand in the evil day, and having done all, to stand.'"

Hearing the verses from her father's lips made her squirm. "Mama made us learn the whole passage when we were young. She would ask us each morning if we had put on our belt of truth, our breastplate of righteousness, our shoes of the gospel of peace, our shield of faith, our helmet of salvation, and our sword of the Spirit." As she said it, a little of the weight on her shoulders fell away. She hadn't followed through on that for so very long. *Oh, Mama . . .*

"Your mother was a wise woman. The very best."

She could agree with him on that.

"I guess the question is . . . what are you going to do now?"

She didn't want to take any spiritual advice from this man. No matter how right he might be. But the memory of Mama made her squirm. What would she say right now? Probably the same thing.

"Don't waste your life believing the enemy's lies, Whitney. You're too good for that. You know better. Don't abandon your family like I did."

"I am *not* abandoning my family."

"Aren't you?"

She sputtered and words failed her.

"Mr. Powell?" A miner stood off to the side. "That man you were askin' 'bout? He's awake."

"I'll be there in a few minutes."

"It's okay, Dad. Go see if you can find Stan. That's more important right now." Besides, she didn't want to finish this conversation.

"*You're* important, Whitney. *This* is important." Dad's shoulders slumped a bit. "This is the first time we've really talked—"

"I know. And I will think about what you said. I promise." She lifted her chin. "But you and I can talk later. Stan may not have the luxury of time."

"All right." Dad surged to his feet and brushed the snow off his pants. He peered down at her. "I love you, Whitney. I know I've failed you. But I love you."

Then he followed the guy back to the camp.

Whitney fixed her gaze on the horizon and tried *not* to think about all her father had said. But it didn't work.

He'd spoken a lot of truth.

The question was, was she ready to listen?

Mama's lilting voice whispered through her mind: *"Put on the armor of God, my sweet. Every day."*

———

Chris walked up to the man's cot and squatted beside him. He didn't look too good, but at least the man was awake. "You say you know Stan Robertson?"

"Yeah . . ." His voice was scratchy and hoarse.

"Do you know where he is?"

The sick man closed his eyes for a moment. When he opened them back up, he shook his head. "Stan's dead."

As much as he'd expected the news, his heart still plummeted.

"We was lookin' for gold together last spring. Stan got in a fight over a claim and got hisself killed. By the time the lawman got here, the murderer was long gone." A coughing fit took over the man. When he calmed, he closed his eyes again. "I'm sorry."

"You certain it was Stan Robertson?" How was he going to break the news to Ruth? Especially without proof.

"He talked about his wife and kids a lot. Her name was Ruth. Said they lived in Colorado."

Oh no. It was Stan all right. "Did you bury him?"

"Yeah. I'll draw ya a map. Felt bad not knowin' how to contact his kin. But a few of the other fellas and me had a service for him."

"That was kind of you. Thank you." Chris waited for the

man to finish scrawling the crude map and then took it and stood. "His wife will be grateful to know he was taken care of in the end."

"Wish I had better news to tell ya. I even went and looked for his belongings after we buried him, but someone had already taken off with 'em."

"I appreciate what you've done. Thank you. Get some rest and get better." Chris nodded at the man and put his hat back on. A nudge in his spirit made him think of the men he'd witnessed to at the last camp. The lost and dying were all around him. Maybe God could redeem his pathetic life after all by using him to share the Gospel.

But first . . . He looked at the map. Best go out and see Stan's grave for himself. He could at least give Ruth that much.

Cain's last letter this morning rubbed Judas the wrong way. Just like *all* the others. But now it felt like a nasty sore was developing.

He didn't have time for this.

But Cain was coming. Had already booked passage on the first ship. Well, Judas would just have to stop that. Somehow. At least he had a few months to come up with a plan. No matter what, he had to keep the preacher from arriving.

He'd be bad for business.

A knock sounded at Judas's office door, and in burst Judge Beck. He rubbed his hands together as he sauntered toward Judas's desk. "You're going to love this idea."

"Oh?" He doubted it but leaned back in his chair. "I'm listening."

The judge made himself comfortable in one of the chairs.

"The plan is simple. When people arrive in Nome they have to immediately go before the judge—me, of course—and fill out papers that have to be filed with the District of Alaska. They'll pay a price for entry into our beautiful district. Then you and I can split the money between us."

"You don't think word will get out we're charging people to come here?"

The man looked as if he hadn't thought it through. "Who would come after us up here?"

Judas quirked a brow at him. "There is law above our heads, Judge Beck. We don't run the whole territory of Alaska. We are owned by the United States Government, after all."

"So you don't think it will work?" The man looked defeated.

"No. I don't." Judas didn't try to hide his sarcasm. The judge and his schemes. Was the man that desperate? "Having trouble paying off your gambling debts again, Beck?"

The judge sneered at him and stood. "That's none of your business, Reynolds!" The man stormed out of his office and slammed the door.

It made Judas chuckle. Oh, the ideas that man had.

Of course . . . this particular idea wasn't *all* bad.

If Judas added an assessment onto the land deeds people came to buy from him, no one would be the wiser. It was his business anyway. Legal and aboveboard.

If the good judge found out about it, he'd probably want in on it and would say that it was his idea . . . but Judas could deal with that later. Besides, the judge wouldn't be around too much longer.

Time to have a meeting with his workers in the land and deed office.

Eighteen

Six long days had passed, and they blurred together. But at least the men at the camp were improving, and they'd only lost three lives. That was better than Peter had expected when he'd arrived. Whitney had been at his side the whole time and helped him through the worst of it. She'd even made two trips back into town and gotten a report from the other doctors about his patients back in Nome.

She'd also taken him to visit three other camps, where they found sickness as well. But with some instructions and medicine distributed, they'd been able to curtail his greatest fear: an all-out epidemic.

The dogs yapped at Peter as he approached. Whitney had taught him bits and pieces about driving a sled. The commands and so on. He'd even driven one of the sleds himself. And though he took a turn too fast and fell off the sled, he counted it as a success.

He still had a lot to learn, though.

He took off his thick wool hat and ran a hand through his hair. This time spent with Whitney had been difficult. While he couldn't deny his growing feelings toward her, he also had to keep a wall between them so she didn't sense them. He would not fall in love with another woman only to fail her as he did Charlotte.

"Good morning, Peter."

The object of his thoughts appeared in front of him. She held two buckets of food for the dogs and gave him a genuine smile. "You look contemplative today." She poured the contents into the bowls for the dogs, and they lapped it up as fast as she poured.

He allowed a laugh. "Well, I was thinking it might be good for us to head back to Nome today. I think we've done all we can here."

"I was hoping you'd say that." Her eyes were brighter than they had been for some time.

"Do you mind if I test you again this morning?" She had almost a week's worth of the snakeroot in her system. So far, he was pleased with the results.

"Not at all. But it does make my arm cold, so could we do it inside the tent today?" She gave a dramatic shiver.

He smiled. "Of course. Lead the way." He held out an arm and then followed her back to her makeshift tent.

Peter pulled the sphygmomanometer out of his bag and placed the cuff over Whitney's upper arm.

She winced as it tightened, and he watched the mercury manometer.

"Remember, deep breaths."

She nodded.

After several minutes, he'd obtained what he needed. "It seems that your readings are indeed going down. Which is what we hoped for. I would continue with the snakeroot twice a day. How are the headaches?"

"I've had two this week, but then again, I've been too busy

to even think about if my head is hurting." The smile she gave him was more relaxed than he'd ever seen from her. "They haven't been as intense as before."

"Good." His heart twinged when he couldn't tear his gaze away. She was so beautiful. "Thank you for everything you've done to help me. I think we averted a real crisis."

"It's good to be needed. And, to be honest, to do something different. It helped me to get my mind straight again and off of the loss." Her smile faded a bit. "I'm dreading going home knowing that Ruth is going through her own loss right now."

Chris had gone back with another miner several days ago, but he'd told Peter that after she gave up her whiskey to him, they'd had a good talk.

Maybe that helped her too, along with the snakeroot. "That's understandable. You know loss too well."

"How do you deal with it? Loss? You mentioned that you lost your wife and baby—and I guess I don't understand how your other pain isn't brought to the forefront every time you lose a patient." She tilted her head as if trying to get inside his mind. "How do you not push everyone around you away?"

The intensity in her eyes drew him in. He wanted—no, *needed*—to tell her. But what would that do to him?

"I'm sorry I brought it up." She reached out and patted his arm. An innocent enough gesture, but it sent a shock up his arm and jolted his lips loose.

"I lost my wife, Charlotte, and our baby boy six years ago." Had it been that long already? His stomach trembled like an earthquake.

"I'm sorry."

"There are other reasons, too, why I've dedicated my life

to medicine. I lost my father to a farm accident when I was a young boy. My grandmother was a midwife, and in the midst of our grief, she taught me about the use of herbs and plants for healing. It kept me occupied, and her as well, I'm sure. Over the years, we worked together in our small farming community. Eventually, I lost her too, but God had planted the seed in my life to be a doctor."

"How did you meet Charlotte?"

Oh, what a sweet memory. He smiled. He wrapped up the sphygmomanometer and placed it back in his bag. "We were neighbors. Our fathers owned farms next to each other. She began to follow me around when she was barely as tall as the wheat. We were the only two children within miles, so naturally, we did most everything together. She bugged me with thousands of questions every day, and she would say that I was mean to her and stole her ribbons."

"Sounds like the two of you were meant for each other."

Another stab to his heart. "Yes. We were." He shuffled things around in his bag to avoid looking at her. What would she see? That he'd come to care for Whitney so much he couldn't fathom the thought of losing her too? What if he failed her as he'd failed Charlotte?

Peter seemed to be a natural with the dogs and sled. He had a keen sense of balance and managed the team as if he'd been doing it most of his life. Whitney had never known anyone to take to driving a team so easily.

When they were still a good ten miles from Nome, Whitney slowed her dogs and brought them to a stop. Peter did likewise, and when he saw her set her hook, he followed suit.

"I thought this was a good place to rest for the final leg." She pushed back her parka hood and raised her snow glasses. "How are you doing?"

"I think I've got the hang of it, for the most part. Sometimes I'm given to daydreaming, but I learned quick enough that's a mistake. I nearly fell off the sled."

"Yes, you have to be aware of the dogs every minute. They can get easily distracted too, so *you* mustn't. Now's a good time to check each of your dogs. Make sure their feet are good. Check to see that the harnesses aren't rubbing sores on them and are sound all the way around. I had one snap on me once. Made a mess of things."

They went down the line as Peter checked each of the dogs and every inch of the lines. Whitney could see he was meticulous—like a doctor with a patient. She smiled to herself. She liked his no-nonsense manner. He was like her in that. When things required seriousness, he gave it. When there was room for more levity, he gave that.

What's more, and she couldn't believe this was true, she was comfortable with him. She felt *safe* with Peter.

"There, that's done." He straightened and smiled. "All is well!"

"You did a great job."

"I had a great teacher." He waggled his eyebrows at her.

She couldn't help but grin. "Now you may check my team."

"Yes, ma'am!" He walked over to her team and began the inspection.

Whitney followed him and kept her gaze on all that he did. He managed it just as she would have. He was a quick learner.

"That's that. Again, looks good."

She smiled. "Nicely done. You have a real touch with

them." She turned to walk back, but the toe of her boot hit something. Before she realized what was happening, she started to fall.

Peter reached out in a flash and caught her. As he pulled her to his chest, Whitney looked up to find her lips inches from his. Their eyes locked, and for a moment Whitney was paralyzed. But not in that fearful way she had known with Garrett Sinclair.

Although she did find herself trembling.

He stepped back and righted her as if nothing had happened. The perfect gentleman.

For the first time, she wasn't grateful. In fact, as unbelievable as it was . . . she was disappointed.

"Thank you." She forced her thoughts into place. "We better get moving."

Hurrying past him, she straightened her coat and then pulled the hook for her sled from the snow. "Let's go!" she commanded her team.

Peter would have to catch up. She needed a moment to clear her head. No doubt the dogs would be straining at the harness to follow her. After several breaths, she glanced back.

Peter was fine. He'd managed to maneuver quickly, and his team wasn't too far behind.

Her feelings were so muddled. What had happened? That moment in Peter's arms had been . . . well . . . amazing. Wonderful.

They took a turn, and without her thoughts on the task at hand, she nearly lost her balance when the basket listed to the left.

That was close. She needed to focus. Plenty of time to think about what happened later.

A shout rent the air.

Whitney glanced back to see the dogs pulling an empty sled.

"Whoa!" she called to her team. It took a moment, but they halted. She threw out her hook and grabbed hold of Peter's lead dog almost in the same motion. "Whoa."

Peter was already on his feet and running after the sled. He caught up to them and grabbed the hook from his sled and set it in place, then made his way toward her, dusting off his clothes as he walked. "Sorry about that."

"Are you okay? You're not injured, are you?" She put a hand to her chest.

"Nothing's wounded but my pride." His smile stretched across his face, and he shook his head with a laugh.

"What happened?" She'd nearly lost control on that turn as well.

Peter brushed more snow off his arms and legs. He gave a shrug. "Daydreaming." He returned his gaze to hers and gave a sheepish smile. His hat was askew, and it made him look like a little boy who'd gotten caught with his hand in the cookie jar.

Whitney broke into laughter. Had he been daydreaming about the same thing she had? Their closeness was hard to forget.

What would it have been like if he'd followed it with a kiss?

Morning light broke through Whitney's window. She pushed up to sit in her bed and blinked away the vestiges of sleep. It was so good to be home. What time was it?

Swinging her legs over the side of her bed, she stretched and then looked at the clock. After eleven in the morning! Good heavens.

She jumped up and raced around to gather her clothes. A knock sounded at her door.

"Come in." She pulled her dressing gown over her frame and tied the sash.

"Morning, sis." Madysen peeked through the doorway and then carried in a wooden tray. "I brought you some eggs and biscuits." Her tiny feet padded around the bed toward her.

"Thank you. I can't believe I slept this late."

Maddy set the tray on the end of the bed. "Oh, I can. It was late by the time you made it home last night, and from what Dad told us, you probably haven't slept the past week."

She shrugged. "I have to admit you're right. But it felt good to help Peter minister to those men." Whitney climbed back up on her bed and tugged the tray closer as her stomach rumbled. "Thank you for this."

"You're welcome." Maddy climbed onto the bed facing her. "You look rested."

Whitney pushed her hair out of her face and realized her braid had come undone in the night. She must have slept hard. "I *feel* rested."

Her youngest sister leaned forward and grabbed her hand. "It's good to have you home."

With a squeeze, she patted Madysen's hand. "I can honestly say I'm glad to *be* home." She sighed. "I'm sorry for my behavior lately. I don't know what's been wrong . . . but Dad and I talked."

"Wow. Like . . . *talk* talked?" Her sister's eyes were wide. "That's a first." Her hand shot over her mouth. "Sorry."

"That's all right." Whitney shrugged and let out a small laugh. "I guess it is pretty shocking after how I've treated him. But yes . . . *talk* talked."

"Are things better between you?"

"I'm not sure. I haven't seen him since. But I will admit that he gave me a lot to think about. That and, well . . . Peter."

"Does that mean that you've come to care for the good doctor?" The sly grin on her sister's face caught her by surprise.

"No." She put a hand to her chest. Even if she admitted it was true, there wasn't any way he could ever feel the same for her. Not after what he'd shared about Charlotte. Whitney could never measure up to his soul mate. "Not like that. But he *is* a good friend." It was best for her to keep reminding herself of that. "Besides, I've allowed Judas to court me."

For the first time in several days, her mouth watered with the craving for a swig of whiskey.

Ever since she'd handed over her flask to Peter and the reality of her actions had hit her square in the face, she had been able to push it from her mind. So why had it come back with such a vengeance now?

"He asked about you several times while you were gone."

Whitney refocused on her sister. "Who?"

"Judas, silly."

"Oh." She took a bite of biscuit to cover her lack of interest. She might be courting the man, but that didn't mean she was in love with him. In fact, she'd hardly thought about him while she was gone. What did that say about her?

A change of subject was in order. "How's Ruth doing?"

"Losing Stan hit her hard, even though I think a part of her expected the news. Dad has been so gentle with her, but Eli and Bethany also took it hard. They grew up with their uncle around. Ruth cries herself to sleep every night and misses her children terribly. That's the one thing that I think can fill the hole. But you know as well as I do there's no chance she will be able to see them until the first ship comes in and she can go home."

Whitney gasped. "She won't leave, will she?"

"At this point, I think she wants to be with her children. And who could blame her?"

"I can't imagine what she is going through." Whitney rubbed her forehead as the throbbing in her head started up. "Could you bring me some hot water?"

"To wash your hands?"

"No. I forgot to tell you that Peter thinks my headaches are made worse by hypertension. Something to do with the pressure in my blood? Anyway, he's had me grinding up snakeroot into a powder and mixing it with hot water. It seems to be helping, and I have to admit, I'm feeling better than I have since the attack."

"That's great, Whit." Maddy hopped off the bed. "I'll bring you a cup of hot water right away."

"Thanks, sis." While she was gone, Whitney dug into her food.

A light tap on her door. "Whitney?"

Eli's sweet voice.

"Come on in."

He opened it a crack and sent her a smile. "I heard you were back."

"I am." Her cheeks lifted with a smile. "It's good to see you."

He ventured in another foot. "I've been helping John with the dogs."

"Thank you. I bet they love attention from you." She pointed her fork at him before taking another bite.

His nod was enthusiastic and made his hair fall into his eyes. Poor kid. He needed a haircut. "Do you think you could teach me about driving the sled so maybe I could help you raise and train your next litters?"

"Ah . . . so John spilled the beans, didn't he? You know we've got three pregnant mamas."

Another nod, with a grin that almost reached his ears.

"I would love to teach you. As long as you get your schoolwork and your other chores done." After she took a sip of orange juice, she lifted her glass to him. "How about I meet you out there in an hour? We'll get started right away."

"Thank you! I'll be ready." He ran out the door and almost knocked Maddy down.

Her sister watched their younger brother as he ran. "You made his day brighter, that's for certain." She offered a piece of paper. "This arrived for you."

As she took the envelope, she hoped it was from Peter. Maybe he needed her again.

But when she unfolded the paper, she found an invitation to dinner from Judas. Why was she disappointed? A rich, kind man wanted to spoil her with another lavish meal. She should be ecstatic.

She held up the paper for Maddy to read.

Her younger sister's eyebrows rose almost to her hairline. "Well . . . are you going to go?"

NINETEEN

A week had passed since Whitney turned down Judas's invitation to dinner, citing that with Ruth finding out about her husband, the family was deep in mourning. Guilt had riddled her for the exploitation of Ruth's pain, but she hadn't been ready to face Judas quite yet.

Then this morning, another invitation came. She'd gone straight out to the dogs and began mucking the stalls. Maybe clarity would descend on her with the hard work.

Peter had been correct in his diagnosis: As long as she took the snakeroot morning and evening, she felt better. But the whiskey bottle under her bed still called her name. And a few times, she'd given in. Much to her shame.

Shaking her head against the condemning thoughts, she shoveled out the soiled hay twice as fast. It made her arms and back burn. The best thing she could do was to lock the bottle up and give the key to someone else.

"Have you decided how to respond?" Havyn propped her elbows on the fence.

Whitney put a hand to her chest. "Gracious, you might

be growing in size, but I think you're getting stealthier. You scared me."

Havyn's laugh echoed through the barn. "Maybe you were deep in thought. I don't think there's any way I'm stealthy. If anything, I'm growing clumsier by the day." She wiggled her eyebrows. "Now back to the question . . ."

"Can't get anything past you, can I?"

"Nope."

She let out a long sigh. "All right. What do you think about inviting Judas out here for dinner?"

"We've had him over hundreds of times over the years. That's not a problem at all."

"I know. But this time, it would be different . . . don't you think? Since we're courting and all?"

Havyn waved it off. "I think it's a perfect idea. Especially if you're thinking of him seriously . . . we better get used to having him around."

"All right then. Decision made. I'll send a note back inviting him here for dinner." But she didn't want to. Not really.

"I'll let the family know." Havyn waved and headed back toward the house as if nothing was strange or awkward.

Whitney's stomach did little flips inside her. Why was she so nervous?

Hours later, she'd worked herself into a frenzy. Head throbbing, she headed to the bath chamber inside the house. Maybe a long, hot soak would ease the tension.

In the tub, her thoughts went back to Mama. And then Granddad. Then images of Garrett Sinclair tortured her. As she shivered in the water, she couldn't get the thought of his tight grasp on her out of her mind.

So she scrubbed her skin as hard as she could with the

soap. Then dunked her head and scrubbed her hair. Envisioned washing him away like that dirt.

What she really wanted was to go back to her room and hide for the rest of the evening. Tuck the bottle of whiskey into bed with her and try to forget her troubles.

God, help me. Please.

Silence greeted her. She wanted to think that He'd abandoned her too. It was easier to be angry that way. But after she'd talked with Dad about her drinking, she could feel her heavenly Father chiseling away at the wall she'd built around her heart.

Whitney wanted to be normal again.

Wanted to feel things again.

Wanted to be free of this anxiety and pain.

So why must she go through it over and over? It didn't make any sense.

With a long exhale, she got up out of the tub and dried off. Judas would be there soon. Thankfully, her sisters were preparing the meal because she really didn't have the heart or the energy.

When he'd first asked to court her, she'd thought it would be a good idea. She wanted to fall in love like her sisters. But nothing sparked with Judas. He was their old family friend. All the money and power he held just didn't matter to her.

Nothing really seemed to matter right now.

No. That was a lie. Peter mattered. Helping him had mattered.

She shook off the thoughts. Tonight was not about Peter. Time to wrap her mind around Judas Reynolds coming to dinner.

Dinner had been lovely, with the whole clan that made up his intended's family now. At least, that's what Judas hoped to convey to the mob of people that were entirely too goody-goody for him.

"Lovely dinner."

"Thank you for the lovely time."

"Delicious. The food was divine."

His cheeks hurt from all the smiling and cooing he'd done.

So why did Whitney still seem . . . distant? She should have fallen in line with his plan much sooner than this. And frankly, he was running out of patience.

First, there was Ruth and her sad eyes. Then Powell's other children, who were sweeter than ice cream and begged for his attention. John and Daniel sat there smiling and nodding through the entire performance. As if that was how everyone acted every meal.

What was *wrong* with these people?

It was time for him to put the next part of his plan into action. Wiping his mouth with his napkin, he leaned back and turned toward Whitney. "My dear, might I escort you on a brisk walk outside in the moonlight?"

She looked to her family and then glanced back at him. "That would be nice. As long as it's not too long. I find myself quite tired."

"Of course. But I find myself in need of some exercise after that *lovely* meal." There was that word again. Once they were married, he'd have to keep these visits to a minimum.

The racket around the table increased as they stood and everyone gathered plates, said their "good-nights" to him, and continued to chatter on incessantly. Was it a farce, or did these people really like each other that much?

He kept a pleasant expression glued to his face as he and Whitney gathered their coats and gloves and headed out the door.

She kept several feet between them as they walked toward the pond. "It's probably best not to disturb the dogs tonight. They'll get too excited to see me, and then the rest of the animals will be wide awake with their noise."

"I'm pleased to get some time alone with you."

She picked up her pace, but didn't respond. Ah, so she was being coy, was she? He could be patient. After all, he'd waited this long.

Once they were a good bit down the lane, she stopped and turned toward him. "Judas, there are some things I need to say."

"Of course, my dear. Feel free to tell me anything."

"I'm not convinced I'll ever be able to love you. Not the way you'd want a wife to love you. In fact, I'm not sure I can ever love anyone because I feel so broken right now."

"That's completely understandable." He dared to step a bit closer to her. "You've been through a lot this past year."

"Maybe our courting isn't such a good idea. I don't think it's fair to you, and I'm not ready."

He'd better get a handle on things and fast. "Whitney, I don't want you to feel any pressure from me, but most people don't go into marriage with a great love between them. That comes with time. I'm sure if we were to seriously speak of marriage, we could build our love a little at a time. You must know that I care for you, and I believe that you care for me too. Neither one of us is getting any younger, so there's no need to rush the romance now. We could marry and spend the rest of our lives falling in love."

Her eyebrows shot up to the fur hood of her coat. With a

step back, she held up her hands. "I don't want to get married to you right now."

He'd pushed. Too fast. "My apologies. That's not what I meant. I'm simply stating that you don't have to have expectations that we will fall in love right away. Let me take you out to dinner again. We can take our time getting to know one another as more than family friends." Hopefully that would smooth things over for her.

She seemed to weigh his words in her mind. "As long as you understand where I'm coming from. I wouldn't want to hurt you in any way."

"Of course, my dear. No pressure from me, all right?"

She nodded.

"So how about dinner tomorrow evening?"

"That would be nice."

Judas drummed his fingers on his desk. There *had* to be a way to apply pressure to the situation without making Whitney run the other way. Patience was definitely not his virtue. Once he decided on something, he went for it. And expected immediate results.

Loud thuds erupted outside his office. Bolting from his chair, he charged for the door. Who would be here at this hour?

When he yanked the door open, he saw two men engaged in a fistfight.

"What is going on here?" His booming voice caused the two to separate and turn toward him.

"He's tryin' to steal my land!" The younger one was wiry and short. Judas remembered him from the deed office.

"Am not—you're the one who's the thief!" The second man was older and yanked a piece of paper out of his pocket.

"Lookee here, Mr. Reynolds. This here's my deed to the property."

"Oh no you don't." The young one shoved past him. "I got a deed too. Right here."

"Gentlemen, gentlemen." He used his best authoritative and soothing voice. "Come into my office so we can sort this out."

But what he wanted to do was kick both of them out onto their keisters. Nevertheless, their squabble had piqued his interest—and an idea took shape as he sat at his desk. "Now please. Let me see each of your deeds."

The two continued to whisper argue with each other while he looked over the papers. Both appeared to have valid deeds. And yet, one deed was ten years older than the other. Well before the gold rush had hit Nome.

Very interesting.

"Fellas, I'm going to hold on to these to ensure their safety and demand that you both appear before Judge Beck in the morning. I'll let him know you are coming. Until then, I suggest you go home and get some rest."

"But—"

"Hey, that's not—"

"I insist, gentlemen." Judas got up from his chair and pushed them both out the door and then closed it behind them.

Then he went back to the desk and studied the papers one more time.

This would work perfectly.

TWENTY

The morning was almost balmy after the frigid temperatures the last six weeks. Even though it was only February, Peter looked forward to spring. Because then maybe this sickness would be past. He took long, steady strides throughout town, taking the time to savor his walk.

He'd held his breath for days waiting to hear that more cases had sprung up, but so far, so good. He'd spent a good deal of time checking his herbs and tonics and tending to the small indoor gardens he kept in his office. Pretty soon, he'd need to hire someone to help out because he wouldn't be able to keep up with all of it.

As he made his way the length of town and back, he prayed for every person he knew by name and then the others he didn't. God had brought him here for a reason, and he wanted to be about the Father's will, even if he didn't understand what it was.

As he prayed for the town, his thoughts quickly shifted to Whitney.

Funny, he thought about her even more now that he'd shared about losing his wife and child. The fact was, he didn't think of Charlotte nearly as much as he had in the past. Even the bad dreams were gone.

Whitney. Her striking eyes that noticed everything. Her deft hands helping him tend to the sick. Her depth of care for people, showcased in the sorrow and anxiety she'd dealt with after her own losses.

The woman had gone through so much upheaval the past year, and yet it seemed as though nothing could shake her. At least, that's what she conveyed to everyone.

The fact that she'd allowed him into her innermost struggles touched his heart. And when she'd handed over her bottle of whiskey for him to use at the gold camp, he'd wanted to cheer.

She never asked for it back.

Her eyes had become bright again. Her blood pressure had lowered.

Thank You, Lord, for showing me the signs of her hypertension.

If he hadn't put the pieces together, she might be in a much worse place right now. A little niggle at the back of his mind warned him that it wasn't over, though. Whitney could very well be struggling with her dependency on the alcohol.

The jangling of a harness brought his attention around.

Without even thinking about it, he'd struck out on the road toward the Bundrant farm.

Mr. Norris from the Roadhouse sent him a wave. "Dr. Cameron, it's good to see you this morning. What brings you out here?"

"I was out on my morning constitutional, and I guess my thoughts distracted me. Where are you headed?"

Norris brought his sleigh to a stop. "I'm on my way out to the Bundrant—um, well I guess it's the Powell, no maybe . . .

Roselli?" He shrugged. "You know what I mean. I'm headed out to Chuck's farm to pick up the milk, cream, and butter for the Roadhouse."

"Would you mind if I tagged along?" He didn't have anything pressing this morning, and it would give him a good excuse to check on Whitney and Ruth.

"Not at all. Hop in."

The ride out to the farm passed in a flurry of words. Peter had no idea the man was such a talker. He learned a good deal about what was happening in town. Including that there were rumored to be a couple of cases of measles in Nome. Two miners had apparently come in from the gold camps to try to find claims elsewhere, but they were now sick.

Add that to his ever-growing list, and he'd have plenty to keep him busy. On top of trying to get out to the farm as often as he could to work with the dogs.

Norris shifted the conversation to the menu at the Roadhouse. As he talked about the different foods he was hoping to introduce to entice the crowds to keep coming since he didn't always offer the musical entertainment of the Powell sisters anymore, Peter's stomach rumbled.

"Seems as if Whitney needs to take a break for a while."

"Wait. What did you say?" His full attention on Norris now, Peter wasn't sure he'd heard correctly.

The man chuckled as they pulled up to the farm. "My wife is always telling me that I talk too fast and mumble. My apologies. What I was saying is that Madysen and Havyn are the ones who've been playing out at my establishment and it's only on Fridays now. Seems Whitney needed to take a break. Ya know, with the loss of Chuck and all."

Peter blinked at the man. "Oh." How had he not known this? Of course, she'd been out at the gold camps with him a lot lately. He'd expected her sisters had played without her during those times, but hadn't expected to hear that she was taking a break. Was she quitting? "Thanks for the ride, Mr. Norris. I greatly appreciate it." Peter jumped off the sleigh.

"Not a problem, Doc. Good to see ya." He pulled ahead to the milking shed.

The question now was, where was Whitney? There was a good deal he wanted to discuss with her. He walked over to where the dogs' kennels were, hoping to find her there.

Sure enough, she was there in the middle of them. Crouched on the floor while the dogs vied for attention.

"Good morning, Whitney."

"Peter, I didn't think we had a training session this morning." Her expression was puzzled.

"We don't. But I hitched a ride with Mr. Norris out here and thought I'd check in on Ruth." It was partially the truth. Fact was, he was more interested in *her* than Ruth, but he kept that thought to himself.

She stood up and brushed the straw from her coat. "I'm glad you did. She hasn't had much of an appetite. We're concerned about her."

"Losing a spouse will do that." He squatted next to several of the dogs and rubbed their ears.

"She said that even though she'd tried to convince herself that Stan was gone, she really didn't believe it until she heard the news. I guess no matter how much we attempt to brace ourselves for bad news, we can't be prepared for what loss can do to our hearts and minds."

Peter watched her carefully. How was she handling this new tragedy in their family? "I can imagine that it has taken its toll on you as well. How are you doing?"

Her brown eyes shot to his. Looking straight through him.

"I'm not drinking, if that's what you're implying. I gave you my bottle, remember?"

He held up his hands in front of him. "I remember. And thank you for that, by the way. But I was asking more about your anxiety. Has this caused your own grief to resurface?"

"It never went away, Peter. Granddad has been gone but a short time." Her shoulders slumped a bit. "I'm sorry. I shouldn't get so defensive with you."

"It's all right. I did the same thing each time I lost someone." As long as she continued to open up to him, he wouldn't have to fret and question as much about her. Grief and anxiety were cruel beasts that could send the sweetest people into the darkest depths.

"I appreciate your friendship. Thank you for listening."

"Of course." Oh, to share more with her than just friendship. He waited for the guilt to strike . . . but it didn't. "You know, I think you're helping me to heal too. So I should be thanking you for your friendship as well."

She tilted her head as she looked up at him. Their gazes locked for several seconds. "You're a good man, Peter Cameron."

While she was being open, he decided to ask another question. "What's this I hear about you not playing with your sisters at the Roadhouse anymore?"

She squinted at him. "Ah, Mr. Norris." With a shake of her head, she put her hands on her hips. "I needed a break."

"I thought music was important to you?"

She groaned. "Not you, too, Peter."

"What do you mean?"

"My sisters are already hounding me about this. And Ruth. And Dad. And John and Daniel."

"I didn't want to hound you. Just thought you might want to talk about it."

The look she sent him made him step back with a chuckle. "I take that as a no."

Her lips pinched together.

Several silent seconds passed, but he couldn't let it go. She was gifted by God with her talent. "Isn't music like breathing to you? Your mother poured everything into teaching the three of you, and now you're going to throw it away?"

"You're so exasperating!" Her hands flew up. "I'm *not* throwing it away. I don't *deserve* it! Don't you see that?" Her face reddened after the words were out. She turned back to the dogs.

"Whitney . . ." He sighed with her name. "I'm sorry. I didn't mean to push so hard. But you don't really believe that do you?"

"I don't know what I believe right now. That's why I said I needed a break."

"Fair enough." He stepped over to her and placed a hand on her shoulder. "I'm still your friend, and if you need to talk, I'm here."

She nodded but didn't look up at him.

"Maybe I'll go check on Ruth now." He moved away with slow steps, petting each dog as he passed them. Great—he'd probably pushed her even further away.

She walked over to the wall where she kept the harnesses hung. "Why don't you stay for lunch after you've visited with Ruth. . . . Then after that, would you like to take the dogs out for a run? They need exercise, and it would save me time if you ran one sled and I ran the other."

It was an olive branch and he'd take it. "I'd love to."

"No falling off the sled this time. No daydreaming."

"I make no promises." He watched her for several seconds, but she never turned to look at him. That was all right.

He'd take one step at a time.

The afternoon had gone much better than the morning. Why was it she always let Peter's words get to her? At least she'd caught herself before she unleashed her temper on him. Again. That man seemed to bring out the worst in her . . . *and* the best, if she was honest.

All through the rest of her morning chores and into lunch, she couldn't get her mind off his probing questions. Everyone else had questioned her too, but it was different coming from him. The truth was, Ruth had actually guessed it first.

Yes, she was punishing herself by taking away music. But she deserved it.

As soon as she and Peter took the dogs out, though, things got better. The beautiful weather and fresh air mended her weary soul. The dogs loved Peter, and she had to admit it had been the best day she'd had in a long time.

When they arrived back at the barns, Havyn and Madysen were waiting for them, smiles covering their faces.

Maddy bounced on her toes. "Sounds like you two enjoyed yourselves. We could hear your laughter all the way from the house."

Whitney smirked at Peter. "He fell off the sled twice. Day-dreaming."

"She took you around the turn by the manure pit, didn't she?" Havyn put a hand to her stomach. "I fall off every time."

Peter grunted and looked at her. "Oh really? So you did that on purpose?" He dramatically brushed snow from his coat.

"Maybe." Laughter bubbled up and burst forth. "But it was so funny!"

"I'm glad you can laugh at my expense—"

"Whit said you were daydreaming." Havyn quirked a brow. "What about?"

Peter glanced at Whitney, brow raised as if daring her to answer. Whitney laughed even harder.

"What is so funny?" Judas stood behind her sisters.

Whitney fought a frown. When did *he* arrive?

Oh! She sucked in a breath and looked down at the watch pinned to her shirtwaist. "Oh goodness, Judas. I didn't realize it was so late." She put a hand to her hair and rushed past them. "Let me go change, and I will be right with you."

"Mr. Reynolds, would you mind if I hitched a ride back to town with you two?" Peter's words floated over to her as she raced to the house.

How could she have forgotten about her dinner plans with Judas? How had she let the time get away from her?

"Wait up!"

Madysen's voice came from behind her. Whitney looked back and slowed her steps.

"Havyn is going to take the men into the parlor and keep them company until you're ready. I'm here to help you get your hair tamed."

She reached up and put a hand through her hair. Her curls were all over the place. Of course—she'd been outside on the sled for hours. No wonder she was such a mess. "Thanks, Maddy. I need every bit of help I can get."

"Are you getting serious about Judas? I mean, I don't want to pry, but after he came out here last night, you two talked quite a bit, and then you're going to dinner with him again this evening . . ."

The insinuation hung in the air.

"I don't know." It was honest. She'd told Judas that she didn't love him last night. He seemed fine with it. She couldn't tell her sister, but she truly hated being the last one unmarried. It made her more certain than ever that there was something wrong with her.

Then there were her feelings for Peter. They had nothing but friendship between them, but her heart was starting to long for a more intimate relationship. Peter had done nothing to make her believe that was what he wanted, but if she was feeling that way about him, how could she continue with Judas?

"Well, there's no need to rush into anything." Maddy bustled around her with a comb.

Her sister began to chatter about the sheep as Whitney readied herself for the evening out. Goodness, their family was quite the circus when it came to their animals. Between Havyn and her chickens, Maddy and her sheep, and Whitney with her dogs, they had enough stories to entertain a crowd for a month.

Within minutes, she at least *looked* like a lady. It would have been better if she'd taken the time to bathe, but Judas understood they lived on a farm. He would have to accept her the way she was if he wanted to continue their relationship.

Maddy turned her to face her and smoothed the front of Whitney's dress.

"Do I smell too much like dog?" She grimaced.

"Eh . . . not too bad." Her sister reached for the perfume Dad gave her for Christmas. "With a few sprays of this, he'll never notice." She giggled.

"Thanks, Maddy."

With a swish of skirts, she hurried to the parlor. Peter and Judas both stood and smiled at her.

In that moment, the differences between the two men were startling. She looked back and forth between them.

Stop. It wasn't wise to compare them. Both were her friends.

"You look magnificent." Judas beamed at her. "I hope you don't mind, but I've offered to give the good doctor a ride back into town." He held out his elbow for her and escorted her toward the door.

"I don't mind a bit."

After bundling up in their coats, they climbed up into the sleigh, which was cozy indeed with her sandwiched between the two men.

"Hope I'm not squishing you." Peter nudged her with his shoulder.

No matter what she tried, she couldn't quit comparing the two men as they spoke about the weather, politics, businesses in Nome, and church. While she never would have guessed that the two had that much to talk about, it was interesting to hear them so eager to speak their minds. Judas didn't surprise her, but Peter had never been one to share so many opinions.

And why were they both being so . . . upbeat? Their lively conversation—if she were to be frank—exhausted her.

When they dropped off Peter at his office, though, she missed his presence.

"I'll see you tomorrow!" Peter waved at her. "Thank you for the ride, Mr. Reynolds."

"You're welcome, Doctor." Judas tipped his hat, then turned to her. "Now, my dear. Finally, I have you all to myself."

For some reason, that didn't hold the appeal he probably hoped for. But she sent him a smile anyway.

At the restaurant, they were escorted to the same private table. Judas held out her chair for her, and she situated herself.

None of this was right.

Her shoulders were tense. Her neck was tense. Pretty soon, a headache would rear its ugly head. What was going on with her?

"Wine?" Judas held a bottle over her glass. When had he gotten that?

Perhaps a little would help ease her nerves. "Yes, thank you. But just one glass."

"Of course." He filled her glass. "So tell me how things are going out at the farm."

She took a sip, and the liquid warmed her. She could already feel herself relaxing. So she took another, longer sip. "Busy as usual. The farm keeps us hopping, that's for sure."

"I'm so glad that you have such a prosperous venture." After he gave their orders to the waiter, he leaned his arms on the table.

It flattered her that a man of such prestige would give his attention completely to her. "You knew Granddad for many years. He was a smart man and provided well for us." She lifted the glass again and drank. She should stop. The nudging she felt in her spirit confirmed it.

But she needed it.

Just to get through the evening. This would be the last time.

Their conversation circled around to every area of the farm. But the more she sipped on the wine, the harder it was to keep her focus. Was that normal?

"Tell me, Whitney, I know Chuck owned prosperous mines

before he brought you to Alaska. Did he ever think about mining here once the rush hit?"

She shook her head as she finished the last bite on her plate. "No. He hated mining towns. Didn't want us to be raised in them. Especially not after what happened with our dad."

"So where did his gold come from? Surely, he didn't bring it with him." Judas smiled.

"Oh, but he did." The thought made her laugh, and she put a hand to her mouth. "He didn't like banks. So he brought crates of it up to Alaska. Labeled them as books."

"Crates, you say? That was indeed clever." He lifted his own glass and downed the rest of it. "Surely, when the gold rush struck here, he must have at least panned the river on your property out of curiosity."

"Not that I was ever aware." She shrugged. "Why would he need more gold? The farm more than took care of us."

He lifted his napkin to his lips. "Oh, I don't know. Chuck was a savvy businessman, so I thought for sure he would have at least tried."

"I doubt it. Granddad was done with gold when we left Colorado." She let out a sigh and stared at Judas. It had been a pleasant enough evening, but she still had no feelings toward him. A wave of exhaustion hit her. "Would you mind taking me home? I find myself quite tired."

"Of course. It's been a long day."

He helped her with her coat and walked her out to the sleigh.

As she sat next to him on the ride, the first few moments were silent.

She thought back over the evening. And cringed. Once again, she'd had too much to drink. Oh, she'd told Judas one glass, but she saw him refill hers when he refilled his own. And she didn't stop him. What did that say about her? She tried to clear her mind and sat up straighter.

"It has been a delightful evening, wouldn't you say?" His hands were on the reins, but he scooted closer to her.

Alarm bells went off in her mind.

He stopped the sleigh. "Would you mind if I kissed you, Whitney?" He leaned closer.

She put a hand up between them. "I don't think that's a good idea, Judas. I want my first kiss to be at my wedding."

He didn't pull away and let his grin broaden. "Then . . . will you marry me? Because I love you and want you to be my wife."

Leaning back as far as she could, she pushed him away. "I *don't* love you, Judas. I have great admiration for you, and you've always been a good friend to our family, but I don't think I can marry you."

"Love will come, my dear. Most people don't fall in love like your sisters did. Most people marry for convenience or outright desperation. In our case, neither of those is needed, but I *do* love you. I'll lavish you with whatever you want. You'll always come first in my life." He moved closer again.

She pushed him back. "That's not how God intended marriage to be." In fact, *God* should come first. As soon as she thought it, her heart twinged. Yes, she still believed that God should be first . . . even though she certainly hadn't put Him in that place in a long while.

Father, I'm so sorry. I'm such a mess. Please . . . help me to get back on the right path.

Every inch of her heart ached as if she were shredding it to pieces in front of her. *What have I done? You are Almighty God. I need You in control of my life again. On the throne of my heart. Please. Forgive me.*

A soothing rush of warmth filled her middle, and then, as if the Potter were molding her heart back together, she felt whole again.

Her breath caught. God still loved her. No matter how hard she pushed Him away. No matter how much she blamed Him for the difficult times in her life.

"All right." Judas's voice brought her back to the moment. He straightened and picked up the reins. "I won't push. I'll give you some time to think about it."

She didn't need time to think about it. Of that she was certain.

They rode the rest of the way in silence as the aurora above them wove across the sky in waves of green and yellow.

Back at the farm, Judas helped her down from the sleigh. "I hope you'll reconsider. I'd marry you tomorrow, and you would make me the happiest man alive."

How did they get to this place? Did he really love her? She couldn't imagine that he could think she'd developed feelings for him in such a short amount of time. She pasted on a smile, not wanting to crush him after his sweet attention. "I'll think about it."

"Good. I look forward to seeing you again soon." He climbed up into the sleigh and put the horses back into motion.

As she watched him drive away, she went over the evening again. Had she given him any indication that she was falling in love with him? Not that she could remember. Clearly, the wine had clouded her judgment, but she knew now for certain.

There would be no future for her with Judas Reynolds.

She didn't want to hurt him, but she had to be truthful. Oh, what kind of mess had she gotten into this time?

One thing was clearer than anything else.

She had a bottle to dump down the drain.

TWENTY-ONE

Halfway through her pregnancy and Havyn already had to use the facilities multiple times a night. Not fun. Especially since she really enjoyed her sleep. John had teased her about that ever since they got married, and now here she was, waking up grumpy every morning.

She looked at the clock on her way back to their bedroom. Already five in the morning? She let out a moan. Might as well stay up. She'd have to start breakfast soon anyway.

Padding her way to the parlor, she yawned. At least she could get some prayer time in before the house teemed with activity.

When she entered the large room, movement on the settee startled her, and she gasped.

"Sorry, Havyn. It's me."

Whitney sounded so forlorn.

She took the chair across from her sister. "Couldn't sleep?"

"No." Whit stared out the window.

"Wanna talk about it?"

A shrug.

Whitney's long hair hung in curls that scattered over her

shoulders and back. Even in the dark, she was beautiful. Havyn studied her for several minutes. When Whit was ready, she'd talk.

Her older sister let out a sigh and lifted something from beside her. As she turned it, it reflected the sliver of moon from the night sky. "I need your help."

"All right." She leaned back in the chair.

"I came out of my room to dump this down the drain." Havyn waited.

"I could blame everyone else and all that's happened for why I started drinking . . . but that would be a lie." She leaned forward and set the bottle on the table in front of her. "I realized something tonight."

"What's that?"

"That I stopped putting God first in my life. Actually, it's been quite a while since I've done that. Long before we lost Mama. And when I couldn't deal with everything that happened, I tried to fill that hole in my life with something else. Anything else. Whatever it took to numb me." She gave a harsh laugh. "I've been whining and complaining in my mind about being broken and feeling numb. But I was doing it to myself the whole time."

Havyn watched and held her breath.

Whitney let out a sigh. "Funny . . . it took Judas Reynolds proposing to me for me to see the truth."

"*What?*" If she hadn't been expecting, Havyn would have jumped out of her chair.

Whit held up a hand. "Don't worry. I told him no. But he still wants me to think about it." Then she waved her hand back and forth. "That's not the point here. He said he loved me and would give me everything I wanted—that he would put me first in his life. That's when it hit me. Even though

I've felt abandoned by God all these months, have lashed out at Him for my suffering, I knew in my heart that no one deserves to be first in anyone's life but Him."

Havyn scooted to the edge of her seat. "Mama made sure to remind us of that every day."

"It took me long enough to realize I had caused my own misery." She stood up and walked over to the piano. Sliding her hand over the lid, she looked at Havyn. "Peter and Ruth both asked me why I was punishing myself by not playing anymore. . . . I didn't have a good answer. I keep thinking about Peter talking about the ways he's failed the people he loved. I felt that way too, but I tried to help him see that he hadn't failed. Maybe I need to see that for myself, too. Life is difficult, and I won't always manage to do the right thing"

Havyn got up and went to wrap her sister in a hug. "None of us have handled things perfectly, Whit."

"I need you to forgive me, Havyn. I'm so sorry for my behavior. For lashing out at you and Madysen when you found the whiskey. I know you confronted me because you love me. But I couldn't see it at the time." Whitney took her hand. She reached down for the bottle she'd left on the table. "Will you help me get rid of it?"

Nothing could contain the joy coursing through her. Her sister was back. "Of course." She gripped her sister's shoulders and fixed her gaze on her. "Look at me."

Whitney did.

"Maddy and I will love you, no matter what. And we're always here for you. I promise. You don't have to carry all of this on your own. Mama would scold us if we let you."

Her older sister laughed at that. "You're right. She would." She headed for the kitchen. At the sink, she poured the remainder of the bottle out.

"I'm sure that was hard. Especially since it helped with your headaches."

Whitney shook her head. "No. My headaches were just an excuse. Once Peter discovered they were caused by hypertension and started me on a treatment, they got better. I don't need the alcohol for that pain anymore, but I can't say that it doesn't call to me. Now I understand why dad drank so much. It numbs you. Helps you forget." She turned to Havyn and gave her the empty bottle. "But I don't want to forget anymore. I'm ready to move forward, no matter how painful it may be. Life is still beautiful and worth living."

Havyn threw her arms around her sister and let the tears flow. "I've missed you."

"Me too."

As her sister pulled back, Havyn saw great big tears fall from her eyes. Healing had begun.

No matter the losses, no matter the trials . . . they were whole again. Together.

Family.

Thank You, God.

It wouldn't be long now. Whitney would come to her senses and see that marrying him was the best choice for her.

Soon he'd have a beautiful wife on his arm, her family fortune at his disposal, and perhaps even a child on the way.

Judas stared out the window and let himself dream. He'd built quite an empire here.

Nome was his.

He took a long sip of his coffee and turned back to his desk. Now to see what else was on his morning docket.

Two more letters from Cain. So far, Judas hadn't come up with a decent plan to stop the man from coming. But he had other more pressing matters at the moment.

He opened his financial ledger and double-checked the numbers.

A knock at his door brought his nose up out of his ledger.

The door opened and Whitney walked through.

He stood. "What a nice surprise!" Walking around his desk, he held out his arms.

But she didn't come any closer. Instead, she held up her hand. Just like she had last night. "Judas . . . I need to speak with you." She pushed the door closed. Her shoulders lifted with a deep breath.

"Of course. I am always at your disposal." Perhaps she needed his advice on something out at the farm. Exactly what he wanted. To get involved enough to find out the true wealth of their enterprise.

"I've come to give you a final answer. I can't marry you."

For a moment, he thought he hadn't heard her correctly. "Pardon me?"

"I can't marry you." She looked down at her hands and then back up at him. "It's not that I don't care for you—I do. As a friend. It was very nice that you asked to court me, and our time together was lovely. Thank you for that. But I won't marry you."

He stepped forward.

"Please. Don't try to convince me otherwise. My mind is made up." And with that, she slipped out the door.

As it clicked behind her, Judas narrowed his eyes.

This wasn't the end of the discussion. He still had plenty of cards to play. A winning hand.

No one turned Judas Reynolds down.

———

Pounding from somewhere made Peter sit up straight in bed. He wiped his hands down his face and listened. There it was again. He hadn't dreamed it.

Jumping to his feet, he grabbed his robe from the end of the bed and then raced to the door.

When he opened it, Daniel was standing there. "We need you to come quick, Peter. It's Bethany. She's spiked a high fever, and we can't bring it down."

He nodded and went to pack a bag. This wasn't good news. Five more cases had erupted in Nome, and even though he'd tried to quarantine the men from the rest of the town, he'd known it had likely been too late.

Dressing as fast as he could, he prayed that no one else in the family would get it.

"I brought a horse for you." Daniel took his bag and tied it to his saddle.

Peter mounted and gave him a nod. "Let's go."

They pushed the horses as fast as they dared through the deep snow and made it to the farm in less than fifteen minutes.

"You go in. I'll take care of the horses."

"Thanks." Peter took his bag and went in.

Whitney stood there, tears in her eyes. "She hasn't had the measles. I asked. She's terribly hot."

He stared deep into her eyes. "I'm here. In a day or two, she'll be right as rain." He prayed his words were true. "Take me to her."

Havyn and John stood out in the hall.

Peter stopped and looked at John. "You need to keep your

wife away from this sickness. It could be very dangerous for the baby."

John's face turned very serious, and Havyn put a hand to her mouth. "I didn't think about that." With a hand to her expanding stomach, she winced. "I'm sorry we won't be able to help."

John took his wife by the arm. "We'll move into the room I used as a foreman right away." He turned to Havyn. "Don't worry, darling. There's plenty of family to help. Let's just keep you and the baby healthy."

Peter gripped John's shoulder. "Keep her away from the house. You keep your distance as well and keep your hands washed." He turned and looked at the rest of the family gathered outside of the room Bethany shared with Ruth. "If this is what has been spreading through the villages and now Nome, we need to take it very seriously. I need everyone's help to keep things clean. Wash your hands. Regularly."

They all nodded.

"Who's with her now?"

"Madysen." Whitney said. "We were going to take turns sitting with her."

"Since you live in close quarters, you all might get sick. My highest priority right now is to help Bethany's fever to break, but second to that is to ensure that Havyn doesn't get it."

Whitney's chin lifted. "We'll do whatever you need us to do."

"How many of you have had the measles?"

"We all have." Whitney answered for the group.

That, at least, was in his favor. But the influenza had proven deadly, and none of them were protected from that.

At that moment, a terrible cough came from the other room. "Keep hot water boiling on the stove. I'll need as many rags as you can find. Keep them boiled and clean. I'll have to use them for poultices that need to be changed out regularly."

He moved into the room and saw young Bethany, flushed and sweating. "Why don't you take a break, Madysen."

She nodded and joined the rest of the family in the hall. All except Whitney. She came in and opened his bag. "Let me help you."

He nodded. "I want to listen to her heart first."

She dug in his bag and handed him the stethoscope.

After he examined her, he turned to face Whitney. "We'll need to get some tea brewing right away and some poultices ready. Why don't you get her changed out of this wet night-gown and I'll go work on those things."

"Of course."

Three hours later, they'd worked side by side with precision, in perfect harmony. Something he hadn't had in years. But the young girl's temperature was finally coming down. "Thank you for your help, Whitney. Your gifts never cease to amaze me. Will you sit with her while I go speak to the rest of the family?"

She touched his arm. "Thank you."

He dipped his chin. "It's not over yet, but I'm hopeful."

Walking down the hallway to the parlor, he tried to wrangle a thousand thoughts scrambling for attention. First and foremost, how good it was to work side by side with Whitney. Second, he'd barely skirted this sickness wiping out the villages and gold camps. But now, it was here. And there were a lot more people in Nome.

Everything got quiet as he walked into the room and approached the family. "It's not as bad as we thought. She's strong, but everyone needs to be vigilant."

"How's her fever?" Chris twisted his handkerchief in his hands.

"She's sweating, which is a good sign. The fever started coming down after I applied the elderflower tea and some apple-cider vinegar compresses to her forehead and feet. It's the cough I find most worrisome now."

Dark circles under Chris's eyes accentuated the tears that pooled there. "Can I see her?"

"Of course, but remember to wash your hands before and after seeing her. Talk to her and encourage her to keep fighting the fever."

Eli stood up and grabbed onto his dad.

That was when Peter noticed Ruth. She hadn't said anything in a while. Her face had paled considerably. "Ruth, how are you—"

"I fixed some sandwiches for everyone. They're in the kitchen." Madysen's entrance into the room interrupted his question.

Then Ruth fell off her chair and onto the floor.

Twenty-Two

Three days had passed since Ruth's collapse. Now Daniel, Madysen, and Eli were sick as well. Peter stood over the basin as he washed his face. He'd used up the last of his tea on them.

Thankfully, Bethany was improving, but so far she was the only one. This respiratory influenza was taking its toll on the household. Thank God there was no sign of the measles. But the two so often seemed to go hand in hand with this new horrible sickness. Since 1900, how many lives had been lost?

He worried most about Ruth. After losing her husband and being separated from her children, she simply didn't seem to have the will to live. But he needed her to fight—

"Peter?" Whitney's voice came from behind him.

He turned and dried off his face with a towel. The weariness in her eyes must certainly match his own, but she had been so strong. At his side every moment he needed her. There was no denying his feelings for her had grown ever stronger— ever constant. One day—after this crisis was over—he'd tell her.

"We're out of the vinegar as well as mustard." They'd made so many poultices, it was no wonder.

He stepped closer to her. "Do you think you and your father can handle taking care of everyone here? That way I can run into town and restock from my office and the mercantile. I need to check on my patients in town as well."

"Sure. Whatever you need." She looked like she had more to say, but she clamped her lips shut. "Should I harness a team for you? I think you'll be able to manage them just fine on your own."

He reached up and moved a curl from her face. The smile in her eyes was enough to keep him energized for days. But as much as he wanted to bare his soul then and there, now was not the time. "Thank you. I appreciate your faith in me. I'll head out right away."

When he brushed past her in the doorway, their hands touched. She captured his fingers, squeezed them, then turned and walked away.

An hour later, he'd gathered up what he could from his office and loaded it on the dogsled. The pups had been perfect on the journey back to town. He headed to the mercantile Daniel's father owned to see if they had more vinegar and mustard in stock.

As he entered the familiar building, he narrowed his eyes. The atmosphere was different. And Martin Beaufort wasn't behind the counter. As Peter walked through the store and picked up what he needed, his eyebrows raised. What was going on with the prices?

He headed for the counter. A stranger stood behind the counter, wearing an apron and helping a customer.

"But why is it so much more?" The elderly gentleman

held out a sack of beans. "I've been buying the same bag of beans for years!"

"With new management came new pricing. It costs a lot of money to get supplies up here. That's why Mr. Beaufort lost the business. He couldn't make his payments."

Peter couldn't believe his ears. What was going on? Beaufort lost the business? That was odd. Daniel hadn't said anything about that. What if he didn't know? And who owned the mercantile now? When his turn came, he stepped up to the counter. "I couldn't help but overhear. You say there's new management?"

"Yes, sir." The man smiled.

"Might I inquire who it is?"

"Of course, sir. Mr. Reynolds owns it now. He loaned Beaufort money to keep the store afloat for over a year. When the man couldn't pay, the ownership reverted to Mr. Reynolds."

Peter clamped his jaw shut. So Reynolds was behind this.

He handed the man behind the counter his list. He'd pay the extra charges for now and figure out what to do later. "Can you load these things onto the dogsled outside the door?"

"Yup." The clerk took the paper and looked over the list.

Peter headed for the door. "I'll pay you when I get back."

He walked out of the store and went to the house behind it. He prayed Martin and Granny still had a place to stay, at least. After he knocked on the door, a cough greeted him from inside.

He opened the door. "Hello? Everyone all right?" He made his way into the parlor and found Granny sitting in a rocking chair, a quilt up to her chin.

"Sorry, Doc. I'm not feeling too well."

He rushed to her side.

"Don't be concerned about me. Martin's the one who's really sick." She pointed to the back of the house.

"I'll be right back." Peter quickened his steps and found Martin in the bed. The man was delirious with fever.

"He took my store . . ." he mumbled. "He took my store . . ."

"I'm sorry, Mr. Beaufort." He covered the man back up and went to put some water on to boil. As much as he wanted to confront Judas Reynolds at this moment, these people needed his attention more. Which was good.

Because he was quite certain he'd punch the man in the face if he saw him right now.

Whitney sat by the fireplace and stretched her aching muscles. Everyone was asleep, and Peter had come back from town with supplies and wanted to check his patients. Something was clearly bothering him because he hadn't stopped frowning since he got back.

She hadn't seen Havyn and John since Bethany first got sick. John had been handling the entire farm by himself, with the help of the hired workers.

Thank heaven Havyn was well, if not a bit restless.

Then there was Dad.

He'd helped Whitney take care of everyone. Never balking at anything she said. Never scolding her when she got short with him.

Guilt had nudged her many times. So far, though, she hadn't done anything about it. Which was wrong. She'd have to make things right with him once and for all. And soon.

Good thing she'd dumped out the rest of the whiskey.

Admitting that she would've given in to the temptation was awful. But true.

If only Mama was still here. She could really use her shoulder to lean on right now.

"Mind if I join you?"

Peter's husky voice broke the silence of the room. He was leaning against the doorjamb, his arms crossed over his chest. The deep frown still creased his forehead.

"Not at all." She scooted over to give him room to sit.

"You look deep in thought."

She shifted her attention to her hands. "I guess I was. I was thinking about my mother and how much I wish she were here."

"That's understandable. Especially at a time like this."

"I miss her every day. I realize that I wasted so much of the time I had with her and wish I could get some of it back." She dared a look at him.

Their eyes met and his softened. "After my mother died, I battled those same thoughts. I thought of the ways I hadn't been there for her. How I could have been a better son."

"I definitely could have been a better daughter." How many times had she exasperated her mother with her strong will and independence? The woman had been a saint . . . but Whitney hadn't truly understood until Mama was gone. "She was my confidante and confessor. My guide and encourager. I always thought I was so strong, but once she was gone, I knew I hadn't been the strong one. Not really. I'd relied on her for everything."

Peter put his elbows on his knees and clasped his hands. "Hindsight always helps us to see the what-ifs and could-have-beens. But it's not a good place to dwell. Charlotte was my best friend since childhood. We'd known each other so long, and then . . . she was gone. I didn't know who I was without her."

His words struck her heart. It had been the same way with Mama. "Same here. Who am I now? And I have no idea how to let her go." She clamped her hands between her knees and squeezed.

"I'm beginning to see that maybe it's not about forgetting and letting go . . . maybe it's more about giving ourselves permission to love again. So you can allow yourself to love your father . . . and maybe a husband one day."

"And you . . . a wife?" Did she really just say that out loud?

"Yes." His eyes bore into hers. Searching. Caring.

The connection between them was like a jolt of lightning. And she wanted nothing more than for him to take her into his arms—which made her glance down and then back up. Still there. Her stomach swirled. "We know how to go straight to the tough parts, don't we?"

"That's what good friends do." He raised his eyebrows at her and stared.

Good friends. Why did that no longer seem like enough? Was he taking his own words to heart? Would he be able to love again one day?

Why did it matter so much to her? Did she want to open up her heart to Peter? As the thought took root, she swallowed. Hard.

Yes. She did. Already had, if she was honest. Did she love him?

"You really helped me, Whitney. Helped me to see that my losses weren't about my failing the people I loved. I sat down and reasoned with myself. I've seen badly injured men who had no doctor to help them at all survive and come through just fine. Equally, I've seen men with teams of doctors die despite having so many learned men working to make them well. It isn't about me and what I can or can't do. It's about accepting that in all things God has a plan and it is His will and way—not mine."

His words went straight to Whitney's heart. "Yes." It seemed very clear now. "And even though we don't like what's happened or approve of it, we need to hold fast and maintain our trust in God Almighty. After all, what is the alternative?"

"Life without Him."

They sat in silence, gazing into each other's eyes. Words weren't necessary to continue the discussion. And there was something so very right about it.

Peter pushed up to stand, breaking the connection. "I need to get back to town. I just wanted to check on everyone and make sure you had enough supplies."

"Oh?" She stood with him.

"The other two doctors had symptoms of the sickness, and many in town are sick. I'm afraid we've got an epidemic on our hands."

"I'm so sorry. Do you need my help?" As much as she wanted to stay with her family, she longed for him to say yes.

"You're needed here to take care of your family. But I would greatly appreciate your prayers. I wish I could be here to help, but I know they're in good hands." He reached for her hands. "I'll come back and check on everyone in a day or two."

She clasped his, and they held on for several seconds.

"Take care of yourself." The timbre of his voice was low. Intimate.

She didn't want to release his hands. "You too. I'll be praying for you."

He let go and took a deep breath. "Well, I better be going."

"I'll walk you out."

But after he put on his coat and hat and opened the door, they were greeted with the howl of the wind.

"Oh no! Another storm."

He shook his head. "I still have to get back to town. Too many people need me."

Whitney walked out and looked at the sky. At least she could still see the barn. *Lord, please take care of him.* "You better take the dogs and a sled. They'll fare better in this weather than a horse." She took the halter of the animal and headed to the barn. "Come on. You'll need to hurry before this becomes an all-out blizzard."

Twenty-Three

Judas paced his office.

There'd been no word on anyone from the farm in several days. He sure wasn't going to risk going to the hospital to find out anything. Not with that horrible disease rampaging through the ranks of men. He'd sent his secretary several times, and that was good enough.

Better to put someone else's life at risk rather than his own. He was too important to the town.

The ticking of the clock blended with his steps and began to get on his nerves.

This was ludicrous. He had plenty to keep him busy.

Besides, Whitney would surely come to visit him soon and beg for his assistance for poor, dear Martin. As soon as word reached her—and he made sure that it would—she would come to her family's rescue, and he would be obliged to help her once again.

The door opened, and his secretary entered. "These arrived for you." She placed a few packets on his desk.

Rubbing his hands together, he dismissed her and opened the first large envelope.

He perused the document.

Perfect.

Nothing would stand in his way now.

Not even Miss Whitney Powell.

———

Ruth moaned, and Whitney wiped her brow. "I know it's hard, Ruth, but you need to fight this fever. Please." She lifted a cup to the woman's lips and tried to coax her to drink. "Just a sip or two. You can do it."

The frail woman swallowed.

"Think of your kids, Ruth. And how much you want to see them again. Take another sip for me. . . ." She held the cup and waited. *God, I don't know what to do. Please help.* Ruth swallowed and relaxed in Whitney's arms. It took everything out of her to drink, it seemed.

Shuffling at the door made Whitney peer over her shoulder. "Hi, Dad."

"Any improvement?" His shoulders were slumped. Neither one of them had slept in more than a day.

"Not much. But I did get her to drink a little water."

"That's good." A chair scraped across the floor, and he sat down next to her. "Bethany and Eli are weak, but they're sitting up and teasing back and forth."

"What a relief. I'm glad you put them in your room with each other. Laughter truly is the best medicine." The prodding in her heart to talk to her father wouldn't go away. "Thank you for your help."

"You're welcome. I wish I could do more."

The tense set of his jaw, the weary lines on his face . . . it showed that the man before her wasn't anything like the man who'd walked away from his family all those years ago. This man was caring. Giving. Sacrificial.

"She has so much yet to do . . . so much love to give. I've been praying God would heal her. Not just of this disease, but of her broken heart." Dad's voice cracked as he reached forward to take his sister-in-law's hand. "I would trade places with her in an instant if I thought I could give my life for hers. I owe her so much."

How should she respond? She understood the feelings he expressed, the ache in her father's voice. Wouldn't she be willing to give her life for one of her sisters? It all made sense. "Keep praying for her, Dad."

He turned to look at her, a sheen of tears in his eyes.

"You really are a different man now." The last vestiges of ice she'd held around her heart for her dad shattered into little pieces. "I'm so sorry."

He opened his arms to her and welcomed her into them.

"Please forgive me for the hateful words I've said to you or thought about you. I had no right to hold the past against you." She sobbed against his chest.

"Oh, daughter. I forgave you long ago. I hope you can forgive me as well."

"I do, Dad. I'm so sorry it took my stubborn heart so long."

"I love you, Whitney. Always have. Always will. I'm sure I'll fail you again, because the only perfect Father is the one above, but I hope you'll continue to forgive and love me through it."

She nodded against him. Finally feeling free of the chains that had kept her bound for so long. "I love you too, Dad."

He held her for several minutes and stroked her hair. Just like he had done when she was a little girl. She looked to the ceiling. *God, please tell Mama we're a family again.*

If only Maddy and Havyn were with them right now. But

Maddy was fighting a horrible cough, along with her husband, and Havyn was still quarantined from the rest of them.

Whitney took a deep breath. "You know, I just thought of something. As soon as the storm is past and one of us can make it to town, I think I need to send a telegram and offer to pay for Ruth's children and mother to come up on the first boat. That way, we can tell Ruth about it and try to give her a reason to fight."

"That's a great idea." Dad teared up again. "Thank you for offering."

Footsteps sounded in the hallway. Rapid. Hurried. The quiet of the moment shattered, and she pulled away from Dad as her heart raced. *Please, God. Not more bad news.* Whitney turned to the door and saw John.

"Whit, we've got a problem."

"What is it?" She got to her feet and swiped at her face.

"The team of dogs that Peter took to town returned with the sled. But there's no sign of Peter."

TWENTY-FOUR

All night Whitney prayed. No matter how much she begged God for sleep, it didn't come. The thought of Peter out lost in the snow tore her heart in two. He had to be all right. He had to be.

What would she do without him?

They hadn't had a courtship or romance. They'd had a friendship. A tumultuous one at that, because he didn't mince words with her.

Something she appreciated more each moment as she rubbed her gritty eyes. God knew exactly what she needed in a . . . *friend*. It was all too clear to her now that she cared deeply about him. Couldn't bear the thought of losing him.

As soon as John told her the news, more bad news followed. Most of the workers had come down with fevers, leaving John to keep the farm running on his own. Though they'd taken precautions, the sickness found them anyway.

The storm was still blowing, which meant no relief could come either. From the villages or from town.

If her family wasn't sick, she would be out there looking for Peter right now. Storm or no storm.

Soft footfalls sounded behind her.

"How are you holding up?" Dad's voice sounded as full of grit as her eyes felt.

For the first time since she was a child, she needed—and *wanted*—comfort from her father. "I'm so worried. What if he didn't make it to shelter?"

He sat down beside her and patted her knee. "The only thing we can do is pray and give this over to God. Our hands are tied, Whit. I wish I could do something to fix this, but I can't. Neither can you. It's in times like these that I have to remind myself over and over that God is in control. He doesn't need my help. But we need His."

He was right. They had to pray and encourage everyone to fight the sickness.

At least Bethany and Eli had shown more improvement last night. It had lifted her spirits when she thought for sure she would spiral down after the news of Peter.

Lord, we need Your help.

"Why don't we pray together?"

Deep calm washed over her. She hadn't prayed with just her dad since she was a little girl. "I'd love that."

Coughing and moans filled the air in the Roadhouse. Thankfully, Mr. Norris had the foresight to open his establishment to the sick as soon as he'd heard the hospital was full and the other doctors were sick.

Peter walked through the makeshift aisles between pallets on the floor. How long had it been since he'd left Whitney at the farm?

His mind went over the past few days, and they blurred together.

"You look like you need some sleep." Norris brought him a cup of coffee.

"I'll sleep when it's over." Not only was the sickness raging, but so was the storm.

The owner of the Roadhouse shook his head. "Nope. That's not gonna work for me." He gripped Peter's shoulders and steered him toward the back. "I set up a cot for you. Now give me a list of what to do and I'll come get ya if I need ya."

He would argue, but he was the one who'd preached to the man—just yesterday, was it?—about the importance of sleep so they could keep going and care for the patients. So Peter rattled off directions for the man and allowed himself to be led to a little room.

"It's not much, but it will give you some time to yourself." Norris patted the cot and tossed a pillow and blanket onto it. "At least it's better than the floor, where I found you last time."

Which was better than what the poor men crammed into the Roadhouse had. The hospital was equally overrun. He'd tried to get over and visit a couple times a day, but he and the nurses caring for the sick were relying on prayer—and waiting for the sickness to run its course.

God . . . You are the Great Physician. Please heal our town, and please stop this storm. We need help.

Bolting upright, Peter blinked. What had woken him? How long had he been asleep?

The last thing he remembered, he'd been praying for God to tame the storm and to heal their town. A tiny window in the room gave Peter a glimpse outside. Still daylight. But which day was it?

He got up and went to the window.

Plump snowflakes floated down in a gentle curtain. Nothing like the blizzard that had raged for days. He looked at his watch. It had only been half an hour. No wonder his body was begging for more sleep. But God had given him the gift of the storm passing. Now he could send word to the farm.

"Everything all right?" Norris spoke from the doorway. "I heard a noise and came to check on you."

"I had been praying for the storm to clear and woke up to see that it had." He rubbed a hand down his face. Exhaustion and relief fought to be foremost in his mind. "I need to get word to Miss Powell that I'm all right." Norris was the one who'd found him staggering into town in the storm.

The man obviously understood. "I'll send someone as soon as I can. But you look like you could fall over any second. Get back to sleep, Doc. I'll take care of letting her know."

"Thank you." In that moment, weariness overtook him. He lay down on the cot and tucked the pillow up under his head. The sound of a door closing registered in his mind, but his eyes were already shut. His thoughts drifted back to Whitney. If he hadn't been so busy with the sick, he'd be beside himself with concern for her dogs. When he fell off the sled in the storm and they took off back toward the farm, he'd prayed they would make it home safely. It had been a wonder that he even made it to town on foot.

Whitney.

She was sure to be concerned. Hopefully she wasn't sick. *Lord, please heal that family.* Then there was the news about Martin . . . but how could he tell them at the farm? With Daniel sick, it was best to keep the news to himself for now. Otherwise, he'd try to get into town and argue with Judas.

Faces of the different men inside the Roadhouse—men whose names Peter didn't know—flashed through his mind, and he prayed for each one, until he no longer had the strength to fight the sleep that overtook him.

———

The days had blended together. How long had it been since her dogs returned without Peter? There'd been no word from him, and she'd prayed with every ounce of her being that he'd made it to town. Dad prayed with her each chance he had.

This new relationship with her father sure did seem like a miracle to her. Something she couldn't have ever dreamed would happen. Especially with how she talked to him just a few weeks ago. But God was the God of miracles and second chances. She shouldn't be surprised. But she was. Each moment.

"Whit!" Eli came into the kitchen, where she was stirring a pot of soup. It was so good to see the boy up and on his feet, but he definitely needed fattening up after days of the fever. "Yutu just came in to help John. He said that he came from town first and had a message from Mr. Norris that Dr. Cameron made it in safe, and he was the only doc that wasn't sick."

"Really?" Her breath left her in a great whoosh, and her legs felt like they wouldn't hold her any longer. She grabbed a towel and wiped her hands on it. He'd made it to town? She closed her eyes and went to the nearest chair. *Thank You, God.*

"Yep." Her younger brother took a slice of bread. "Can I eat now? I'm hungry."

They laughed together, and she put a hand to her heart. "Of course. Eat as much as you want."

"Come on, sis. Eat with me." He pulled her to her feet.

Wrapping her arms around him in a great big hug, she smiled over the top of his head. "I'd love to."

Peter was all right! She couldn't wait to see him for herself.

And find out what happened. What sent the dogs running home without their driver? It didn't make sense. But she was so thankful. For days, she'd had such worried thoughts. What if he'd taken ill and . . . died?

She banished the negative thoughts. It was time to rejoice and be glad.

Today was a new day.

As she delivered soup to everyone, her heart soared. Peter was alive! And little by little, the household was coming back to a state of normalcy. Maddy and Bethany were on the mend too.

Poor John. The man must be running ragged trying to keep the farm going. The adults who contracted measles seemed to have it the worst, and most of them ended up with the respiratory sickness too.

Whatever this was, it was no wonder it killed so many people back in 1900.

Peter had taught them well, though. He'd taken precautionary measures and shown them exactly which tea and poultices would help.

Thank You, God, for Peter.

Though Ruth was still sick, she hadn't gotten worse, which Whitney counted as a blessing. The woman simply didn't seem to have the will to go on. And that broke her heart. She'd told her friend several times that she was sending a telegram to her family. But no response.

She entered the sickroom with a tray of soup and bread. Not that she expected Ruth would eat much of it. Whitney had managed to spoon only a few scant bites into the woman's mouth the past few days. But she was determined to try. Again.

She took hold of Ruth's hand.

Lord, how can we reach her?

How many times had she poured out her heart to the Lord the past few days? It seemed like a constant conversation was taking place with her heavenly Father. Something she didn't want to give up once this trial was over. She'd promised herself she would keep her focus on the Lord, but that was harder to put into practice than simply saying it.

"How is she doing?" Maddy's soft voice made Whitney lift her head.

"Her pulse is better. No fever. But she doesn't seem to want to wake up." Whitney patted Ruth's hand. "I don't know what else to do."

"Havyn has an idea." John entered the room and gave each of them a hug. He walked over to the window and opened it a few inches.

Havyn waved from outside, her smile wide, a beautiful glow about her.

Cold air swept through the room. Cleansing. Fresh. "She suggested you sing to Ruth." John gripped both of their shoulders.

From outside, Havyn started:

> When peace, like a river, attendeth my way,
> When sorrows like sea billows roll;
> Whatever my lot, Thou hast taught me to say,
> It is well, it is well with my soul.

Whitney and Maddy looked at each other and joined in on the refrain.

It is well, it is well
With my soul, with my soul
It is well, it is well with my soul.

The next few verses they sang together, in perfect harmony. Just like at the Roadhouse. Chill bumps raced up and down her arms. This was so right. So perfect. The yearning to fill her life with music again flowed through Whitney. She stood up and wrapped an arm around Maddy.

By the time they reached the final verse, she had tears streaming down her cheeks.

And Lord, haste the day when the faith shall be
  sight,
The clouds be rolled back as a scroll;
The trump shall resound, and the Lord shall
  descend,
Even so, it is well with my soul.

They sang the chorus twice at the end, and then Whitney looked at Havyn. "I love you, sis."

"Love you, too! Both of you!" She blew a kiss and walked away from the window.

"Whit, look!" Maddy squeezed her.

When she looked down, Ruth's eyes were open.

"Ruth!" She scrambled to her friend's side. "You're awake." She hugged her and gave her a huge smile.

"I am." Her hoarse whisper was one of the most beautiful things Whitney had ever heard. "I thought I heard angels singing."

"It was just us. We've been worried . . . I'm so glad you woke up."

Ruth nodded. "I was in a battle, that's for certain." Her voice was barely audible. "Wasn't sure I would win, but here I am." A long swallow was followed by a deep breath. "Did you say my children were coming, or did I dream that?"

Whitney's heart overflowed, and she grabbed Ruth's hands. "We're sending a telegram today."

Ruth closed her eyes, and a single tear slipped down her cheek. "My babies . . . I didn't think I'd ever see them again. Thank you. From the bottom of my heart."

Maddy went over and closed the window and then put her hands on her hips. "Whit, I'm not very strong yet, but I think it's time you headed into town to check on the good doctor."

TWENTY-FIVE

Calling to her dogs to go faster, Whitney leaned forward on the runners, pushing off with one leg to help them get momentum. The sooner she could get to town, the sooner she could see Peter.

And she *would* see Peter. When she closed her eyes, she could see him. Bent over one of his patients. Giving that ever-understanding smile and encouragement.

The trek into town had never seemed so long. The storm had dumped several more feet of snow, and the dogs struggled in some of the areas where it drifted and swirled. "You can do it. Let's go!" Her voice rang out across the wide-open expanse.

She gazed out around her. This was home. To think that a few months ago, she'd thought of leaving with Maddy and that wild man with his follies and frolics. All to escape the horrible rumors a bad man had spread.

She swallowed against the tears that formed a lump in her throat. Just this morning, she'd found a note from Mama shoved in her Bible at the book of 1 Peter. It had been too long since Whitney had picked her Bible up and read it. Their mother had been great at leaving them notes here and there. And there'd been no better time for Whitney to read 1 Peter than this morning.

In her loopy script, Mama wrote about the encouragement she'd gained from reading the epistle that focused on joy through suffering. How her mom must have suffered the last few months. Struggling with asthma and not wanting to worry anyone . . . then succumbing to whooping cough. Yet, she'd always been full of joy for them.

Always.

Whitney had decided this morning to try to memorize a few verses Mama had underlined. No time like the present to put it into practice. She lifted her voice to the sky. "'Wherein ye greatly rejoice, though now for a season, if need be, ye are in heaviness through manifold temptations: that the trial of your faith, being much more precious than of gold that perisheth, though it be tried with fire, might be found unto praise and honour and glory at the appearing of Jesus Christ: Whom having not seen, ye love; in whom, though now ye see him not, yet believing, ye rejoice with joy unspeakable and full of glory . . .'"

That was what she could remember at the moment, but it was enough. Actually, it was exactly what she needed. Regret poured through her that she hadn't held fast like she should have. That she hadn't rejoiced with joy unspeakable . . . but Christ didn't expect her to be perfect. He wanted her to come to Him with her burdens—all the hardships, all the filth and junk that weighed her down—and lay it at His feet.

Forgiveness was a beautiful thing. She was a long way from where she needed to be spiritually, but she'd made the start back in the right direction. Maybe God would let Mama know that all her hard work, everything that she'd poured into her girls, was not in vain.

Thank You, God for giving her to us.

The dogs yipped as they reached the outskirts of town. "Whoa." She slowed the team to a stop. Where to? The hospital? Peter's office?

The streets of the town were much quieter than usual. Was it the storm or the sickness?

Mr. Norris had sent word to them about Peter, so maybe she should head to the Roadhouse. She turned the dogs toward the beloved building, keeping their pace slow as they meandered through the streets.

A sign on the door of the Roadhouse said it was a hospital.

"Haw, haw!" She turned her team around and then parked them in front of the Roadhouse. After she set the hook, she ran up the steps and into the familiar building.

But there was nothing familiar about it.

Pallets lined the floor. Pallets filled with men. Many resting. Some propped up. Several coughing.

She wove through the maze and searched the faces. So many she knew from the times they'd played and sung on the very stage in front of them.

What a nightmare. So many sick!

For the next several minutes she walked among the men and yearned to pray over each one of them. God knew. He knew her heart. Knew each of the men lying there.

She ached to find Peter, but she hadn't seen him anywhere. Maybe he was at the hospital?

"Miss Powell." Mr. Norris's voice stopped her, and she turned around. "What are you doing here? Is your family well?"

"We are, thank you. I came looking for Dr. Cameron."

She swallowed past the dry lump in her throat. "Have you seen him?"

"He's in the back resting. Poor man hasn't slept or eaten much in days." Mr. Norris held out an arm. "I'll take you to him."

Her heart had almost stopped its pace when Mr. Norris said Peter was there. Then she let out a long breath she hadn't realized she'd been holding. At this point, a nod would have to suffice, because she couldn't speak.

She wanted to run but walked behind the owner to the back.

Norris tapped on the door and then opened it an inch. "Dr. Cameron, I've got someone here who wants to see you."

The groggy baritone of Peter's voice made her heart sing. Without thinking another thought, she pushed through the door.

"*Peter!*"

———

At the sound of Whitney's voice, Peter bolted upright on the cot. Oh, how he'd longed to hear that the last few days.

He'd barely made it to his feet when she barreled into him and wrapped her arms tightly around his waist.

Mr. Norris chuckled from the doorway. "I'll leave you two to catch up."

Peter, still dazed from sleep and by the woman who'd dashed into his arms, nodded at the man and wrapped his arms around Whitney.

The tension in his shoulders eased as he allowed himself to relish the moment. They fit together perfectly. Her red curls under his chin.

"It's good to see you." His voice was gravelly, and he cleared his throat.

She laughed against his chest. "I'm so glad you're alive. When the dogs returned without you, I thought the worst. But with everyone so sick and the storm . . . there wasn't anything I could do but pray for you."

He hugged her a bit tighter. "That's the very best thing you could have done."

"I know. But I still worried. Even though I tried not to."

"I'm glad to hear the dogs made it back all right. I was pretty concerned about them."

In that moment, he wanted to hold her forever. Not exactly an appropriate thought as they stood in a secluded room by themselves. With reluctance, he released her.

Her head dipped, and she clasped her hands in front of her. "Peter . . . there's something I need to tell you."

A catch in her voice made his heart pick up pace. "The dogs *are* all right . . . aren't they?" If he had been responsible for any of them getting injured, he'd never forgive himself.

"They're fine." She smiled. "It warms my heart that you care for them the way you do. But if I'm going to get this next part out, I need you to listen."

His eyebrows raised. "Certainly." There was nowhere to sit except the cot, and that didn't seem appropriate to offer to her, so he stood there and slid his hands into his pockets to keep from fidgeting.

"You know that Judas Reynolds asked to court me. And I dined with him on multiple occasions . . ." She began to pace.

Peter braced himself. Surely she wasn't about to say that she had agreed to marry the man! *Please, God, no.* As much as he had tried to deny it, he had fallen in love with Whitney.

"It became clear to me that it was a mistake."

He let his breath out.

"Judas is not the one for me. I've come to care for someone else." She stopped her movement and stood barely a foot in front of him.

Their eyes connected.

"Peter . . . it's you. I know we are in the middle of an epidemic—a crisis for the town—so I don't want you to think that I have any high expectations. But . . . I had to tell you the truth."

For several seconds, he stared into her eyes. The love he saw there made him want to scoop her up in his arms and go find the pastor. He'd never thought he could deserve another chance at love.

But he shouldn't get ahead of himself. He hadn't even proposed yet. Gracious, they hadn't even courted. "Whitney, I—"

"Dr. Cameron." The young boy who helped Mr. Norris sweep the floors of the Roadhouse burst into the room, out of breath and waving at Peter. "It's Mr. Beaufort. Granny sent for you."

He closed his eyes and winced. "Tell her I'll be right there."

"I'm coming with you." Whitney nodded at him.

"All right. Promise me we'll finish this conversation later?"

"Promise."

As he grabbed his bag and coat, he paused. "But I'm afraid I have some bad news to share about Martin."

"Is he dying?" She followed him out the door.

"He might be . . . yes. But there's something else." Once they were outside of the Roadhouse and out in the brisk air, he offered her his arm. "If I'm walking too fast let me know."

"Of course. Just tell me what's going on with Martin."

"The day I went back into town for supplies? I found that Martin was sick. But before that, I found someone else running the store. Judas *took* it, Whitney. Apparently, Martin owed him a good deal of money and when he couldn't pay, Judas took the store as payment."

She'd never been so furious in her whole life. "I'll meet you at Granny's in a few minutes. There's something I need to do."

"Whitney—"

Holding up a hand, she shook her head at Peter. "No. Don't try and stop me. This is something I have to do. Please. Go take care of Martin."

She marched off down the street, letting every bit of anger within her boil to the surface. Was this how Judas reacted to her turning him down?

Storming into the Shipping and Freight offices, she waltzed right past the secretary and flung open Judas's office door. "You took Martin's store? How *could* you?"

He sat behind his desk, looking entirely too content. "Why, Whitney, what a lovely surprise." He stood. "Please . . . have a seat."

Her hands fisted at her sides. "I don't want to have a seat, Judas. I want to know why you took the mercantile from Martin!"

His hands came up, and he moved toward her. "It was just business. Calm down and we'll talk about it."

"No." She squinted at him. "I will *not* calm down."

"He owed me a great deal of money. And asked for extension after extension. Ultimately, he simply couldn't make the payments." He went behind his desk and opened a drawer, then pulled out some papers. "See for yourself."

"I don't care what your papers say. How could you? Especially now when there's an epidemic? Did you know that he's sick? *Really* sick?" That was when she saw it. Triumph. In his eyes. How had he fooled them all?

"It couldn't be helped, Whitney. You must understand that I can't allow for someone to go without paying for this length of time. Everyone else in town who owes me money would then think they could do the same as well, and then where would my business be? How would I get shipments in if I couldn't pay? The town relies on me."

His request for pity wouldn't work. It was all fake. His seemingly heartfelt expression. The overly sincere tone of his voice. Awful man—he was playing a part! Right there, in front of her. After all these years, it didn't make sense. "So you took the store?"

"I had to. Surely, you must understand." He came around the desk and set the papers down. "Please, read them and see. Martin signed them himself."

She snatched the papers up and perused them.

"You know . . ." Judas stepped closer to her.

The hair on the back of her neck stood up.

"There is a way I could give the mercantile back to Martin, and it wouldn't damage my reputation in town. That is . . . if you agreed to marry me, then Martin would essentially be family. I'm sure we could work out some sort of deal."

A shiver went up her spine, and she tossed the papers to the floor. "Some sort of *deal*?" That's how he saw her? A bargaining chip? To what end? She stared at the man she'd known for half her life. Or had she?

Had any of them really known him? Rage built inside her

like a tidal wave. Granddad . . . oh, if he'd known . . . he'd have sent Judas to jail.

"Of course. I would do anything for you." He reached for her hand.

She moved it away. Searching his eyes, she couldn't find anything of depth. It was like Judas hid behind a veil . . . like he wasn't even there. Instead of emotion, what she saw was . . .

Darkness.

Father, protect me. She stepped back and shook her head. "You're a fine actor, but no, Judas. I will not marry you. Not ever. Not for any reason. And it sickens me to think that you have done this to more people than Martin."

With one swift step, he grabbed her arm.

Smack! Her other hand stung from the contact with his cheek. "Let. Me. Go." She ground out the words through her clenched jaw.

He stepped back and held his hands up. "Whitney, please. You must know how much I care about you." The tone of his voice made her want to scream. How had they all been blinded by him?

"No. I don't believe you do. Especially not after this." She fled the room as fast as her feet could carry her.

When the door slammed shut, Judas slapped his palm down on his desk and then threw everything on it to the floor.

His secretary came through the door. "Mr. Reynolds, did you need me?"

With a deep breath, he straightened and adjusted his waistcoat. "Yes . . . yes, I do. Please send a message to Judge Beck informing him that I need to see him immediately."

"Yes, sir."

The door closed again, and he sat in his chair. So it had come to this. He knew, when he set his sights on Miss Whitney Powell, what she was made of. How stubborn she was. How loyal. How . . .

Naive.

So this came as no surprise. Not really.

His reasoning extinguished his anger. After all, in the end, he would have what he wanted. He always did.

Several minutes later, his secretary came through the door and announced the judge.

"Good to see you, Judge Beck." Judas beamed at him.

"I came as soon as I received your message." The man lifted his chin and sat in a chair. "What can I do for you? Have you reconsidered one of my proposals?" The smarmy man lifted his eyebrows.

"No. But you *are* going to help me, and I promise you, it will be profitable for you."

"I'm listening."

"You are going to meet me out at the Bundrant farm this afternoon. And you will back up everything I say."

"Of course. Shouldn't I just accompany you?"

"No. I'm hoping to stay a good deal longer."

"Oh." The judge straightened his cuffs. "And what will you give me in return?"

"Five thousand dollars."

Beck tilted his head and smirked. "What time shall I meet you there?"

TWENTY-SIX

I was so mad at him, I could have spit on him." Whitney leaned up against the sink in the kitchen and faced her sisters.

Madysen's eyes were wide. "Maybe you misunderstood . . . that could be a possibility, right? I mean . . . we've known Judas forever."

But Havyn shook her head. "I haven't wanted to think ill of him, but John and I have talked a good deal about stories we've heard the past few months. We thought it amounted to rumors, that people wanted to speak ill of Mr. Reynolds because he was so rich. I certainly would have never thought a man could pull the wool over Granddad's eyes, but I'm beginning to think that Judas did. And the whole town's eyes as well."

That lying snake. Her hands squeezed into fists at her sides. "What are we going to do about this? I mean, we can't allow for the mercantile to be taken away from Martin . . . can we? Judas can't get away with this. He can't."

At the bitterness in her own voice, Whitney swallowed hard. She fought against the anger building in her chest. *God, what do we do?* She steadied herself and rubbed her eyes. "You should have seen him. Granny was beside herself because Martin has lost the will to live. I left Peter with him, but I don't know if I did any good."

"Sounds like Judas taking over the mercantile has already been done." Their pregnant sister winced. "I hate to say it, but what *can* we do?"

"We could offer to pay off the debt. Maybe all Judas wants is the money." Even as the words left Whitney's mouth, she knew it wouldn't work. Not after his shady offer to help Martin *if* she agreed to marry him. For some reason, Judas was using *her* as a pawn . . . but to what end?

The outside door shut, and heavy footsteps approached. John peeked into the kitchen. "Just wanted to let you ladies know that Reynolds and Judge Beck rode up. I need to wash up before I can see them."

"Rode?"

"Yep. They both came out on horses. Now I better go change before the whole kitchen smells like manure." John leaned in and kissed his wife.

Knock, knock, knock.

With each thud, Whitney wanted to throttle someone. *Lord, get a hold of my temper. Please.*

"I'll go let them in." Maddy pasted on a smile. "Whit . . . no spitting. Promise?"

"I make no guarantees." At least her sister had broken the tension . . . it helped to laugh, even if it was halfhearted.

"I'll make some tea real quick and be out to join you in a jiffy." Havyn scooted toward the stove.

"All right." With a deep breath, Whitney squared her shoulders and sent another prayer for control to heaven and then walked toward the parlor.

Maddy offered the men seats and asked them about the weather.

"Good afternoon, gentlemen. To what do we owe this pleasure?" If Judas could be an actor, then so could she.

"I'm afraid I'm the bearer of some bad news." Judas appeared to be broken over the matter, but Whitney now knew better. It was all an act.

"Go on." Whitney took her seat.

"It seems another party has come forward with a deed for your land and is claiming ownership."

What did he say? "You mean . . . *this* land?" She pointed to the floor.

Maddy surged to her feet. "Excuse me for a moment." She came by Whitney and whispered into her ear. "I'm going to get the men."

She gave a slight nod and narrowed her eyes at Judas. "You can't be serious. Our grandfather purchased this land more than a decade ago."

"Sadly, I am quite serious." Judas pulled a piece of paper out of his pocket and laid it on the table in front of the settee. "Here's the deed, which I asked Judge Beck to investigate." He turned to the judge.

"It's legitimate." The man's mustache twitched as he nodded.

She took a long glance at each of the men before her, then reached for the deed and read it. It looked like any other deed. Clearly, the man had paid someone off. Well, he wasn't going to get away with it. She had no qualms confronting the man for his deceit all these years. "We have the deed for this land, so this must be a forgery. It's fake." Just like the men before her. She handed it back.

Judas came out of his chair, his face red, his eyes wild. "Don't you see the situation here? You could lose your farm."

A wave of calm flowed through her. "Our fate is in God's

hands, and I don't believe He'd let us lose the farm or be swindled by a tyrant." She couldn't help throwing in the last part. *God, please help me keep my temper in check. But You know I want to throttle him.*

"Lose the farm?" John's voice came from the doorway, then he strode over. "What is going on?"

"It seems Mr. Reynolds and the judge have come to inform us of a deed that has *mysteriously* come forward, showing that someone else owns our land." Whitney couldn't help the sarcasm. But at least she wasn't losing her temper.

"Oh? I'd like to see this so-called deed." John held out his hand.

The paper was handed to him, and he studied it. "This must be a fake. I've seen the real deed."

"It's not a fake." Judas's face became a deeper shade of crimson as he lifted his chin. "The man staked a claim, even had a small shed he'd built on the property and lived in. That makes it a homestead with improvements."

Ha! Caught in his own lies. "There was no shed on the property here. Nor was there any evidence that anyone had *ever* lived on this land." She knew the facts.

"It doesn't matter." Judas lifted his chin, his eyes mere slits. "The records show that there was."

"I'd like to see those records." John's voice was calm but firm.

Thank God for her brother-in-law. "Yes, please let us see those records." For some reason, she smiled.

"I'm losing my patience." The ever-proper Mr. Reynolds looked as if he might explode at any moment. He pointed his hat in the direction of the judge, who still sat in his chair watching the discussion. "I interrupted Judge Beck's very busy schedule and asked him to come out here so that you could understand the seriousness of the situation. Now I'm on my way back into town to see if I can purchase this deed from the man and help you save the farm. The least you could do is offer up your appreciation to me for bringing the matter to your attention."

John stepped forward and put a hand on Judas's shoulder. "While we appreciate you coming out, you still haven't shown us any proof that the deed you're holding hasn't been forged."

Judas stepped out of John's grasp and pointed to his partner in crime. "You missed the part where the judge verified it's legitimate."

"Oh?" John turned toward Mr. Beck. "Is that so?"

Beck looked back and forth, but something in his eyes was squirrelly. "Um . . . yes."

Whitney almost laughed at his meek tone.

"I see. Well, in that case, we will come into town and investigate this ourselves. If anyone is going to buy the deed to the land—it will be us. *If* your claims are found to be true."

She and her sisters would need to grab Granddad's letter immediately and find where he'd stashed everything. If it took every penny they had to buy the farm to make it legitimate, they would. She was about to say as much when John raised a hand. She clamped her mouth shut.

"Are they true, Judge?"

The man hemmed and hawed and cleared his throat. "I wouldn't be here if they weren't."

Judas took a step even closer until he was nearly toe-to-toe with John. "Oh, they are true. And you're going to need my help."

John didn't flinch. In fact . . . he smiled.

Judas spun and looked to her. "Miss Powell, if you would accompany me outside, there is something I need to discuss with you."

"I don't think that's a good idea." John crossed his arms over his chest.

Whitney placed a hand on her brother-in-law's arm. "It's fine." No, it wasn't, but she had to do something to get Reynolds away from the farm.

"I'd best head back to town. I have several things to attend to." Judge Beck stood and walked toward the door, looking over his shoulder as if afraid they'd set the dogs on him.

Which wasn't a bad idea . . .

John touched her elbow. "Do you need me?"

Whitney looked to Judas, whose face held a smile that sent chills down her arms. "No. I can handle this."

"All right, but I can't say that I like it." John released her, and she led Judas to the door. "I'll be right here." The words he pointed to Judas. The glares between the two men could start a war.

Once outside, Judas watched the judge ride away and then turned to her. He inched closer to her, and his voice was low. "It would be in your best interest to cooperate, Whitney. Things could get ugly. For your whole family. You can't risk losing the farm and you know it."

With her arms tight across her chest, she shook her head at him. How had they ever thought this man honorable? "God has this under control. We will be fine. Granddad would never have purchased this property if there was another claim to it, and you know it."

In an instant, he grabbed her arms. "I'm not going to play any more games. You're going to marry me, and you're going to do so *immediately*. If you don't, then I'll see that you and your family are left with nothing. I'll destroy Daniel's family and that goody-goody doctor as well."

The venom is his voice sounded like it sprang from the depths of hell.

"Let go of me, Judas."

When her voice cracked, he smiled. "Good. It's about time you realized you need to be afraid of me." He pulled her even closer. "Now, let's get this straight. You will meet me tomorrow at noon at my office. Ready and willing to marry me. If you don't . . . well, people you care about will die. Plain and simple." He put his face up to hers until their noses touched. "I'm going to enjoy this. And so are you."

He released her and slapped his hat on his head. He got on his horse and looked down at her with a sneer.

"Tomorrow. At noon."

Madysen had a bad feeling in her stomach. Even though Whit had said she could handle Judas alone, it didn't sit right with her. So she headed toward the door.

It opened.

Whitney stood there. Her face ashen.

"What happened?"

"I need to sit down." Her older sister put a hand to her stomach.

Madysen led her back into the parlor where John, Havyn, and now Daniel stood waiting.

Once Whit was in the chair, she put her face into her hands. Then she looked up, tears brimming. "It's so much worse than I expected. I can't believe I allowed this to happen!"

"What?" Everyone asked at once.

Maddy gripped Daniel's hand. He was still so weak—would he be able to handle this? But she desperately needed him with her.

Havyn pulled a chair closer to their sister. John stood right behind her.

"The deed . . . all of this that he just told us? It's to get me to marry him." She stood up. "I'm guessing he wants Granddad's farm." Her eyes widened. "I bet he took the mercantile from Martin as part of the plan too. The man is evil. Pure evil. How did we not see this?" She put a hand to her forehead.

"The mercantile?" Daniel looked down at Madysen and squeezed her hand. "What's going on?"

As Whit told them everything—from Peter going into town to get supplies and discovering the mercantile run by someone else, to Martin and Granny being sick, to her going to Judas's office to confront him, to his threat outside just now—it made more sense. The man had lost his mind, or so it seemed. Who would act this way? Do these horrible things?

But the dread built in Madysen's gut. "What are we going to do?"

Everyone began to talk at once.

Then someone whistled. They turned toward the sound. Dad stood there, his hands on his hips. He stepped toward them, a deep furrow in his brow. "Let me get this straight. Judas Reynolds is trying to swindle my family?"

If steam could come out of a man's ears, Madysen imagined she would see it at that very moment. "Dad . . . we're all upset. But we've got to keep our heads about us. No one needs to go off and lose their tempers." She grimaced at her sisters. "Even though we all would be prone to do just that."

"Fine. I won't lose my temper. But I'm going to pay him a visit."

Whitney reached their father first and grabbed onto him. "Oh no, you're not."

And the discussion started up again.

"Before we do anything, we'd best get on our knees and pray about it." Daniel's voice cut through the chatter. "It's not just our livelihood on the line here."

Madysen looked up at her wonderful husband. *Thank You, Father for this man You've given me.* "I agree."

"And then," her husband continued, "I need to go visit my dad and Granny. You can discuss what we need to do as a family, but my father is sick and he's lost the business he loved."

"Of course. As much as I want to barrel into town and take matters into my own hands, I know that's not right. Thank you for being a voice of reason." John drew them into a circle. "Let's pray right now. And like Whitney said to Judas earlier, we know that God has got this under control. We have to wade through the muck and mire together and keep our eyes on Him. He will deal with Judas Reynolds."

"Let's join hands." John took his wife's hand on one side and Whit's on the other.

After a good hour of prayer together, Madysen was more refreshed than she had been in a long time. Tears had flowed down her cheeks, and she'd heard sniffles from others as well.

"We really should do this more often," she said after Daniel's "amen." He'd had to sit after only a few minutes, but his voice had grown stronger as they prayed.

"Agreed." Havyn smiled and hugged her husband. She turned to their older sister. "You gonna be all right, Whit?"

"I'm fine. I'm mad, but I'm fine." She pulled her hankie out of her pocket.

Daniel wrapped an arm around Madysen's waist, and it made everything right with the world. Oh, how she adored this man.

He gave her a squeeze. "Are you ready to head to town? I'm still not very strong, though, so I might need you to drive the sleigh."

"I am. And I'll help however you need. Just let me grab the basket of goodies we've put together for Granny and your dad." Madysen ran to the kitchen. Her poor husband. The sickness—whatever it was—had taken its toll on him. In fact, today was the first day she'd seen him stand for longer than five minutes. And he'd dressed and shaved.

She heated a few extra bricks and gathered up some more things to bring to Granny. Peter said that she was doing better, but Martin was still quite sick. If there was any way to help ease the load on the older woman so she could tend to her son, Maddy wanted to do it.

Once they were settled into the sleigh, Daniel already looked worn out.

She took the reins. "Why don't you rest while I drive us into town. That way, you'll save energy for your visit with Dad and Granny."

He nodded and leaned his head back as she urged the horses into motion. Within minutes, his head rested on her shoulder. But she didn't mind. Being married to this man had brought her more joy than she could have ever imagined. Now if only Whit could find that same joy.

She'd seen the glances between her older sister and the good doctor. They'd been friends for many months now, but it wasn't until Peter's last visit that Madysen had hoped to dream of a future between the two of them. Peter carried a burden from the past. Whit had told them about the loss of his wife and child. And their sister carried her own burdens. But didn't they all?

Every single person on the planet had flaws and problems. But by God's grace, they could make it through to glorious freedom in Christ.

She hated to be nosy . . . or a matchmaker for her sister, but it was time for Whit to have the same happiness.

She deserved to love.

And to be loved.

No one defied him.

The terror on Whitney's face as he left made the corners of his mouth lift. She knew who was in control, and he would relish making her pay every day for the rest of her life for *ever* rejecting him.

Everything he wanted was about to be his.

His horse's hooves pounded through the snow as Judas pushed his mount harder and faster.

Sweat beaded on his upper lip. Olivia's face appeared before him. He swiped the apparition away with his hand, but it returned. Eyes shimmering with tears.

And then he heard her voice.

"God has made it clear to me, Judas, that we are not supposed to marry. I love you. I'm sure I will always love you . . . but you've become . . . obsessed. I thought you would become a preacher like your father, but all you talk about is money and power. Do you even believe in God and His Word?"

No amount of persuasion had changed her mind. She'd rejected him. Humiliated him. Just like God.

He'd vowed that day that no one would *ever* do that to him again. No one.

The memory made him sick to his stomach. "It doesn't matter. She was a worthless fool." As he said the words, he went cold. Had the blood drained from his face? What was happening?

He leaned closer to the horse's head, spurring the animal again.

He didn't need God. Didn't need Olivia. Didn't need Whitney. Didn't need *anyone*. He was a self-made man. In control—

His arms went numb. His hands could no longer hold the reins. His knees grew so weak, he couldn't grip the saddle. His legs went limp, and his feet slid from the stirrups—

He was falling.

He slammed into the snow on the ground and lay there. The world tilted.

Judas.

Who said that? He scanned the horizon. Tried to shake the fogginess from his mind.

Judas. I didn't reject you. I love you. I'm calling you to repentance. I've been waiting for you to turn your heart to Me.

The voice in his head was clear and strong.

"Shut up!" He struggled to a sitting position, tried to ball his fists, but nothing happened. So he spit into the snow. "I don't need You."

My child . . . you do.

"No!" He shouted to the air around him. "I don't need You in this life *or* the next!"

As soon as the words were out, pain shot through his chest and down his arm.

I love you, Judas. Turn to me. Redemption is yours.

No. He wouldn't do it. Wouldn't give in. He'd spent his entire adult life rejecting and ignoring God.

Redemption.

The word, like a whisper from a lover, repeated over and over in his mind.

As his strength left him, he fell back into the snow and was transported back to the church of his youth. Dad up in the pulpit shouting down to the congregants. Mom and the rest of the family jammed into the front pew.

Over the years, the few who had the guts questioned why a preacher would give his sons biblical names with such negative connotations. Cain, Ananias, Judas. Their father would chuckle and preach at them again. "Everyone is born a sinner. It will be God's miraculous power that redeems my sons *and* their names."

After a particularly troubling day at school, one time—and only one—Judas asked why his father would want to give bullies an open invitation to tease his children. It had been pure torture growing up with the name of the disciple who betrayed Jesus.

He'd received swift punishment for questioning his father.

Later, he sat in his room, tears streaming down his face, and swore that he wouldn't give his father the satisfaction of winning. There would be *no* redemption of his name.

Shutting his eyes against the memory, Judas let out a moan.

Turn to Me.

No.

As sharp pain overtook his senses, he clenched his jaw and held on to his anger. This was God's fault.

No! You can't do this! I say what happens in my life. Do You hear me? I do!

The lone horse in front of Madysen looked familiar. Wait a minute. That was Judas's horse.

She slowed the rig. "Oh my goodness! Daniel, wake up!"

"Hmm?" He sat up.

"Look! It's Judas." She pointed to a large snowdrift in front of them, where Judas lay.

Jumping down from the sleigh, she went to the man's side.

Daniel joined her. "I think he's still breathing. I don't have a lot of strength, but we've got to get him up into the sleigh and into town. Can you help me lift him?"

She nodded and grabbed Judas's feet. Together they got the man into the sleigh, and then Madysen tied his horse to the back. Once she was seated again, Daniel gave her the reins and she put the horses back in motion.

Daniel wrapped an arm around her. "You better hurry, he's awfully cold." He let out a sigh. "You know what, while you drive, I'm going to pray for him."

TWENTY-SEVEN

Oh, for a good night's sleep.

It had been days since he had the chance. Peter rubbed a soapy hand down his face in the washroom at the hospital. At least the two other doctors were up and around now.

A knock sounded at the door.

He grabbed a towel and dried off his face and then opened the door.

"Dr. Cameron?" One of the nuns who was working as a nurse nodded at him. "Dr. Miller asked for an update on the patients. What would you like me to tell him?"

As he gave the nun the information he knew off the top of his head, a bit of relief flowed through him. Things were looking up. Most of the patients seemed to be on the mend. Perhaps the worst was behind them.

"I'm going to go home, get cleaned up, and get some rest. Can you and your staff handle everything?"

"Yes, Doctor. You definitely deserve a break." She nodded and left.

The first thing he wanted to do was see Whitney. After her

confession to him, he'd thought of her constantly. There was no denying that he had strong feelings for her as well. But what if he failed her as others had?

No. That was the enemy talking again.

As he left the hospital, he shook off the thoughts. God had been working on his heart a lot lately. He'd shown Peter that he'd built a wall around himself to keep from failing anyone else. And He'd shown Peter how foolish that was. God had ordained his life, and while there would be times when he wouldn't be able to cure or help, he could always pray.

Watching Whitney work through her own struggle had taught him so much. Her honesty with him was beautiful. Bold. Unashamed. He needed to be more honest as well. Stop putting up facades. Admit to his struggles and do his best for the glory of God. And, just as was true for Whitney, healing wouldn't come overnight. It would be a journey.

He walked toward his home and office, letting the frigid air in and out of his lungs.

"Peter!"

He turned. Daniel and Madysen stopped their sleigh in the street.

"Come quick!" Maddy waved toward him. "It's Judas."

What? He ran to the sleigh and peered in. "What happened?"

"We don't know. We found him in a snow drift after he left the farm."

Peter winced. "Was he trying to convince Whitney to marry him again?"

"Worse. He came to tell us that someone else held a deed to our property and then threatened her when she wouldn't agree to marry him." Madysen had tears in her eyes. "We can't let him die like this, Peter. He has no one. He needs Jesus."

In his flesh, Peter didn't want to help this man that had treated Whitney with such manipulation and deceit. But Madysen was correct. *Lord, help me.* "Get him inside, and I'll see what I can do."

"We need to head over to Granny's to check on them. Will you send word?"

"Of course."

An hour later, he walked to the Beauforts's. Oh, how he needed the fresh air. Madysen opened the door, her eyes filled with concern.

"I'm afraid it's not good news. We haven't been able to wake him, and from what we can ascertain, he's had a heart attack."

Madysen put a hand to her mouth.

Daniel's shoulders lifted in a heavy sigh. "What should we do?"

"Pray. There's nothing else you can do. I'll keep an eye on Judas, and if he wakes, I'll send a message out to the farm."

Watching them go, he looked to the ceiling. He wouldn't get to see Whitney again today like he'd hoped.

Because he'd be caring for a man who'd threatened her. But Madysen was right. The man needed Jesus. And Jesus could turn life around for anyone.

Even Judas Reynolds.

All right, God. Show me what I need to do to help heal this man.

Whitney dressed in her best dress. When Maddy had returned last night and told the family about Judas, and that

Peter thought he'd had a heart attack, her first reaction had been relief. Then guilt rushed in. Such thoughts were not honoring to the Lord. No matter what Judas had done, Jesus had died for his sins, the same as He had for hers.

By five in the morning, after a restless night, she'd paced her room for an hour and then itched to play the piano. She'd padded to the parlor and opened the lid, revealing the ivory and black keys.

"It's all right if you want to play. We're awake."

Havyn's voice.

She'd turned around to see her sisters and their husbands huddled by the fire.

Maddy smiled at her. "Please play for us. We've simply been praying for Martin, Granny, the town, and yes, even Judas."

As nerve-racking as it had been to think of an audience surrounding her the first time she came back to the instrument, she pulled out Chopin's *Nocturnes opus 32* and everything else vanished. She felt more refreshed by God in that thirty minutes of playing than she'd had in a year. She'd thanked her heavenly Father over and over again as she'd played and cried.

When she finished, she knew she had to go to town and see Judas.

Now that she was on her way, she was nervous. Her whole family had piled into the new three-seat sleigh they'd purchased after Maddy's wedding. Whether they all came to give moral support or to see Judas for themselves, she wasn't sure. But she was glad they were with her.

When they reached the hospital, she climbed out of the sleigh first. "Please. I'd like to see him alone." She turned around and didn't give anyone the chance to respond.

At the entrance, she asked the kind nun for Mr. Reynolds's room number. Everything was a bit of a blur as she walked down the hall to his room.

She opened the door.

He was pale. His eyes were closed.

"Judas?"

No response.

She crept closer to the bed and fidgeted with the button on the front of her coat. "It's not quite noon, but I'm here."

His eyelids fluttered.

She took a deep breath. "You demanded that I come, but I'm not here because you demanded. I'm here because I care about where you will face eternity."

This time he moaned.

"Judas?"

His eyes opened to slits. "Whit . . . ney . . ." His voice was weak and breathy.

"I won't marry you, Judas. And I will fight you about this other deed on our property. But I can't in good conscience let you lie here in the hospital and not tell you the truth."

"God is . . . punishing me . . ."

She bit her lip. How many times in the past couple days had she wanted to punish this man? But what he said wasn't true. Praise the Lord for His mercy and grace. "That's not how God works, Judas. Just like Jesus did with the thief on the cross next to Him, He's offering you hope. Forgiveness."

"I've spent my life defying God. He took everything . . . *everything* from me. I hate Him." His breaths came in large gasps. "There's no . . . forgiveness for me now. I don't want it."

"Yes, there is." She stepped closer and grabbed his hand. No matter what he'd done, Jesus still loved him. Something she was supposed to do too. Closing her eyes for a brief moment, she pictured her mama. What would she say? "His desire is that *none* should be lost. He loves you, Judas. He loves every single one of us the same."

"It's too late. . . . I was born lost. I'll die . . . lost too . . . that's how it has to be. I'm in . . . control." He shut his eyes.

"Don't say that." Oh, if only Maddy were here. She was the one full of mercy. Ready to help people no matter what they'd done. *God give me the words. Please.*

A sound at the door made her look over her shoulder. Peter stood there.

Judas gasped and let out a groan. "Your God couldn't stop me."

"Stop you?" What was he talking about?

He yanked his hand away and fisted it in the blanket. "*I* took the store." His eyes bulged. "That fool believed his God would help him. But *I* won!"

Her eyes burned. "Judas, please—"

"I'll have the farm too. I'll own it! I own *you* . . ."

She shut her eyes against the words. "No. Stop this nonsense. All you have to do is believe, Judas. Have faith. You know the truth."

"Doesn't matter." He shook his head and paled. The man who had always been larger than life shrank against the bed. Terror filled his eyes.

"It does matter. I'm worried about your soul."

"My soul . . . is black. . . . Not . . . worth . . . sav—" His eyes closed, and a long breath came out of his lips. Then nothing.

Peter rushed to the bed and put his head to Judas's chest. "Come on, Reynolds. Fight! I know you've got it in you. Breathe!"

Whitney stepped closer and placed her hand on Peter's shoulder. Moments passed.

Nothing.

"He's gone." Peter's shoulders slumped.

A silent tear slipped down her cheek. "How could he refuse God like that at the end?"

"I don't know. But I'm glad you were here to speak to him." Peter wrapped an arm around her shoulders.

She put both hands over her mouth and cried. The hateful thoughts she'd had for the man over the past few days rushed into her mind.

Forgive me, Father.

She leaned her face against Peter's strong chest and wept for Judas. And the loss of his soul.

Peter walked into the Roadhouse and scanned the crowd. Whitney waved to him from the front. Making his way through the tables surrounded by people, he gave her a smile.

Nome had recovered in more ways than one over the last month. The sickness was gone. Many people had died, like in the epidemic of 1900, but many more had survived.

He'd spent every spare moment he had out at the farm. Working with Whitney and the dogs. Taking long walks with the woman he loved.

When Daniel and John approached him about building him a house on the farm, he'd asked if it could be big enough for a family. When the two men had given their hearty approval, Peter couldn't wait for the day when he could ask Whitney to marry him.

The day had finally come. At least he hoped tonight would be good. It depended on what happened in this meeting.

Judge Beck had taken over Judas's freight business, stating that Reynolds had left it to him. Many people in the town called him a liar— especially those who had owed Judas money and now supposedly had to pay the judge.

That was why they were at the Roadhouse. The "good" judge had called a town meeting.

Peter made it to Whitney's side and greeted the rest of her family. "Any idea what all this is about?"

John shrugged. "Mr. Norris said that the judge is trying to save face with the town."

The object of their conversation appeared on the stage and held up his hands. "Quiet, please. Everyone." He nodded and smiled as he gazed around the room. Clasping his hands behind his back, he took several steps back and forth across the stage. "I want to make things right."

The crowd hushed until they could hear each other breathing.

"I know how many of you owed Mr. Reynolds money. Many of you feel that he swindled you into the debt."

Affirmation filled the air.

Beck held up his hands until they quieted again. "But I'm here to tell you that even though Judas left everything to me, and told me that I would also acquire the repayments, I've decided to release everyone of their debts."

That got the crowd riled up into another uproar, but this one was of cheers.

"Please . . . let me continue." The judge put his hands on his lapels. "It seemed right, since the good Lord above has blessed me with this gift from my dear friend, that I offer the forgiveness of debt to each of you."

Funny how the man was trying to sound humble and yet his chin lifted with every word. Was he trying to win favor with the town so he could go on manipulating like Judas? His chest puffed out with every cheer from the crowd.

"It is my heart's desire to see our beautiful town of Nome prosper in the coming years. And Reynolds's Shipping and Freight will continue to be a cornerstone of our home."

John leaned over to Peter. "Somehow I don't think Beck is any less corrupt than Judas."

The crowd cheered for the man on the stage.

Peter shook his head. "I have a feeling you're correct."

Since they were at the front of the room, it would be hard to sneak away with Whitney as he'd hoped. But she'd brought the dogs to town for him so they could drive them home together.

That was good. It would give him the opportunity he'd been praying for.

He pulled his watch out of his pocket and watched the second hand tick around the face.

"Just a minute, Beck!" A booming voice from the back caught everyone's attention.

The sheriff stood there, holding a paper high. Two deputies stood at his side.

The hall hushed as the three men strode to the stage and joined Judge Beck.

The man went ashen.

When the sheriff made it to the center of the stage, he held out the paper again. "This here is a telegram from the sheriff of Portland, Oregon, stating they have verified that a man named Cain Reynolds—a preacher—is the brother of one Judas Reynolds. Judas's only living relative and thus—" he pointed his words to the judge—"Judas's sole heir."

This sent the crowd into another tizzy. Peter leaned back.

Judas had a preacher for a brother? How had the man turned so corrupt?

"Simmer down." The sheriff didn't need a lot of help getting their attention. "Now, in this telegram, it states that Cain Reynolds wishes to forgive all debt owed to Judas Reynolds, and for his company to be sold to the highest bidder. All proceeds shall be sent to Portland so he can build a new church and provide Bibles for anyone who wants one."

As the crowd cheered, the two deputies grabbed the judge.

"As for you, Judge Beck, you are under arrest for falsifying legal documents, theft, and a number of other allegations that have come to our attention."

Peter looked at John. "Good guess."

As the sheriff escorted the judge off the stage, the crowd scattered and the noise grew around them. The sheriff broke off from the others and approached John. "Mr. Roselli. Might I have a word with you and your family?"

"Of course." Havyn's husband waved them all to gather.

The sheriff nodded to the women and then to each of the men. "Ladies. Doctor. Beaufort." He smoothed his mustache. "Judge Beck came to me earlier today stating that he had legal claim to your farm. Showed me the deed. Rest assured, it's clear it's a forgery."

John held out a hand to the lawman. "Thank you, Sheriff. When Reynolds first showed it to us with the judge, we knew it couldn't be real."

"Happy to be of service. I look forward to the day when our town is rid of the corruption." The sheriff placed his hat on his head and walked away.

This was his chance. Peter offered a hand to Whitney. "Care to take the ride in the moonlight now?"

"I'd love to."

He nodded to the rest of the family. "I'll have her home at a decent hour. I promise."

He walked her through the mass of people and out to where her dogs and sled sat. "Your chariot awaits."

Whitney's bright laugh rang through the night. She set her feet on the footboards.

"Mind if I drive?" Not waiting for an answer, he lifted the hook and stepped up behind her, putting his arms around her, his hands over hers on the handle. "Let's go!"

The nearness of her took his breath away as he drove the sled through the town and out to the north, where a beautiful aurora-filled sky awaited them.

Once they were away from the cacophony of Nome, he called out, "Whoa."

The dogs slowed and the sled came to a stop, but he didn't move.

For several seconds he watched the sky move in beautiful waves of greens and yellows. Then he stepped back a few inches and turned her around to face him. "Whitney . . ."

She gazed up at him, her gorgeous hair framing her face. Those brown eyes searching his.

"I don't have a lot to offer you. But I believe our future is together." He got down on one knee, and her eyes widened. "I love you. I haven't been whole for a very long time, but you fill all the empty spaces when nothing and no one else could. I pledge to honor you and love you with all my heart. Will you marry me?"

"Yes!" She threw herself into his arms.

Nothing in this world could be better.

Epilogue

June 15, 1905

With a nod to Peter, Whitney squeezed her sister's hand.

"Havyn . . . it's time to push." Peter's voice was calm and soothing.

"Are you certain it's not too soon?" Sweat beaded on Havyn's forehead.

They'd expected the baby in July, but Havyn had been large for some time now, so Peter said he thought there might be a chance at twins. Though he'd heard only one heartbeat.

His reassuring smile was all Whitney needed. "Your baby is coming now. God's perfect timing, so don't you worry. Simply focus on pushing when the contractions come."

Havyn's head bobbed up and down. "I didn't mean to mess up your wedding, Whit. We had so much to do today, and I was supposed to help." Tears pooled in her eyes.

"You haven't messed up a thing. The wedding will still happen tomorrow, and we'll put you and the baby into

Granddad's wheeled chair and roll you in." Whitney winked and kept a grip on her sister with her right hand while using her left hand to wipe a cool cloth over Havyn's forehead. "I'm right here. Nothing is more important than this right now."

Butterflies took up residence in her stomach. She and her family had helped birth hundreds of animals, and the miracle of new life was always exciting. And now . . .

It was time for the first of their family to bring in the next generation.

Excitement filled her heart. Tomorrow was her wedding day, and today she'd have a niece or nephew.

Thank You, Lord. Please give Havyn the strength she needs and keep our new little one safe.

"Here we go." Peter's demeanor held strength and peace. All at the same time. God had used everything he'd been through to make him an even better physician. What a blessing it was to know and love this man. To think that she was marrying him . . . *tomorrow!* "Big push."

"*Ahh!*" Havyn's long cry turned into a powerful grunt. Her face went from pain to determination. Then back to pain.

"Keep breathing. You can do this." Whitney had no idea if what she was saying was encouraging or not, but she'd promised to be here for Havyn while Madysen kept everyone else busy with preparations for the wedding.

"Almost there. You're doing a great job." Peter's encouragement steadied her nerves. Exactly what they needed right now.

After several more contractions, Peter nodded to her and spoke softly to Havyn. "One more big push."

Havyn moaned. "I don't know how much I've got left."

The contraction must have hit, because she squeezed Whitney's hand so hard she thought it might break.

"*Ahhh!*"

Peter scooted back with a big smile on his face. "Havyn, it's a girl."

Her sister relaxed against her. "She's all right?"

The baby let out a lustful cry.

With a laugh, Peter nodded. "I'll say. She's healthy and breathing well . . . and she's a *big* baby."

"Look at those chubby cheeks!" Whitney watched as Peter passed the baby to Havyn. "And she has red hair!" Her squeal couldn't be contained.

Havyn's face showed her pure awe. "I told John that if it was a girl, I wanted to name her after Mama." She looked up at Whitney.

Whitney's eyes watered. "Melissa. Mama would be so honored."

"Melissa Joy," Havyn said. "To remind us to grab onto God's joy each and every day."

"I love it." Sweet tears rolled down her cheeks. *Oh, Mama, can you see this? You would be so proud.*

"Would you go get John for me so he can meet his daughter?"

She nodded.

Peter's smile stretched across his face as he beamed at Havyn. "Good job, Mama. Looks like we were a bit off on the due date, but she's healthy." He wiped his hands on a towel and gave Whitney a long look.

So much passed between them without a word spoken. The blessing and miracle of birth. The relief that both mama and baby were well. The joy of getting married tomorrow. The hope for their own future.

They'd come a long way together. And she wouldn't change a thing. Even the hard lessons learned. Because she'd found this man and for the first time understood unconditional love.

———

Whitney walked through the double doors of the brand-new church building. Even though the furnishings hadn't been built yet, the crowd didn't seem to mind standing. They split down the middle to allow her passage.

Today she would marry the man she loved.

Then they would take the dogs out into the wilds and camp under the stars for several days. It was the perfect honeymoon.

As she stared at him, she loved the way he smiled at her.

A small cry drew her attention away.

The congregation laughed at the newest member of the family making her presence known.

Up at the front of the room stood her family.

John and Havyn with baby Melissa. Daniel and Madysen. Ruth with her kids who'd arrived from Colorado. Eli and Bethany. She could almost picture Granddad and Mama looking down from heaven and smiling.

Their family was growing. The farm was thriving. The future would certainly hold trials, but she wouldn't want to face it with anyone else.

"I'm so proud of you. Thank you for asking me to walk you down the aisle." Dad leaned in and smiled down at her.

"Thanks, Dad. I know I haven't been the easiest to get along with, but thank you for forgiving me and showing me what true grace really means. If you hadn't come back, I don't know how I would have made it."

Tears gathered in his eyes, and he blinked several times. "Oh, you would have done fine. You always have."

Whitney turned to him. Even though her sisters were playing the piece she was supposed to be walking down to, this was important. "No, Dad. *I* haven't. I know I made you think that I didn't need you—that I didn't need anyone. But that was a sham. Remember when I was little and one of the mines collapsed? It shook the ground like a huge earthquake. You used to always talk about how unshakable I was because I stood in the middle of the street with my hands fisted at my sides and didn't fall down like the rest of the town. From that moment on, I took it on as my job to be strong for everyone else. To take care of others. To be ever constant, in case anyone needed me. But if I've learned anything this past year, it's that the only One who is ever constant is God. That means I need to rely on Him and not myself. For too long, I did it my way. But not anymore."

He wrapped her in a big hug. "You're right, sweetheart. Thank you for the reminder."

Turning back to the front, she gave Peter a smile. They had wanted to inaugurate the church with their wedding. After everything the town had been through the past few months, they needed something positive.

"Let's get you down to your groom."

She nodded and walked in step with her dad.

When they reached the front, she looked deep into Peter's eyes. His words from last night flooded her mind. After the house had settled down from the birth of baby Melissa Joy, he'd given her a piece of paper. On it, he'd drawn a triangle without a base.

"What's this?"

He wrote her name at the bottom of one side and his name at the bottom of the other.

"I still don't understand."

Without a word, he kissed her forehead and then wrote God up at the top of the triangle. "You see . . . the only way we can get closer together is for each of us to get closer to God." He traced each side of the triangle from their names up to the top. "I vow to you now, Whitney Powell, and for the rest of my life, that I will do my very best to keep my focus on God first. And if I falter, I need you to point me back in the right direction. That's the only way I can love you the way God intended."

As if Peter knew her thoughts, he put his index fingers together and made a triangle without a bottom. "I love you."

"I love you too." She threw her arms around him and kissed him with all the love she had within her.

The crowd cheered and laughed.

Pastor Wilson cleared his throat. "Dearly beloved . . ."

Note from the Authors

We want to thank you for joining us for Havyn, Madysen, and Whitney's stories in *Forever Hidden*, *Endless Mercy*, and *Ever Constant*. It has been a roller coaster of a ride for these characters, but we've learned so much. We pray that you have as well.

Alaska is very near and dear to us, and as always, we portray it as accurately as we can. After living in Alaska for several years, it's very important to me to make sure the details are correct. Alaskans are *very* proud of their state and its incredible uniqueness. Anything that is fictionalized in the setting of *Ever Constant* is done for a purpose.

We wrote about the heyday of Nome, and during the short-lived gold rush the population was in the tens of thousands, but soon after this era, the number of people who made Nome their permanent home dwindled down to the hundreds. Today the population is 3,850.

In this story, we included a thread that is difficult for many people: addiction. Whether it is alcohol, drugs, food, pornography, or anything else, addiction is very real for the majority of the population. If you are struggling with an addiction of any kind, please know that you are not alone—there is help and hope. We are praying for you. Here are a few places to start to get help: www.lighthousenetwork.org, www.teenchallengeusa.org/about, and www.celebrate recovery.com.

Don't forget to keep up with us online and via our newsletters and blogs. We absolutely love to hear from our readers.

And we've loved hearing your chicken stories (we've even gotten some great sheep, sled dog, and cow stories). But if you have any great chicken stories you want to share via Facebook, Twitter, or Instagram, please tag us and use the hashtag #chickensforkim. Who knows what the #chickens forkim campaign will accomplish—and you never know what shenanigans we will be up to next.

We can't wait to share with you our next series, which is set in Kalispell, Montana, starting in May of 2023.

Until next time,
Kim and Tracie

Acknowledgments

Tracie and I would like to once again thank our incomparable team of creatives, designers, editors, marketing gurus, publicists, and all-around-brilliant people who make up the publishing team at Bethany House. Dave Long and Jessica Sharpe, thank you for all you do for our stories. Amy, Noelle, Brooke, and Serena, we love-love-*love* what you do for us. Hannah, your insight and great catches are invaluable to us. And to everyone else at BHP, thank you. From the bottom of our hearts. We treasure you and appreciate all the hard work that goes into getting each book baby out into the hands of readers.

To the woman who makes me work my tail off but makes me love story and writing even more—Karen Ball: You. Are. The. Best. I absolutely love the editing process, and that is what truly makes the story come to life. So very thankful to work with you!

To our husbands and families, we wouldn't be able to do this without you. We love you more than you could ever imagine. Thanks for all the encouragement, the support, the flowers, the food, and the times when you left us alone with our characters so we could get the story done.

And to Almighty God, the One and only Ever Constant, we love You. Thank You for giving us the gift of story.

Readers, we can't do this without you. Thank you for journeying along with us again.

Grabbing onto joy,
Kimberley

About the Authors

Tracie Peterson is the award-winning author of more than one hundred novels, both historical and contemporary. Her avid research resonates in her many bestselling series. Tracie and her family make their home in Montana. Visit www .traciepeterson.com to learn more.

Kimberley Woodhouse is an award-winning, bestselling author of more than twenty-five books. A lover of history and research, she often gets sucked into the past, and then her husband has to lure her out with chocolate and the promise of eighteen holes on the golf course. She loves music, kayaking, and her family. Married to the love of her life for three decades, she lives and writes in the Poconos where she's traded in her role of "craziest mom" for "coolest grandma." To find out more about Kim's books, find her on social media, and sign up for her newsletter, go to www.kimberleywoodhouse.com.

Sign Up for the Authors' Newsletters

Keep up to date with Tracie and Kimberley's news on book releases and events by signing up for their email lists at traciepeterson.com and kimberleywoodhouse.com.

More from Tracie Peterson & Kimberley Woodhouse

When Madysen Powell's supposedly dead father shows up, her gift for forgiveness is tested and she's left searching for answers. Daniel Beaufort arrives in Nome and finds employment at the Powell dairy, longing to start fresh after the gold rush leaves him with only empty pockets. Will deceptions from the past tear apart their hopes for a better future?

Endless Mercy
THE TREASURES OF NOME #2

You May Also Like . . .

When her grandfather's health begins to decline, Havyn is determined to keep her family together. But everyone has secrets—including John, the hired stranger who recently arrived on their farm. To help out, Havyn starts singing at a local roadhouse—but dangerous eyes grow jealous as she and John grow closer. Will they realize the peril before it is too late?

Forever Hidden by Tracie Peterson and Kimberley Woodhouse
THE TREASURES OF NOME #1
traciepeterson.com; kimberleywoodhouse.com

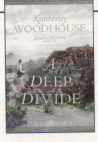

When her father's greedy corruption goes too far, heiress Emma Grace McMurray sneaks away to be a Harvey Girl at the El Tovar Grand Canyon Hotel, planning to stay hidden forever. There she uncovers mysteries, secrets, and a love beyond anything she could imagine—leaving her to question all she thought to be true.

A Deep Divide by Kimberley Woodhouse
SECRETS OF THE CANYON #1
kimberleywoodhouse.com

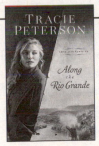

When bankruptcy forces widow Susanna Jenkins to follow her family to New Mexico, what they see as a failure she sees as a fresh start. Owen Turner is immediately attracted to Susanna, but he's afraid of opening up his heart again, especially as painful memories are stirred up. But if Owen can't face the past, he'll miss out on his greatest chance at love.

Along the Rio Grande by Tracie Peterson
LOVE ON THE SANTA FE
traciepeterson.com

◆ BETHANYHOUSE

More from Bethany House

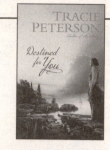

After scarlet fever kills her mother and siblings, Gloriana Womack is dedicated to holding together what's left of her fractured family. Luke Carson arrives in Duluth to shepherd the construction of the railroad and reunite with his brother. When tragedy strikes and Gloriana and Luke must help each other through their grief, they find their lives inextricably linked.

Destined for You by Tracie Peterson
LADIES OF THE LAKE
traciepeterson.com

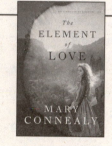

After learning their stepfather plans to marry them off, Laura Stiles and her sisters escape to find better matches and claim their father's lumber dynasty. Laura sees potential in the local minister of the poor town they settle in, but when secrets buried in his past and the land surface, it will take all they have to keep trouble at bay.

The Element of Love by Mary Connealy
THE LUMBER BARON'S DAUGHTERS #1
maryconnealy.com

A very public jilting has Theodore Day fleeing the ballrooms of New York to focus on building his family's luxury steamboat business in New Orleans and beating out his brother to be next in charge. But he can't escape the Southern belles' notice, nor Flora Wingfield, who has followed him determined to win his attention.

Her Darling Mr. Day by Grace Hitchcock
AMERICAN ROYALTY #2
gracehitchcock.com

⬥ BETHANYHOUSE